PRAISE FOR
THE SHADOW SKYE TRILOGY

"A story fantasy-loving young readers
may not even know they've been waiting for."
—*The New York Times Book Review*

"A gripping story and a dark one."
—*The Wall Street Journal*

"Thrilling, strange, and brutally involving."
—*The Guardian* (UK)

★ "The narrative gallops along, with hefty doses of humor,
tenderness, and violence, until the storylines meet on a
final page that will leave readers desperate for more."
—*Kirkus Reviews* (starred review)

"Readers will be swept up in this story of unique heroes,
new voices, and Scottish mythos. This is a natural next
step for fans of Rick Riordan and mythology."
—*School Library Journal*

SHADOW SKYE

BOOK ONE

THE GOOD HAWK

JOSEPH ELLIOTT

WALKER BOOKS

THE
GOOD HAWK

WITHDRAWN

Text copyright © 2020 by Joseph Elliott
Illustrations copyright © 2020 by Anna and Elena Balbusso

First US paperback edition 2021

Library of Congress Catalog Card Number 2019939811
ISBN 978-1-5362-0718-7 (hardcover)
ISBN 978-1-5362-1516-8 (paperback)

21 22 23 24 25 26 TRC 10 9 8 7 6 5 4 3 2 1

Printed in Eagan, MN, USA

This book was typeset in Fairfield LH.
The illustrations were created digitally using mixed media.

Walker Books US
a division of
Candlewick Press
99 Dover Street
Somerville, Massachusetts 02144

www.walkerbooksus.com

FOR RICHARD

PART ONE

SKYE

AGATHA

THE WIND IS ON MY NOSE AND MY EYES STING. I BROUGHT two cloaks today because I am clever. I pull them together with my hands. The tops of my fingers are numb but I don't mind because it is my job and it is an important one.

I look at the sea. The waves are chopping up and down. Sometimes I follow a wave from as far away as I can see, all the way to where I am. I look at it and keep my eyes on it and try not to let it out of my eyes when it comes close and more close until it crashes. It is a hard thing to do and I am good at it.

When I was only young I wanted to go on the sea so much. I asked the Anglers and the Seals lots of times to take me on their boats but they wouldn't. They shoved me away and called me a "good-for-nothing nuisance," which is rude. I made the plan to do it myself and climbed up the wall when no one was looking and down the other side. It was a hard thing to do but easy for me because I'm good at climbing. The waves went on my legs and my face and I laughed because I liked it and it tasted like soup. Then a bigger wave came and I couldn't hold on anymore and I fell. I could have drowned but one of the Hawks saw me and my arms splashing. "You stupid, stupid girl." he said when he pulled me out. "You stupid, stupid girl." I'm more clever now and I wouldn't do it again.

After it happened I didn't want to go on the boats anymore. I stayed inside the enclave and didn't look at the sea until they gave me my *dreuchd*. I was very happy that day because they made me a Hawk, which is my duty and an important one. One day I will save someone from drowning too like when the Hawk saved me.

"You look cold."

It is Lenox who says that, who is another Hawk. "Go into the turret and warm up. I lit a fire," he says as well. His eyebrows go scrunchy when he talks. They are big ones and black.

"I don't—want to," I say and shake my head. I don't like going in the turret because when I'm inside I'm not looking at the sea which is what I should be doing.

"Go on, little girl, it's for your own good," he says, and he pushes my back. I hate it when he calls me "little girl" because I am not a little girl. I am fifteen so he shouldn't call me that. I do a big frown so he sees it.

When I am in the turret, I kick the fire because I don't want to be there and bits of it fly up to the walls. It's a small room in a circle. I should not have kicked the fire. Now it might go out, which would be bad. I scrape the bits with my shoe and add some more sticks to make it big again. Even though I didn't want to come, it is nice to be hot and I move my fingers which is nice as well. I undo my first cloak and the other one underneath so I can reach the pocket on my top where Milkwort is. He is warm which is good because I was worried he would be cold. I put him next to the fire because he likes it there. In my trousers is some bread that I saved. I give some to him and keep some for later. He thanks me and eats it while looking at the fire.

"Don't get too close," I warn him.

Milkwort is my friend and a vole and a secret. No one knows about him. Except Maistreas Eilionoir. I don't know how she found out. She is old and knows everything. When she found out she pulled me into her bothan and told me to get rid of him.

"You could be severely punished for this," she said. She was holding on to my arm tight and it hurt a lot even though she is old and her hands are small.

"I know," I said, and I tried to pull my arm away. People think that I'm stupid but I'm not stupid.

"Get rid of it. Before someone finds out who isn't as forgiving as I am." She let go of my arm and I rubbed it and then I left.

"All right, Aggie, my turn."

The voice is a surprise to me. I must have been staring at the fire for longer than I thought. It is Flora who is there and it is her turn to come in. I am in panic because she may have seen Milkwort. My eyes look to where he was. He's not there.

"I need to do up my cl-cloaks. Give me one—one moment, will you?"

"Of course."

It is lucky that Flora turns away so I can search for Milkwort without her seeing. I want to call for him, but Flora will hear me if I do that, so I only do it in my head. Talking to animals is not *dùth,* which means you shouldn't do it. He is nowhere by the fire and there is nothing for him to hide behind. He wouldn't have run away. He would never leave me. Then I spot him in a gap between the stones in the wall. It was clever for him to go there. I hold out my hand. He jumps onto my arm and behind my neck and into the pocket again. That was close. I do up my cloaks the quickest possible.

"I'm done," I say to Flora.

"Thanks," she says, and she smiles and comes in and I go back onto the wall.

I like Flora because she is nice. She's my friend. She is a girl like me but her hair is light brown and she is taller. When she was made a Hawk I helped by telling her all the things you have to do to be a good Hawk, like how to tell the difference between a dolphin and a deathfin and the best way to spear a spider crab and what the five chimes mean and how to ring them properly. I am good at helping.

The sea is a gray color today with only a bit of white. It looks like broken rocks. When I am looking I have to do walking as well. Otherwise the blood will freeze inside you. That is what Lenox says.

It is one hundred and seventeen steps to walk along this part of the wall which I know because I counted them. I can walk it without looking at my feet which is good because it means I can look at the sea the whole time and don't miss a single thing. When I reach the other side I turn and walk back and then back again the other way the whole day.

Behind me is the enclave. That is where we all live which is

Clann-a-Tuath which is my clan. It is the best one. There are other clans but they are far away on the other parts of the island. I can't even see them from the wall. That is because Skye is a big island. We are on the north part. Inside our enclave are lots of bothans made of stone which is where we sleep, and a big wall all the way around which means we can see everything that's all around us. Some people might want to come into our enclave but they are not allowed which is why I have to do the looking on the wall to stop them if they try.

It is getting darker now. You have to look more hard when it is darker because it is not so easy. There is something there, on the sea. I saw it because I looked so well. It is far away and it is small but I think it will be a boat. I keep it in my eyes until it is a little bit closer and then I know that yes, it is a boat. I do not know who is in it. Maybe it is a Seal boat coming back. That would be good.

I walk to the turret and keep looking at the boat still. All of the turrets have a set of chimes outside them so we can do warning and send messages with the sounds. I pick up the hammer and am going to hit the First once at the top which means I can see a boat and it is people but I can't see who it is yet, but the sound comes out before my hammer hits the metal. It makes me jump because I am not expecting it and I am confused how it made a sound without me hitting it first. Then I know that the sound didn't come from my chime. It came from a different chime, from one of the other turrets, and was hit by someone else. It is confusing in my head because I was expecting one sound and then I heard a differ-ent one so it is hard to remember what it was I heard. It could have been the Second but no, I think it was the Fourth. That is very not good. The Fourth is for danger and two hits at the top means it is a ship and it is going to attack. My heart is going fast. When you hear the Fourth the most important thing is that you have to act quickly. If you don't then people could die because it is serious. I look in the turret but there is no one there and I can't see anyone farther on the wall either. Who was it that hit the chime? I look back at the sea. The boat is coming in fast now and I am the only one who can stop it. I have to stop it. It is my duty and important and I have to protect my clan.

I run to the launcher and wind back the claw until it clicks. The arrow is already inside. It is a big one and a metal one. I've got the flint in my belt because we always have to have it. I take it out and try to light the moss on the arrow, but it won't do it because it's all wet from when it was raining. I shake my head and tear the moss off and throw it in the sea. I need something else. I look up and it makes me yell because I see how close the boat has gotten. Think, think, I need to think. Then I know what to do.

I kick off my boot and take off my sock quickly so quickly. I tie the sock to the end of the arrow with one knot and then two knots so it won't come loose. It is a clever plan. The sock is hard to light because you have to hit the flint so fast. My hands are all shaking. I try to do it lots of times and then I do it. The fire goes all big because of the animal fat on the arrow. In my eye there is someone and it is Lenox on the wall far away. He is waving at me to go faster. He knows how fast I need to be because the boat is so close now. I slide the launcher over, making the middle of the boat line up with the tip of the arrow like I was taught.

"Agatha, no!" Lenox's shout is an echo, but my finger has already pressed the trigger. Why did he tell me no?

The arrow goes up into the sky. The boat is more close now so I can see the people inside. That's strange. I squint my eyes because what I see isn't right. I can see their faces and it's not right because I know them.

It means the boat is one of ours. I have done a terrible mistake.

JAIME

THE BOAT LURCHES, MAKING MY STOMACH TWIST. I OPEN my mouth to retch, but all that comes out is a hollow whimper. I tighten my grip on the boat's side. Sharp scabs of paint flake away beneath my fingers. I'm sure the other Anglers are giving me pitying looks behind my back. I'm trying. I'm really trying. I hope they know that.

I reach up with one hand and pull my hood over my face. The wind whips it straight back off again. Sleet lashes my cheeks and trickles down my neck.

"You look like you've been grabbed by a gannet," Aileen says as she steps beside me.

"I feel like it too," I reply in between heaves. If a gannet did try to take me right now, I would probably let it.

"Can I get you some water?" Even with rain spewing down and the boat being tossed from side to side, Aileen still manages to look graceful.

"I'm fine," I say, shifting away from her. I'd rather she didn't see me like this.

"On the plus side, you appear to be attracting more fish. We've caught loads since you started emptying your guts." She's trying to make me smile. I really don't want to. "I've no idea why," she continues. "It smells *awful*."

The sides of my mouth betray me and start twitching upward.

"That is definitely a smile!" she says. "I knew I could break you."

"It's not," I say, forcing my mouth into a knot.

"It gets better with time," she says. "I promise."

Although Aileen is roughly the same age as me, she was given her *dreuchd* about six months ago, so she's already had six months' practice. I'm sure she was great at it, even in her first week. She gives my hair a gentle ruffle, then leaves me to my misery. I watch as she slips back to her place and casts her line into the sea. She says something to the Angler next to her that makes him laugh. How does she do that? Make people laugh so easily? It's one of the reasons everyone likes her so much, including me. The only good thing about being named an Angler is that I get to spend more time with her. She's my best friend; she always has been.

Waves strike the side of the boat in a repetitive thud-slap, thud-slap, thud-slap. I look down and immediately regret it. All that deep, dark water. My mind starts rattling through the possibilities of what could be lurking just beneath the surface: giant squid, killer rays, deathfins. . . . I scrunch my eyes closed. *I'm safe in the boat. I'm safe in the boat.* I have to keep telling myself that.

As long as I don't think about what's in the water, I'm fine.

It takes a long time for the weather to improve, the clouds eventually turning from fierce gray to dirty white. As the waves mellow, so too does my seasickness, and I race to try and catch up on all my tasks. As the newest member of the crew, I've been given all the jobs that no one else wants, like untangling the ropes and threading the bait. I work in silence, sitting on my own with my head low.

To make matters worse, we're out east today, which means the Isle of Raasay is directly in front of us: a mountainous strip in between Skye and mainland Scotia. I refuse to look at it. It's where the girl lives, the one who is going to ruin everything. I don't want to think about her right now.

Just before dusk, we start heading back. It's been a long day, but all of my despair melts away at the sight of the enclave. Its walls rise up before us like a welcome beacon. Flecks from the crashing waves make the ancient stones shine.

Home.

My whole body aches to be inside, to be surrounded by the familiar faces of my clan, to feel the spongy earth beneath my feet. To feel safe. From somewhere on the wall, the Second chimes twice to announce our arrival.

"Why have they put *her* on center post?" says the caiptean. I follow his gaze and spot Agatha, one of the Hawks, staring down at us from beside the turret. "And what the hell is she doing now?"

I can just about make out Agatha's arms, pumping at the launcher. She hops about a bit, then ties something to the arrow and sets it on fire.

"She's going to shoot at us. That bloody idiot is going to shoot at us," says the caiptean.

A thunderous twang rings out as the arrow arches high above us. The aim is poor, so the caiptean doesn't bother altering the boat's direction. Instead, he looks up and shouts a string of curses at Agatha. I keep my eyes on the arrow. It tears through the sky like a falling star, its path unstable. A rogue wind catches it, altering its course at the last moment, curving it directly in line with us.

I open my mouth to shout a warning—

Too late.

It rips through the sails before anyone can react, instantly setting them ablaze. The flames lick across the deck and curl up the mast. I yelp, tripping over my long legs in my haste to stand up. The heat is intense, tightening my skin and drying out my eyes. One of the Anglers upturns a bucket of water in an attempt to douse the flames, either not realizing or not caring that it also contains the shrimp-bait. The creatures spill toward me and flit about pathetically, until the fire engulfs them with a series of harsh pops. The smell of scorched fish burns my nostrils.

"Abandon the boat!" yells the caiptean.

What? No. The water is too deep.

People leap overboard in all directions.

I hover at the boat's edge, staring at the water, my legs frozen. I can't do it. I can't.

Someone pushes me from behind. I try to resist, but my knees give way and I tumble into the water.

The coldness hits me like an avalanche of stone. I've fallen in deep. I spin around in circles, but I can't find the surface. My limbs flail in all directions. To my right, a hazy orange smudge pierces the darkness. The blaze from the boat. I kick toward it. Something brushes against my leg. Panic grips my lungs and digs in its nails. I turn. There's nothing there. I turn back, but I can no longer see the boat, no longer know which way is up. I twist my whole body from one side to the other, expecting something to burst out of the darkness at any moment. I'm trapped in the water and I can't breathe. I can't breathe. I can't breathe.

Rough hands find me and yank me upward. Then a new coolness washes over me as my head breaks the surface. I suck in quick mouthfuls of salty air. Above me, flakes of ash rain down from the boat's corpse.

"Where's Jaime? Protect the boy!" people are shouting.

"I've got him," says a voice in my ear. Whoever it is starts towing me toward the wall.

"I'm fine," I say, coughing up seawater. Now that I can see the enclave, I'd rather get there myself. I'm not the best swimmer in the world, but I'm more than capable of swimming a few hundred yards. I also don't want the other Anglers to see me being helped; they already think I'm hopeless. I try to shrug off my rescuer, but he won't let go.

I scan the water for Aileen. I can't see her anywhere. Burning remains fall from the wreckage, sizzling black as they hit the water. When we reach the wall, the caiptean insists that I be pulled over first and that I'm taken straight to the sickbóth.

"Where's Aileen?" I ask, but no one replies.

"It's vital he doesn't fall ill," someone says as I'm hustled across the enclave. "The Ceremony is in less than two weeks." As if I

12

need reminding. Half a dozen people usher me into the sickboth and swamp me in blankets. Once inside, the Herbists fuss around me, drying my hair, feeding me soup.

"Did Aileen make it back okay?" I ask again, raising my voice a little this time.

"She's fine, everyone's fine," says one of the Herbists, placing a sweaty hand on my forehead. "Our main priority right now is you, young man."

I surrender to their care. I've never liked being the center of attention, but I know they mean well. One of them even sneaks me a wedge of hearthcake, covered in thick butter, which helps raise my spirits a little.

"Well, that was dramatic," Aileen says as she saunters through the sickboth door. She's changed into dry clothes, but her rust-colored hair is still sodden from the sea.

"Aileen!"

The Herbists step aside to give us some space. Aileen clasps my fists.

"Thought I'd better check you were still alive," she says.

"Just about."

"Are you all right?"

"I'm fine. Bit embarrassed, maybe. What are people saying? Are they laughing at me?"

"No. Why would they be laughing?"

"Because I'm supposed to be an Angler and I nearly drowned. . . ."

"No one even knows. Or cares. I promise."

"Really?"

"Really really. So stop worrying. And that's an order." She points her finger at me and gives me her best stern look.

"Okay. Thanks." And I mean it. She always knows the right thing to say.

There's a tickle in my throat. I start coughing. There must still be seawater in my lungs. Once I start, I can't seem to stop.

"Are you harassing our patient?" says one of the Herbists, coming back over to check on me.

"Nothing to do with me," says Aileen, holding up her hands.

"Well, I think you'd better let this little mouse get some rest," says the Herbist, patting my back and rubbing my chest at the same time. The cough begins to ease.

"See you in the morning," says Aileen. She can't resist rubbing her knuckles on my head before she goes.

"Good night," I say, knocking her hand away. She leaves me with a big smile on my face.

Not long after, the Herbists leave as well, telling me multiple times on their way out how important it is that I go straight to sleep. Before I have the chance to obey their instructions, there is a knock on the sickboth door and Maighstir Ross enters.

"Jaime-Iasgair. How are you feeling?" he asks.

Wow. The Ceremony really must be a big deal if I'm getting visits from the clan chief himself.

"I'm fine," I say for the thousandth time. "Thank you."

"Very well." He pauses for a moment as if he might say something else, then lowers his head to go back through the doorway. That was brief.

"Maighstir Ross—?"

"Yes." He doesn't take his hand off the door handle.

"I was thinking . . . I was told I have to go to Kilmaluag Bay tomorrow with the other Anglers from my boat, to fish from the shoreline, but . . . I was wondering if I could maybe stay with the Wasps instead?"

His forehead creases. "You want to what?"

"Stay with the Wasps. As part of my training. I thought if I watch how they put a new boat together, I could learn how to fix it, in case anything goes wrong while we're out at sea." I don't know where I'm finding the courage to make such a suggestion. "And also, the bay is quite far; it would probably be better for my health to stay here in the enclave." I let out a pitiful cough to emphasize my point.

Maighstir Ross isn't stupid. He must know that I'm not getting on well as an Angler, but it is not *dùth* to work for a duty other than one's own, so what I am requesting is bordering on unlawful. His face softens and he gives me the faintest hint of a smile.

"Very well," he says, "but you must learn through observation only. You are an Angler now. You would be wise to embrace that fact."

"Yes, Maighstir."

"Now get some rest. We need you fit and healthy for the Ceremony."

The kindness in his eyes disappears the moment he mentions the Ceremony. It was the slightest shift, but I definitely saw it. He blows out the lantern with a fierce breath, plummeting the sick-both into darkness. The door clatters as he leaves.

I try to sleep, but a hundred thoughts itch my brain. Mainly about the Ceremony, of course. The declaration was made a week ago. When they first called me into the meeting circle, my whole body buzzed with excitement. I knew I was about to receive my *dreuchd*—my calling in life. I'd been waiting for it ever since I'd turned fourteen. Being part of a duty and working for the good of the whole clan: that is the greatest honor of all.

My enthusiasm soon faded when they named me an Angler. I had to fight hard to hide my disappointment; all duties are equally important, after all. I'm proud to be an Angler. I am. And the elders would have had a good reason for making the choice they did. I just need to work harder at being better at it.

As soon as the announcement was made, the other Anglers entered the circle and smeared my body with the guts of a freshly killed fish. Not the most enjoyable experience, if I'm honest, but that's the way it's always been. As a result, I was soaking wet and reeking of fish guts when, a short while later, they called me into the circle for a second time. I stepped forward, blood dripping from my scrawny arms. With the eyes of the whole clan on me, I willed myself not to shiver. I'd never heard of anyone being called twice in one night, so I was immediately on edge, imagining the worst. It was Maighstir Ross who made the declaration, his eyes locked on mine. He described it as "a pivotal gesture to ensure positive diplomatic relations for many generations to come." A sickening silence followed, and it wasn't until Maighstir Clyde shouted "May Clann-a-Tuath forever be strong" that everyone raised their fists and started to cheer. Their faces, however, could not hide their confusion.

But it's happening. All the arrangements have been made.

I am going to be married.

To a girl from the Isle of Raasay.

No one wants the marriage to take place, least of all me. Marriage is wrong; everyone knows that. No matter what the elders tell me, it's obvious the only reason I was "chosen" was because I was the right age and the least likely to object. If I'd drowned today, I'm sure they would have found a replacement easily enough.

People keep telling me what an honor it is, but they're only saying that to try and make me feel better. There are six clans on Skye and none of them has allowed marriage for over a century, so I'm going to be the only married person on the whole island. Not even Maighstir Ross could hide his disdain for what is going to happen. No one is going to want anything to do with me afterward, I'm sure of it. I'll be nothing more than a walking reminder of our clan's weakness.

Clann-a-Tuath has always been proud, standing strong against our enemies and our allies, both on the Isle of Skye and over the sea. So why compromise our beliefs now?

There is definitely more to this union than the elders are letting on. Something has made them desperate. Something out of their control. Whatever it is, it can only be something bad.

AGATHA

"I TOLD YOU FROM THE START IT WAS A TERRIBLE IDEA."

"That sort of talking is not going to get us anywhere, Clyde."

"All I'm saying is that this was always going to happen, and if we keep her up there, it's only a matter of time before it happens again."

"I agree, she's proved that she's a liability in positions of trust."

"More than that, we need to discuss punishment. The girl ought to be punished."

There are lots of voices talking so it's hard to know who is saying what. I'm not supposed to be in the elder bothan because it's out of bounds which means I can't go there. That's why I'm hiding. I will be in big trouble if they find me.

"Surely stripping her of her duty would be punishment enough?"

"Come now, it was an honest mistake. She didn't mean any harm." It is Maighstir Ross who said that, I think. He is the clan chief for this moon, which means he is the most important one. There are seven elders and every moon they change who is the chief which is to be fair.

"I know she didn't *mean* any harm, but that didn't stop her from causing it. We're lucky no one drowned. Not to mention the loss of the boat. It'll take the Wasps weeks to replace it."

"Clyde's right. We're living in a dangerous time. We can't chance anything—or any*one*—putting this clan at risk. Especially after what happened to Clann-na-Bruthaich."

"We're not sure what happened to Clann-na-Bruthaich. Not entirely."

"We *are* sure: they were taken by deamhain. Which means we are exposed here. Exposed and vulnerable. Particularly with *her* as our first line of defense." That was Maighstir Clyde who said that. I don't like him very much because sometimes he is a mean one.

"We always knew it was a risk to make Agatha a Hawk, but let us remind ourselves that she has always been one of the most loyal and hardworking members of this clan," Maighstir Ross says.

"She's also a *retarch*, and nearly killed twelve people."

"Clyde, that's enough."

For the first time since the meeting started, everyone is quiet. It's true, I did nearly kill that many people. I didn't mean to. It was only a mistake. Now the elders are deciding what to do with me. I'm here because I want to know. I came up after morning meal when no one was looking. No one lives in this bothan. It is only for meetings. That is why they built it away from the other ones and on the hill. It is a circle shape and all that is inside it is seven chairs and the big chest that is where I am hiding in. The chest had lots of things in it before so I had to take them all out first and hide them outside. That was a clever plan. Then I got into the chest and waited. The elders did not come for a long time so I was waiting a long time. I do not fit very well and it is uncomfortable. I'm glad I left Milkwort in the hole in my bed. He likes it there and he is safe there. If I'd brought him with me he would be squished like me.

"There are three separate matters here," Maighstir Ross says. "Whether we let the girl remain within her duty, what we would do with her if she were to be stripped of it, and, regardless of both, whether a punishment is deemed necessary or appropriate. Let us start with the issue of her duty."

"There has been no recorded instance of a clan member being stripped of their duty, except in cases of exile."

"Can't she remain a Hawk in name, on a quieter section of the wall, perhaps, under heavier supervision?" Maybe it was Maistreas Sorcha who said that.

"She was supposedly under Lenox's supervision yesterday, and look where that got us."

"And can we really spare a pair of Hawk eyes watching over her? They're spread thinly enough as it is. If the threat of the deamhain is real, we need all eyes on the sea."

Why is he saying deamhain?

"So what are the alternatives?" says someone. I don't know who.

"She could retrain as a Wrasse," says Maistreas Eilionoir, I think.

"The Wrasses wouldn't have her—she's clumsy and incompetent. Isn't that why we stuck her up on the wall in the first place? In the hope she might fall off and do us all a favor?"

What did he say? That's not right. It is hard to hear in the chest.

"That kind of talk is not helpful, Clyde."

"I'm not going to apologize for saying what we were all thinking. We didn't make her a Hawk because we thought she'd actually be good at it. We wanted her out of the way. The clan's disgrace. Finally, she has lived up to her reputation."

My eyes are starting to get angry. What he is saying cannot be true. I am a good Hawk, I am a good Hawk.

"I am a good Hawk!"

I have said it out loud because I couldn't stop it. Now no one is talking. There are footsteps walking and then the lid opens. Light from the room is bright. I blink and Maistreas Sorcha is there.

"It appears we have company," she says. Maistreas Sorcha is the youngest one of the elders. She is pretty and nice. She helps me out of the chest which is hard for me because I am tangled.

I step out. All the elders are looking at me. I don't like it so I look up at the ceiling. It is covered in shadows all moving about like they are shadow things. They are not shadow things though because if they were we would be dead. They'd rip us all apart. That is what the shadow things do and you can't even stop them. Also the shadow things are only on the mainland and not on Skye so they wouldn't be here.

Maighstir Ross talks. "Agatha. This is unexpected. I presume you are aware that entry to the elder bothan is strictly prohibited to all but the clan elders?" is what he says.

"I am a g-good Hawk," I say again.

"You have displayed many qualities to attest to that fact, yes," Maistreas Sorcha says, "but you have also put many lives at stake, and that cannot be overlooked." She turns to the elders and then she says, "What should we do with her?"

"Since she's here, she may as well stay to hear her fate," says Maighstir Ross. He looks at me and points his finger. "But you are to remain silent at all times."

I open my mouth to say that's not fair but Maighstir Ross gives me a cross look so I don't say it. Maighstir Clyde snorts. "If you're keeping her here to hold my tongue, Ross, you can think again."

"The time for talk is over," says Maighstir Ross. "The fire is ready. Agatha, make yourself useful and hand me the *bhòt*-stones from inside the chest."

The *bhòt*-stones are what they use for deciding.

"I need to—get them," I say, and I go outside. It is dark outside now so it is hard for me to find the things where I hid them but I do.

"I hid them in the heather," I say when I come back in. I think maybe they will tell me that was a clever plan, but they don't. Maighstir Ross takes the bag with the stones in and then I sit on the chest because there is nowhere else for me to sit.

Maighstir Ross stands and empties the bag of stones into the fire. There are some black ones and some gray ones. He sits down and he says to me, "The flames have died down, but the ashes are still hot, so selecting a stone is a painful experience. This is to ensure that votes are cast only by those who are resolute in their decision. The elders of Clann-a-Tuath have voted in this way for many generations." Then he says to the other elders, "Matter the first. Concerning whether Agatha-Cabhar, here present, ought to be punished for the destruction of one Angler fishing boat plus contents, as well as risking the lives of no fewer than twelve Anglers on board said boat. All those wishing to cast, do so now."

Maighstir Clyde stands up first. He looks into the fire and then puts his hand in at the bottom and takes out a stone. He does not show that it hurts. He has chosen a black one. He throws the stone to the side and sits back down. Some of the other elders do the same thing. The stones that they choose are gray ones. After a bit, Maighstir Ross says, *"Na clachan bhòtaidh deiseil?"*

"Tha bhòtaidh deiseil. Dearbh dhuinn an fhìrinn," say the other elders together. I don't understand it because it is the old language.

Maighstir Ross looks down at the pile of stones and then says, "At a count of one in favor, four against, two abstaining, it is agreed that no punishment shall befall her. *Leig leis.*"

"Leig leis," says everyone else.

Maighstir Ross looks at me and I think he is happy. I am happy that I will not be punished too. He picks up the stones and puts them back into the fire.

"Matter the second," he says. "Concerning whether Agatha-Cabhar, here present, ought to be stripped of her Hawk duty. All those wishing to cast, do so now."

I am not happy anymore. I want to speak or scream maybe, but I have made the promise to be quiet. I am a Hawk. They cannot

23

make me not be a Hawk. They cannot do it, please they cannot.

Maighstir Clyde is the first one to choose a stone from the fire again. The other elders choose their ones too. The only person who doesn't do it is Maistreas Eilionoir. She stays in her seat, watching everyone and me.

"*Seo clach-bhòt ullamh?*" Maighstir Ross says afterward, and everyone answers again. He looks at the new pile of stones. This time they are all black ones.

"At a vote of six in favor, one abstaining, it is agreed that as of this moment Agatha-former-Cabhar is no longer recognized as a Hawk of Clann-a-Tuath. *Leig leis.*"

"*Leig leis,*" everyone says.

What? No. I stand up. They can't do that.

"You can't do that," I shout. "You can't do that!" My teeth are aching.

"Agatha." Maighstir Ross's voice is calm. "I allowed you to stay in the hope that through witnessing the process, you would have more of an understanding of how our decisions are made, and the finality of the outcomes."

"But you can't," I say again. "I am a good Hawk, I am a g-good Hawk."

I need to throw something. I grab a cup and a blanket and everything I can find and I throw them. I don't care who they hit or if they go in the fire. Hands are trying to get me but I won't let them. I pick up the big chest at the bottom and turn it over and it knocks the chairs and they fall. There is shouting. I don't care. I pull and scream and push. Maighstir Clyde is in front of me. He is so quick that I do not know what he is doing until he does it. He punches me in the face and I fall to the floor.

My head hurts and there is blood out of my nose.

The bothan spins.

Then nothing.

JAIME

THE NEXT MORNING, THE HERBISTS AGREE I'M WELL enough to leave. I shove on my boots and run all the way to the Wasps' creation site. I've always been drawn to the place. It's where they make and repair everything the clan needs, from weapons and clothes to beds and cooking utensils. Of course, right now they're all busy working on the new boat. I loiter on the outskirts until one of the Wasps calls out to me.

"What is it, boy?" He's a broad man with ruddy cheeks and grubby fingers. I can't recall his name.

"Maighstir Ross said I could come," I say.

"Speak up, I can barely hear you." Everything he says comes out with a chuckle.

"I'm here to watch," I say a little louder. "Maighstir Ross said it was okay."

"Well, you're not going to see much from way over there." He beckons me and I jog toward him, a smile creeping into the corners of my mouth. "I'm Donal," he says. His small mouth is lost somewhere in the depths of his bright orange beard.

"Jaime," I reply.

"So you want to be a Wasp, eh?"

"No, I'm an Angler." I swallow the word. "I thought if I watch you make the boat it might help me become a better Angler."

"Okay," says Donal in a way that suggests he doesn't quite believe me. "Well, stick with me, lad. I'll show you everything you need to know."

I spend the whole day with Donal and the other Wasps, watching with wide eyes as they forge nails, sew new sails, and shape the wood for the hull. I marvel at their skill, and Donal repays my enthusiasm by explaining everything he does. I'm itching to join in and help. Being with the Wasps is completely different from being with the Anglers. I'm on land for one thing—which immediately makes it better—but it's also much easier to relate to their way of working. They think about every job they do in great detail first, taking their time to consider how best to solve problems and make improvements. I know I'd make a better Wasp than an Angler. If it were up to me, I would change duties in a heartbeat, but of course there is no possibility of that.

Late in the afternoon, everyone stops what they're doing at the sound of a commotion from the Southern Gate. One of the chimes is ringing, but I'm not sure which. I've never been that good at recognizing them.

"What do you think it is?" I ask Donal. He is standing up straight, the hammer he was wielding hanging limp at his side. His nose twitches as he strains his eyes.

"It's the Scavengers," he says. "Looks like they've returned."

The Scavengers! They were sent to find out what happened to Clann-na-Bruthaich, one of the other clans on Skye. There's a rumor going around that the whole clan disappeared without a trace. We're not supposed to know about it, but everybody does.

"Go and see if you can overhear what they say," says Donal.

"Oh," I say. "But it's not *dùth* to stop work before evening meal."

Donal chuckles. "We're not long off finishing, and I won't tell if you don't. Besides, you said it yourself: you're not working, you're *observing*." He gives me a conspiratorial wink.

I don't really want to go, but at the same time I want Donal to like me. He makes the decision for me by placing his large hand between my shoulder blades and giving me a gentle pat. "If you hear anything, come back and let us know."

I nod, scrambling over the framework of the new boat. The Southern Gate is a short walk away. By the time I reach it, the Scavs are already inside. I keep my distance. They glance in my direction, so I duck down behind an old well. The ground is wet with mud, which seeps through my trousers, soaking my knees.

Maistreas Sorcha has come to meet them. She clasps each of their fists but doesn't speak. None of them do. A look passes among them. Maistreas Sorcha beckons them to a communal bothan, right next to where I'm hiding.

They're going to pass right by me! If they catch me hiding, they'll think I'm spying. Which I suppose I am. What was I thinking? This was a terrible idea. I should leave now, before they get too close, but my body refuses to move. They're drawing closer. I slide down farther into the mud and press myself against the curved stone of the well. It stinks of wet algae. If I can slip around it as they pass, maybe I can avoid being seen. They're no more than a few yards away. Now or never. I dig my nails into the gaps between the stones and shuffle to the right as Maistreas Sorcha and the Scavengers approach from the left. I drag myself around, little by little, trying not to make a sound. My palms sweat rivers.

The group passes on the opposite side of the well, talking in low whispers. I strain my ears for any scraps. I hear the phrase "Raasay were telling the truth," and someone else says, ". . . even worse than expected."

Their conversation moves into the bothan. I wait until I hear the door shut before letting go of my breath. I glance up to the wall, hoping I wasn't spotted by one of the Hawks. They're all looking outward. I've gotten away with it. Never again. I scramble to my feet and hurry to my bothan to change out of my mud-streaked clothes. All the while, I can't stop thinking about what the Scavengers said.

What could they have found that was worse than expected? And why did they all look so scared?

AT EVENING MEAL, I SEARCH THE TABLES FOR AILEEN, but she's not there. She must still be walking back from Kilmaluag Bay. I collect my food and approach the long wooden benches where we eat. As I walk past the Wasps' table, a large group of them bursts into laughter. I slow down and smile at Donal and a few of the others. They nod at me and smile back. I'm about to stop and tell Donal what I overheard, but he has already launched into a new conversation.

I move on to the long Angler table. Sitting in the middle is a group of Anglers from one of the other boats, but I don't know any of them, so I sit at the far end on my own and start to eat. Someone grabs my shoulders from behind.

"Where've you been?" The voice is right in my ear, deliberately taking me by surprise. I start choking on a mouthful of stew, and bits of it spray out over the table. "You should really learn some table manners."

I swallow and reach behind me to swipe at Aileen. "Don't do that!" I say.

She effortlessly dodges my arm and then slides in next to me.

"So how come you didn't join us at Kilmaluag Bay? Wanted another day in bed, did you?"

"No, I've been with the Wasps." I can't help feeling a little bit smug.

"What?"

"Maighstir Ross said I could watch them make the new boat."

"You sneaky little . . . Wish I'd thought of that! The trek to Kilmaluag took forever. Was fun being outside the enclave, though. On land, I mean." She tucks her rusty curls behind her ears. She always does that when she's excited. "So really, it's you that missed out. Although I suppose you'll get to leave the enclave for the Ceremony." She covers her mouth as soon as she says it. "Sorry. Forgot we're not talking about that anymore," she says from behind her hand.

"The Scavs came back," I say, changing the subject.

"Really! What did they find?"

"Well, we haven't been told anything yet, but"—I lower my voice—"I was behind the old well as they came past and—"

"You were spying?" Aileen interrupts me.

"No. Well, maybe a little."

"Wait a minute! Who are you and what have you done with the real Jaime?"

"Very funny. Anyway, I didn't hear much, but they all looked pretty worried. They said something about Raasay 'telling the truth' and that what they found was 'worse than expected.'"

"What do you think that means?"

"I don't know, but it doesn't sound good." I chew on the inside of my mouth. "Do you think we're safe here?"

"Of course we are." There's a lump in my throat that refuses to be swallowed.

"But what if what happened to Clann-na-Bruthaich happens to us too?"

"Wait. You're worrying about something and you don't even know what it is? That's bad, even for you!"

She's right; I know I shouldn't be panicking. I can't help it.

"Hey, it's all right." Aileen places her hand on mine and gives it a squeeze. "Trust me, we're safe. We have the best defenses on the island."

That's true.

"There's something else I've been wondering . . ." I say. "They mentioned Raasay; do you think all this has something to do with the Ceremony?"

Aileen presses her lips together and wobbles her head as if to say, *I'm not allowed to talk about it.*

"Stop it," I say, giving her a gentle shove. "If I start the conversation, it's allowed."

She breathes out a puff of air. "So many rules . . ."

"So what do you think?"

"I don't know, Jaime. We've talked about this so much, and we always end up going around in the same circles. Who knows what makes the elders decide the things they do? All I know is that they have our best interests at heart, and we have to trust them."

I do trust them. Of course I do. But that doesn't mean I can't ask them about it. I gulp down the remains of my stew and stand up from the table.

"Where are you going?"

"If the Ceremony is happening, I have the right to know why. The real truth. Not just what they've told me." I hand my empty bowl to the nearest Wrasse. "I'll see you later."

It's a clear night, and the light from the moon spills through the trees as I cross the enclave. I pass two goats chewing on grass, and give them each a gentle rub behind the ears. The late summer air is full of the sweet, nutty scent of wild gorse flowers. I breathe it in until it fills my lungs. I've always loved that smell.

I reach Maistreas Eilionoir's bothan and am about to knock when I hear people talking inside. The first voice belongs to Maistreas Eilionoir, and the second is instantly recognizable as that of the girl who set our boat on fire, Agatha.

"I'm afraid what you want is irrelevant, my dear." Maistreas Eilionoir's guttural rasp contains no trace of sympathy. "It has been decided and there is no other option."

"But I need to be on the w-wall. It's my—my duty," Agatha replies. I strain to catch her words; it's difficult to understand her sometimes.

"Not anymore, it's not. You can either accept the proposal or face exile from the clan. The choice is yours. I'll expect you here tomorrow at first light. Good evening."

Their conversation comes to an abrupt end, and Agatha storms out, swinging the door into my face. I stumble backward, trip on the root of a tree, and fall to the ground.

"J-Jaime," she says. "I didn't—see you. I didn't know you were there." Her tone is defensive, almost hostile.

"It's okay, Agatha," I say.

She tries to help me up but stands too close, making it even harder for me to get to my feet.

"I'm sorry I made you fall."

"Hey, don't worry about it." I smile at her, and her expression changes from remorse to exultation.

"Oh, I'm good. I mean I'm happy. That you're okay."

She reaches out and strokes my arm, which is a bit weird.

"Have a good evening."

"You were on the b-boat," she says with some effort. The look of guilt has returned, fringed with an angry scowl.

"I was," I say, smiling to let her know there are no hard feelings.

"I didn't know it was you," she says. "I heard the chime, but I thought it was a-a different one. I didn't know it, so it w-wasn't my fault and I was only doing my—duty."

"It was a really good shot," I say, focusing on the positive. "If we were an enemy boat, we wouldn't have stood a chance."

The smile that erupts on her face is perhaps the most genuine I have ever seen.

"It's true. You're right, Jaime, you're right."

"I need to speak to Maistreas Eilionoir now. Have a good evening."

"Okay, J-Jaime, I'll go now. Goodbye, Jaime."

She walks away, toward the Gathering. I can see why people get annoyed at her, but it's not fair, really. Besides, from what I just overheard, the elders have stripped her of her duty. That, in addition to the way she was born, probably makes her the one person in the clan even more unfortunate than me.

I knock on the door, and Maistreas Eilionoir barks at me to enter. She's sitting cross-legged on the floor, reading a small leather-bound book. None of the other elders read much, but Maistreas Eilionoir insists that it's important. It's because of her that we're all taught how to do it when we're young. I wait for her to finish her page.

When she looks up, the light from the fire casts shadows across her face. It fills her crevices with dark lines, making her look impossibly old.

"Jaime-Iasgair." She chews my name, her mouth a tight line. Despite her irritable nature, I've always found her the most approachable of the elders.

"Good evening, Maistreas Eilionoir," I say. "I wondered if I might have a word with you?"

"Well, you're here, aren't you?"

"It's about the Ceremony. . . ."

"I worked that much out for myself. What about it?"

"I can't stop wondering why it's happening."

"Maighstir Ross told you: to form stronger ties with the Isle of Raasay."

"I know, but why do we need them? Why now? We've survived without their help for centuries." She's going to reprimand me. I shouldn't be questioning her like this.

Maistreas Eilionoir licks her lips. It does not make them look any less dry.

"What you have been requested to do is no small ask; I appreciate that. And you're a smart boy. So I'm not going to lie to you by pretending there's nothing more at stake than what you have already been told. There are forces at work that threaten every aspect of our existence."

"Are you talking about what happened to Clann-na-Bruthaich?"

"What do you know of that?" she snaps.

"Nothing really . . . just rumors . . ." Maistreas Eilionoir scowls at me. I avoid her glare. "Is it true the whole clan disappeared?"

For a long time, Maistreas Eilionoir says nothing at all. Then her eyes widen a little, forcing back the wrinkles that imprison them.

"I cannot speak of Clann-na-Bruthaich, but I can assure you that what happened to them is most definitely not going to happen to us. The Ceremony is an added precaution; in exchange for your hand in marriage, the Chiefs of Raasay have agreed to provide us with several long-range weapons, which will greatly bolster our defenses."

"And what does Raasay get in return?"

"What they have always wanted: to feel superior to us."

"That's it?"

"We have also agreed to assist each other should the situation arise, although the likelihood of our needing their help is extremely slim. United we are stronger. That is all there is to it."

"So the union is being created out of fear?"

"Clann-a-Tuath does not succumb to fear." A sudden chill fills the room. "I will say no more on the subject. In many ways, I have already said too much."

But you've hardly said anything at all, I think.

"And you're not to breathe a word of this to anyone," she continues. "It would cause panic, and that's the last thing we need."

"Yes, Maistreas."

"Was there anything else?"

I still have so many questions, but it no longer feels like the right time to ask them.

"No," I say.

"Then close the door properly on the way out; it's letting in a draft."

AGATHA

I AM LATE AND SHE IS NOT HAPPY. MY NOSE STILL HURTS from when Maighstir Clyde hit it which was mean.

"Get inside," she says, and I do.

I am late because I went to the wall. I wasn't supposed to do it but I did it. When Flora saw me, I told her the elders changed their minds and decided I could come back and she said okay and was happy. Sometimes lying is okay when it is a small lie. I was doing good walking and good looking on the wall to do my duty. Then Lenox saw me.

"Hello, Agatha," he said.

"Good morning, Lenox," I said, to be nice.

"I don't think you should be here, should you?"

"It's—fine," I told him. "The elders changed their minds and said I could—I could come back to the wall."

"We both know that's not true," he said.

That's when I ran. I am not fast at running so I didn't get very far and Lenox got me. He frowned at me with his big eyebrows and his big nose.

"Look, Agatha, this can go one of two ways. Either you come with me to Maistreas Eilionoir's bothan—which I know is where you're supposed to be—or I sling you over my shoulder and carry you there kicking and screaming. You're not light, so I'm really hoping you choose the first option." I stared at him and didn't know which one to choose. Then he said, "If you can prove to the elders that you are good at doing what you're told, maybe they'll change their minds and let you back on the wall."

He is right. I'm still a Hawk. I'm just having a bit of a break. If I show them I am good they will change their minds. I know it. I also didn't want him to pick me up so I said, "Okay, Lenox, I'll go."

When I am inside Maistreas Eilionoir's bothan she says to me, "You're probably wondering why I convinced the other elders to let you spend your days with me." I am not wondering that. "You could be a real asset to this clan, but you lack discipline and self-control. They will be our first lessons."

"Will you t-teach me how to use the—crossbow under your—b-bed?"

"Absolutely not. Sit."

I sit on the chair that is next to the table. She reaches to a high shelf and takes down a jar. Then she tips all the things inside onto the table in front of me. It is hundreds of seeds that come out.

"Before I was an elder, I was a Reaper, as you may know. Early spring was always my favorite time of year because that's when we started sowing seeds. It never ceased to amaze me that such tiny crumbs could grow into plants big enough to feed us all winter. This is a collection of some of my favorites. Line them up on the table from smallest to largest, and do not move from that seat until you have finished."

"But they're all the same," I say.

"Then your first task is to realize that they are not."

Without saying anything else, she leaves and I am alone. I look at the seeds. I do not want to sort seeds. It is boring and not important. I am not doing it. I want to throw the stupid jar on the floor and smash it. But they will not let me back on the wall if I do that so I don't.

I stand up and look around the bothan at all the things in it. It is a small one. There is the table and a bed and the corner where her fire is. Next to the bed there are lots of books. They look old and falling apart. I touch them on their sides but I do not pick them up. I am not good at reading. They are from the mainland I think. That's where most books came from. They used to make them there before everyone was dead. Only terror beasts and shadow things live there now. It is a very bad place.

I go back to the table and look at the seeds again. Some of them are a bit different. I pick up a few of them and feed them to Milkwort, who is in my pocket. He likes them. It makes me feel better because Milkwort is happy and now there are less seeds to sort too. Maistreas Eilionoir can't find out that he is here. She thinks I got rid of him but I didn't.

I am in the bothan all day and Maistreas Eilionoir does not come back until it is nearly dark. Some of the seeds are in piles I have sorted, even though I still think it is stupid and not important.

Maistreas Eilionoir nods at the seeds and I think she is happy, but then she wipes her hand across the table and all the seeds fall on the floor. I jump to my feet.

"What did you do that for?" I shout.

"Remember who you are talking to," she says and her voice is calm.

"I spent all day doing that and now—now you've—ruined it." I grab the edge of the table and turn it over. I don't care if it breaks. I pick up the chair like I might throw it.

Maistreas Eilionoir holds up one finger and shakes her head a bit. I stare at her and she stares at me. My breathing is all fast and loud. I put the chair down.

"Good. We will not get anywhere until you learn to control your temper," Maistreas Eilionoir says. "When the anger comes, you must learn to let it fade. Pick up all the seeds and then go. We are done for today."

Even though I want to scream at her, I do what she says. The seeds are small and hard to pick up so it takes a long time to do it. When Maistreas Eilionoir is not looking, I put more seeds in my pocket to feed Milkwort later. That will teach her for being so mean.

❧

THE NEXT DAY MAISTREAS EILIONOIR STILL FROWNS AT me, even though I am there on time. She takes the jar and pours the seeds out again. I have to spend all day sorting them again which is even more boring and even more stupid. And the worse thing, before I can finish she comes back in and messes them all up again.

"Why do you keep—doing that?" I shout. I want to hit her I am so angry.

"Let the anger fade," Maistreas Eilionoir says.

"No," I say, because it is her fault and she shouldn't do what she did.

"Breathe in," she says, "as deep as you can. When you breathe out, let the anger out with it."

"I don't want to," I say. I won't do it. It is a stupid thing to do.

"I'm trying to help you, Agatha," she says.

"No, you're not. You're being mean and it's not fair. Why do you—why do I have to sort your st-stupid—seeds anyway?"

"Some things we must do simply because we are told to do them, even though they may seem meaningless or unfair. How can I be expected to hone your talent before you have demonstrated self-restraint?"

I am so cross that it takes a while to hear what she has said.

"What t-talent?" I ask. I breathe out from my nose.

"We will discuss it once you prove to me that you are ready. Now clear up this mess and leave. It's been a long day and I have no desire for company."

I do not want to put the seeds back in the jar but I do it. Some of them I stamp on when Maistreas Eilionoir is not looking. Then I leave and I do not even say goodbye.

I'm late for evening meal so I walk quickly to the Gathering. Two days ago, Maighstir Clyde caught me sitting at the Hawk table and made me move. Now I have to sit at the table with the children. I hate it there because I am not a child.

Tonight some of the children have all colors on their fingers.

They have been painting flags for the Ceremony because I saw them. The enclave looks pretty with the flags flapping. You're supposed to wash your hands before you eat and I know that and they should know it too.

When I am finished, I stand up and I bump into a boy called Wiley because I didn't see he was there.

"Look where you're going, you fat *retarch*," he says.

His friends all laugh.

"I'm not," I say.

Wiley sticks his tongue between his teeth and says "I'm not" which is pretending to be me. His friends laugh again. I want to hit them all for laughing because it is mean but I don't because I think maybe they will hurt me back. To stop from doing it I run to my bothan. It is one of the Hawk bothans where I still am. They'd better not make me move because I won't.

There's no one there when I get inside. What the boy said is still in my head. It makes me nearly cry but of course I don't. I go to the wash corner and pick up the mirror piece. I'm not supposed to look at myself but when no one is around I do it because I'm pretty. My hair is long and dark like seaweed. I pick up the brush and I brush it. I like my hair because it makes me look so pretty.

After I have brushed it, I hold the mirror away from me to see if I am fat. I do look bigger than before, and not because I am older because I am still not tall which I know because I measure on the door to see if I've grown. I press my arms and stomach and also my cheeks and my breasts. I smile at the mirror. It's okay,

I'm still pretty. I wonder if Jaime thinks I'm pretty too. Jaime is so kind. That is why I like him. But soon he has to do the Ceremony which is to marry the girl from the Raasay Island. I don't know why he has to do it. It is bad to be married. After it has happened no one will like him anymore and I won't like him either. Unless I can stop it from happening. That is a clever plan. I will do that for Jaime and then he will be so happy and we will be friends.

The door to the bothan opens and Flora and some of the other Hawks come in. I put the mirror down and give Flora a hug because she is my friend. I ask about what happened on the wall and they tell me.

"Do you want to play *riosg* with us?" asks Flora, and I say yes because I do. It is a game with the stones and it is so much fun and I laugh. One time I even win it and when I do Flora says, "Hey, Aggie, you're getting good," which is kind and also true.

WHEN I GO BACK TO MAISTREAS EILIONOIR'S BOTHAN THE next morning I am not happy because I know she will make me sort the stupid seeds again and I know she will mess them up afterward. But I have to do it so they'll let me be a Hawk again. Then I think that maybe she only messes them because I don't finish doing it quick enough. Yes, that is it. Okay today I will be the quickest ever so she doesn't do it.

I work so hard for the whole day to finish all the seeds and I do it. They are in a long line like a snake back and forth on the table all done. When Maistreas Eilionoir comes in I think she will tell me well done and be happy but she doesn't. She pushes the seeds on the floor again. All the work that I worked so hard to do it. I scream my loudest ever.

"Agatha," she says, but I do not stop screaming. I push the table and I kick it and it is sore on my foot and I kick it again. She says I have to do the breathing but I am not doing stupid breathing.

Maistreas Eilionoir steps over the table and takes both of my hands and holds them. I stop screaming then because it is making my throat hurt. Maistreas Eilionoir is looking at me. The hot inside starts to go away.

"Are you calm now?" she asks me.

I nod.

"Sometimes anger clouds our vision and leads us to poor choices," she says. "Letting go of that anger gives us strength."

I don't even know what that means.

She is going to make me pick up all the seeds again I know it so I let go of her hands and do it. When I am finished she says, "Thank you. You may go now."

I walk toward the door and then I stop and turn. "What does a *retarch* mean?" I ask her.

She looks at me and her face is hard. "Who used that word?" she asks.

"A boy called me it. And Maighstir Clyde said it when I was hi-hiding in the chest."

"Maighstir Clyde was wrong to say such a thing. As was the boy. Tell me his name and I will see to it that he is punished."

"But what does it—mean?"

Maistreas Eilionoir's mouth is all together and she is thinking.

"Sit next to me, child."

I am not a child, but I do not mind it when Maistreas Eilionoir calls me it because I know she says it to be nice and not to be mean. We sit on the floor and my legs are crossed like her legs are crossed.

"It is a word to describe someone who is different, used by people who do not understand what it means to be different," she tells me.

"It is a b-bad word?" I ask.

"The way it was said to you, yes."

"So why did they say it?"

"Have you ever noticed ways in which you are not the same as other people in this clan, Agatha?"

"I'm not very—fast at running," I say.

"That's one difference, yes, but I'm thinking more about the way you look and the way you think. You're fifteen now, aren't you?"

"Yes."

"And do you think you are the same as the other fifteen-year-olds in the clan?"

"I think my hair is pretty," I tell her, because I don't know what the question is.

"It is, yes," she says, and she strokes it a little bit. It is a nice thing that she says and it makes me smile.

She does not say anything else, so I think our talking is finished, even though she still has not told me what a *retarch* means. I stand up and tell Maistreas Eilionoir good night. When I reach the door, she says, "Is the vole with you?" She says it in a whisper voice.

I must have heard her wrong. Does she mean Milkwort? I am not supposed to have him.

"What?" I say.

"Don't make me ask you again. If anyone overhears us, we'll both be in a lot of trouble."

It is true. We will both be in bad trouble. Animals are for eating, not for keeping in your pocket, and definitely not for talking to. This must be a trap or a test. I need to have a plan but I don't have a plan.

"Put it on the table," she orders me.

"Put w-what on the table?" I ask. I think she wants to hurt him.

"Don't play fool, girl."

"I don't have him anymore." It is a lie but I have to say it.

She looks at me and is not happy. "Do you really want to be sorting seeds for the rest of your life?"

I don't know what the seeds has to do with it. Maybe because I fed him some. I know I don't want to do them anymore. I put my hand into the pocket where he is.

"His name is M-Milkwort," I say, and I lift him out. I keep him in my hands so he is safe to protect him.

"What can he do?"

"He likes to eat bread," I say, because I can't say what I shouldn't say.

"Do you talk to him?"

"Um, maybe a little bit."

"And does he talk back to you?"

I don't know how to answer that.

"You need to trust me, Agatha, and know that I am here to help you."

"But animals can't talk," I say.

Maistreas Eilionoir looks at me like she thinks I'm lying.

She walks over to the table where there is a mug of half-drunk tea. She pulls off a button from the top she's wearing and places it at the opposite end of the table.

"Tell him to pick up the button and put it in the tea."

"Why?" I ask. I don't know why she wants her button in the tea.

"Now is not the time for questions."

I put Milkwort on the table. It will be easy for him, but also I'm not sure if I should show it. I take a breath.

"P-put the b-button in the tea, please, Milkwort."

As soon as I have said it, he runs to the button and picks it up in his claws. Then he puts it between his teeth and carries it to the mug. He has to climb up the side of the mug to reach. When his head is over the top, he drops the button in it.

Maistreas Eilionoir's eyes are wide. "Well, I never did," she says.

"Please don't kill him," I beg.

"Of course I'm not going to kill him," she says.

"And don't kill me either. I didn't mean to do it."

"Be quiet. Keep this between the two of us, and no one is going to get hurt. I took a big risk on you, Agatha, but I've never once regretted it. And I have a feeling it's about to pay off."

I have no idea what she is talking about.

JAIME

I WAKE UP WITH SUNLIGHT ON MY FACE, WHICH IS A RARITY, even at this time of year. I stretch underneath the extra blanket, enjoying its warmth. It is still early, and the only sound outside is the chirruping of a few songbirds.

Then I remember. The heat of the sun turns stifling, and my head starts to spin. I throw off the blankets and cross to the vat to splash my face with cold water. Aileen sees that I'm awake and comes over to join me. Her eyes are bright, and her hair hangs in a graceful mess.

"Good morning," she says, slinging a lazy arm around my shoulders. "So, today's the big day."

"It is indeed."

"How are you feeling?"

"I've felt better."

"You never know; maybe you'll like her."

I don't reply. Whether I like her or not is beside the point. She's only nine. Five years younger than me. A child.

48

"Listen," she says, "if she turns out to be that annoying, we'll just push her off the wall and be done with it, okay?"

Despite my mood, I can't help smiling.

"Here, this is for you." She chucks me a small parcel, loosely wrapped in a piece of dirty cloth.

"What is it?" I ask.

"Open it up and find out, why don't you? I would have wrapped it up better, but I figured it wasn't really worth it just for you." She pokes out the tip of her tongue.

I flash her a scathing look, then remove the contents of the package. It is a bracelet, formed from three strips of clunky metal.

"Do you like it?"

"It's beautiful. Did you make it?"

"I got one of the Wasps to help, but mainly it was me."

I slip the bracelet on. It's a little loose around my skinny wrist, but not so much that it'll fall off.

"Thanks." I smile. "I love it." I run my finger along the inter-locking weave.

"What's wrong?" asks Aileen when I don't look back up.

"Nothing," I say, forcing a smile.

"You're worrying again."

"You know me. It's what I do best."

"I've told you before: nothing is going to change. No one will care that you're married. *I* won't care, and my opinion's the one that matters most. You're doing something great, Jaime. For the whole clan."

"But no one knows that. You're the only person I've told about the deal with Raasay."

"Yes, but everyone trusts the elders; they know it's happening for a good reason. No one is going to be anything but grateful."

I just can't see it that way.

"Do you remember when we were little and we used to sneak into the cookboth and steal sweetmeats?" Aileen says.

I smile. "You mean when you *made* me sneak in and steal sweetmeats?"

"I didn't hear you complaining when you were stuffing your face afterward! You used to nearly wet yourself every time, convinced we were going to get caught."

"That is definitely not true."

"And did we ever get caught?"

"No. What's your point?"

"That I'm always right. So if I tell you everything's going to be fine, everything's going to be fine. Okay?"

"Okay."

"Good. Now give me a hug."

I wrap my arms around her, and she squeezes me tight. For those brief few moments, nothing else matters. I'm not thinking about the future or the past. All I feel is safe.

"I should start getting ready," I say, breaking away from her. "I have to meet the girl's parents at morning meal."

"Remember to be nice," she says, flicking my ear.

"Ow!" I flick her back, in the middle of her forehead.

"You really want to do this?" She starts pinching my arms. I squirm away, but she soon has me in a headlock. She's always been able to beat me in a fight.

"Okay, okay, I surrender!"

She lets me go. We're both laughing, out of breath.

"I'm always going to be here for you, Jaime. You know that, right? You've got nothing to worry about."

❧

IT'S ONLY A SHORT WALK FROM OUR BOTHAN TO THE Gathering. I drag my heels, making it take twice as long as normal. I spend the time imagining all the ways I could prevent today from happening: feigning illness, hiding in the food store, scaling the wall and running away. . . .

It's not often we allow people from Raasay into our enclave. They're very different from us. They have all sorts of strange ways and weird traditions. Like forcing marriage. Maistreas Sorcha told me about it: as soon as a Raasay girl turns nine, she is allocated a male, whom she is forced to marry. The couple then stays together for the entirety of their lives. Once the girl turns sixteen, they are expected to have children, and any children they have must stay with them until they too are wed. I'll never understand it. I have no idea who birthed me, nor would I want to know. It is *toirmisgte*—forbidden to be spoken about. I wasn't even aware the words *mother* and *father* could apply to a single person until a couple of years ago. In our clan, everyone cares for one another equally. It is much better that way.

When I reach the Gathering, the visitors from Raasay are already there, talking to the elders while they wait for me. They must have left their island before first light. It is only a small group; I assumed there would be more. One of them laughs, with a forced smile. Maighstir Ross spots me coming and breaks off from what he's saying to introduce me.

"Ah, perfect timing. This is Jaime-Iasgair. Jaime, I'd like to introduce you to clan chiefs Balgair MacSween and Conall MacLeod; Ministear Baird and his assistant, Errol; and your betrothed's parents, Hector and Edme."

The names ricochet off me; I'm far too preoccupied with trying to make a good first impression to remember a single one of them.

"Ciamar a tha thu?" says the man who has been identified as my bride-to-be's father.

"Sorry, I don't speak the old language," I say.

"Is duilich seann cheann a chuir air guaillain!" says Maighstir Ross, and everyone laughs. Everyone except me.

During morning meal, I push the food around my bowl and say very little. Afterward, I'm taken by the ministear's assistant to a small storage bothan not far from the central compound. Today it's going to be used as my preparation room. It's gloomy inside, the air heavy with dust. The walls are lined with moldering crates, and cobwebs have overtaken the corners.

The ministear's assistant, who reminds me his name is Errol, tells me to take off all my clothes. He is a willowy man, with sad cheeks and receded hair. I expect him to go out, to give me some privacy, but he doesn't. I turn away from him and start to strip. He watches me while chewing on the sides of his nails. When I am in nothing but my underwear, he tells me to stay where I am and then leaves.

There are no seats in the bothan, so I stand in its center, tracing patterns in the dust with my toe. I catch sight of my reflection in a metal pot. The image is distorted, making me look even skinnier than I already am. My arms hang at my sides like broken tree branches. I do a hundred ground lifts every day, but my muscles refuse to get any bigger.

Errol returns with a large golden jug.

"This water is from Raasay," he says. "It is important we purify you before the Ceremony. Sit."

I squat and let him wash my body with a clammy rag. His fingers crawl all over my skin, tough and meticulous. It takes a great deal of effort not to shudder at his touch. The ritual takes half the morning. By the time he's finished, I am freezing cold and my body glows an unsightly red from all his scrubbing.

"We're done," he says, handing me an orange robe. "Put this on. It's time to go."

I slip it over my shoulders. It is far too long for me, drowning my hands and feet, and the material makes my back prickle. I look ridiculous. I'm going to be laughed at for sure.

Outside the bothan, it is eerily quiet. The clan has already left for wherever the Ceremony is going to happen, leaving only a handful of people behind to keep watch. As we approach the Southern Gate, the Moths who are guarding it widen their eyes when they see what I'm wearing. *It wasn't my choice,* I want to tell them.

"It suits you," one of them calls out.

They wind open the gate and wish me luck as I pass through. The Hawk on top of the wall nods at me and hits all five chimes in succession, creating a soothing chord that echoes across the whole island.

It is the first time I have ever walked outside the enclave. For some reason, the island looks even bigger from this side of the wall.

In every direction, hills and mountains topple over one another in every shade of green, orange, and muddy yellow. Trying to comprehend the expanse of land stretching out before me makes me feel dizzy.

"Come on," says Errol, twisting my elbow to move me forward. "You don't want to be late."

We walk in silence, first east and then south. Something about Errol's surly demeanor makes it impossible to strike up a conversation. I have no idea how he, a visitor to the island, knows which way to go, but he marches on with confidence, at a pace I struggle to keep up with. The land is rough and uneven, full of rogue stones and unexpected puddles. The weather alternates between sweltering sun and miserable rain, like it can't quite make up its mind how best to torture me. Midges hover around me, attracted by the sweat that is gathering under my armpits and behind my knees.

"Where exactly are we going?" I ask after what feels like forever. We're walking up a steep incline, and I have to gather the bottom of the robe to keep the excess material from tripping me. My legs ache, and blisters are starting to form on both of my heels.

"This is the Trotternish Ridge," Errol says. "At the start of time, warring giants carved out this land with mighty hammers. Some say, on the coldest days, you can still hear their ghosts, bellowing across the hills. We'll keep heading south until we reach Quiraing. From there, we will have a view of Raasay. That is where the Ceremony will take place."

The higher we climb, the windier it gets, and I have to keep dropping to my knees to prevent myself from getting blown onto the rocky crag below. It's a shame I can't look up more, because the view is incredible. The mountains rise and fall in unstoppable waves, punctured here and there with sharp-edged precipices and serene lochs.

In the distance, mainland Scotia looms into view like an unwanted spillage. I've always felt uneasy about the mainland, like it's not quite far away enough. Skye is a big island, but the mainland is much, much bigger. It's actually two countries: Scotia in the north and Ingland in the south. Apparently, we used to trade with them, but not anymore. Not since everyone there died. We're lucky we live on an island; otherwise the plague would have killed all of us as well.

As we draw nearer to Quiraing, we pass strange rock formations, which protrude from the ground like broken fingers reaching for the sky. I pause to take them in. They are at least ten times the size of me, mottled gray and covered in soft lichen. Errol tuts, unnecessarily loudly. I pretend I haven't heard, making him tut again, even louder. I roll my eyes and catch up with him.

Just down from the rocks is a wide, open plateau, where everyone is waiting for me. From here, we have a clear view of the nearby Isle of Raasay, a dark cloud on the shimmering water. Members of my clan are standing in a semicircle, and they click their fingers as I approach. The sound is swallowed by a wind that whistles along the escarpment. Aileen peers out from the crowd and gives me a small wave. I want to wave back at her, but I don't.

I take a couple more steps forward. The semicircle splits apart like the mouth of a whale. I close my eyes, and when I open them again, there she is: the girl they are going to make me marry. She has her back to me, but she's wearing the same color robe as I am, so there's no mistaking her. Even from behind she looks far too young. The ministear stands at her side and beckons me to approach. My breath starts coming in short, sharp gasps. I can't do this. It's too much. I need to get out of here. There's no air. I can't breathe. I have to leave. Now.

I do the only thing I can think of: I turn around and run.

JAIME

I DON'T KNOW WHERE I THOUGHT I WAS GOING. I'M SURROUNDED by hundreds of people, none of whom are going to let me pass. I'm trapped. I manage about three strides before Errol catches me by my shoulders. His nails dig into the robe. "None of that," he hisses in my ear. He spins me around and steers me toward the mini-stear. My legs betray me, walking forward without me wanting them to. He positions me back-to-back with the girl. Her shoulders press against my spine and shake with either anticipation or fear. I reach behind and give her fingertips the tiniest squeeze. She squeezes back, and my breathing starts to settle. At least I'm not in this alone.

The Ceremony consists mainly of speech in the old language, so I have no idea what's being said. Only the people from Raasay join in with the responses. My clan stands by and watches in silence. I doubt they understand what's being said either; no one really speaks the old language anymore, except for the elders. On the couple of occasions I glance up and make eye contact, everyone gives me encouraging looks. They're being friendly enough now, but how will they treat me when all of this is over? Will they still think of me as one of them? The sound of the wind rattles in my ears, which helps drown out the ministear's drawl.

Just when I think it is about to end, the ministear is passed a live hare. He holds it by its ears and, with brutal efficiency, plunges a knife deep into its middle. The hare's hind legs spasm for an uncomfortable amount of time until it dies. The ministear then penetrates the creature with his fingers and pulls out its heart. Maybe it's just my imagination, but I swear the heart is still beating as he holds it in his hands. He slices it in two and offers one half to me and the other to the girl.

"With this heart are you joined. In your own hearts, now and forever," he says.

The finality of his words tears through me.

"*Beannachdan oirbh!*" chorus the people from Raasay and a couple of the elders.

The girl reaches out and takes her half of the heart, so I do the same. It is warm and spongy between my fingers. A thin bead of blood creeps down my wrist. The ministear nods at me, leaving no doubt about what I am supposed to do next. Today is full of fun surprises. What if it makes me throw up? Everyone is staring at me. Waiting. I presume the girl has already eaten her piece. I don't think I can do it. I have to. For my clan. For my clan.

I close my eyes and throw the raw heart into my mouth. A burst of sour metal hits my tongue. I do not chew.

As soon as I swallow, a mighty cheer erupts and fists pound the air. My whole clan is prompted into activity, as if they have been told in advance what to do at this point. A dozen hands grab me and throw me high into the air. The sky spins, and then they're carrying me above their heads, back down the narrow ridge. The whole way down I'm consumed with bouts of panic, imagining what would happen if I slipped out of their hands. It would certainly bring a somber end to the day.

Once we're on flatter ground, I'm thrown around with less vigor, and everyone starts chanting an old òran. It's one of my favorites, and I allow myself to be swept away by the words. It tells the story of our ancestors: how they traveled from mainland Scotia centuries ago and overcame many hardships to thrive here on Skye; how they carved out the entire enclave with their bare hands and built the wall that now protects us; how they established a new, superior way of living, free from the constraints of the corrupt Scotian monarchy. I've heard the chant so many times I know the whole poem by heart. I join in, my voice getting louder and louder as pride for my clan soars through my heart.

There's a section in the middle about the great battle that was won against "the heathens from the neighboring isle." I forget it's coming up until we're all saying the words. It's not very tactful, given our present company. I glance at the chiefs of Raasay, but they're still smiling. It was a long time ago, I suppose.

We arrive back at the enclave and the celebrations begin. I never expected anything like this. The Stewers have prepared a feast, and there is piping and more chanting. The children have made decorations that flap in the wind. Mead—brought by the visitors from Raasay—is passed around in great quantities. It is not often the elders allow such frivolities, so everyone takes advantage, glugging it down their thirsty throats. Eager smiles transform into drunken ones.

People keep coming up to me and grabbing my fists. It's the most popular I've ever been. Maybe Aileen was right; maybe they won't see me as an outcast after all.

There is a slap on my back, and I turn around to find some of the Anglers from my boat.

"You did great today, lad," one of them says, his words slightly slurring.

"Thanks," I say.

"And don't you worry about . . . You're going to be a good, good Angler. The best. We'll see to that."

It's a drunken promise but a heartfelt one. The other Anglers grab my fists in turn and tell me how happy they are that I'm part of their boat. They've never said anything like that to me before. They should drink alcohol more often.

A group of young children runs past, playing a game of wolf and weasel. Their joyful shrieks ring out as one of them gets caught. I use the distraction to slip away to my bothan. Once there, I change out of the robe. I'll probably be reprimanded for taking it off early, but it's too itchy to keep on all evening.

A small wooden heron stands by the side of my bed. I spent the last few nights carving it out of an aspen branch. It's not great, but it's not terrible either. I pick it up and slide it into my pocket.

When I return to the Gathering, it is almost dusk. The last of the sun bleeds out behind a mass of clouds. I wrap my cloak around me to keep out the cold.

"Look, it's Jaime," someone calls out as I pass. "Come play

with us!" I'm pulled into the group of pipers, and someone hands me a set of pipes. I don't want to disappoint them, so I put the mouthpiece to my lips and start blasting out a few notes. The other pipers join in, and we play together while those around us nod their heads and stamp their feet. I'm playing really badly, but everyone's smiling and no one seems to care.

A bass pipe sounds to silence the festivities. From across the enclave Maighstir Ross bellows, "It is time for the couple to set sail for the night. To the Western Gate."

Someone takes the pipes from me, and a surge of hands shoves me forward. The Western Gate is already open. Bobbing on its threshold is a medium-size rowboat, which has been decorated with heather and ferns. Sitting in the middle of the boat, once again with her back to me, is the girl. It's the first time I've seen her since we left Quiraing, and even now, I still can't see her face.

Errol is by my side and explains, "It is tradition for the first night of marriage to be spent at sea. You leave with the wishes of your clan propelling you away and return at dawn, having shared your hopes for the future."

A whole night at sea? Great. Just when I was starting to enjoy myself.

I step aboard. The boat shifts beneath me, making my arms flap, and then we lurch forward after a sharp shove from the crowd. I lose my balance and fall, banging my right elbow. I sit up, hoping no one noticed. I don't look back. I pick up two wooden oars and use them to inch the boat out a little farther. It's designed to be rowed by at least two people, so it is an effort to gain momentum on my own. There is a small sail, but I don't want to risk opening it and exposing my ignorance of how to use it properly.

Eventually, I am aided by the current, which eases the boat away from the enclave. I'm careful not to drift too far out, though; the deeper the water, the more dangerous it'll be. As soon as we are far enough away not to be overheard, I put down the oars. I should say something to the girl. But what? I clear my throat.

"Hello," I say. "I'm Jaime."

She doesn't turn around or make any indication that she has heard me.

"It's all been a bit crazy, hasn't it?" I wobble to my feet and take a step toward her. She turns with a jolt, looking up at me with wide eyes.

"It's okay," I say. "I'm not going to hurt you."

The nearly-full moon casts a pool of silver across us both. Her body is slender, like mine, and she has mousy hair and timid eyes. *Fragile* is the first word that comes to mind. She's too young to be a bride. Her cheeks are wet with tears. I am not used to that.

Crying's not *dùth*. It's a sign of weakness. I have never seen anyone cry before. Other than babies and small children, of course.

"What's your name?" I ask, struck by the absurdity that I am married to someone and don't even know what she's called.

"Lileas," she says. I have to strain to hear her.

"I'm sorry about everything that's happened today," I say. "I can assure you I was against it as much as you were."

"I thought so."

"Oh, I don't mean . . . It's just, well, before today marriage was forbidden on Skye. I presume they told you that?"

Lileas looks at her hands, and more tears drip from her chin.

"Look, I'm not sure how things are going to work out, but my clan is really great once you get to know them. We take care of each other, and no one ever goes hungry. And we have the best enclave on the whole island. I'll look out for you, I promise. We can be friends. Please don't cry."

I reach into my pocket and take out the wooden heron. "I made this for you," I say.

She stops crying long enough to look up at it.

"Don't give her that, Jaime."

The voice leaps from the shadows and scares me out of my wits. Lileas shrieks.

"What on earth?" I say.

Something bounds toward us from underneath the supplies at the front of the boat. I pick up an oar to defend Lileas. It's not until the person stands up straight that I recognize who it is.

"Agatha? What are you doing here?"

"I came to—save you."

"Save me? From what?"

"From the g- girl. You don't want to—marry her."

"What? But I'm already—How did you even get on board?"

"I climbed on. It was a clever plan."

"No, Agatha, it wasn't. You shouldn't be here." As if this wasn't awkward enough already.

"She's not as pretty as me," she says.

Lileas is staring up at her in horror. I shouldn't laugh, but it rumbles out of me. This is all so ridiculous.

"This is Agatha," I say to Lileas. "She's one of the Hawks from my clan." As I'm saying it, I remember that, technically, that isn't true anymore, but it makes Agatha smile.

"I am a good Hawk," she says. "It is an important job and I—I am good at it."

"You need to swim back," I say. "If anyone sees you in the boat you're going to be in big trouble."

"I c-can't," she says. "I don't like going in the water."

"How did I know you were going to say that?"

"I'm good at climbing, though."

"That's really great, Agatha."

"I bet I'm b-better at climbing than you are," she says to Lileas, taking a step toward her, throwing the boat off balance.

"Careful!" I yell, counterbalancing her and almost tripping over my own legs as I do so. When the rocking finally stops, I say, "It's been a really long day. If you can't swim back to shore, I suggest we all lie down and try to get some rest."

"Why do I have to s-sleep on the boat?" Agatha asks.

"Because the clan isn't expecting us back until morning."

"I don't want to sleep on a boat," she says.

"Neither do I! Trust me, it's the last place in the world I want to sleep, but we don't have a choice. Maybe you should have thought about that before sneaking on board."

"I was only t-trying to—help," she says.

I take a deep breath. "Look, you'll be fine sleeping here with us, I promise. Then we'll decide how to smuggle you back in the morning, okay?"

"Okay, J-Jaime."

She sits on one of the wooden benches opposite Lileas and

starts combing her hair with her hands. Lileas edges away from her. I rummage through the supplies and find a tangle of blankets, which I fashion into three makeshift beds. When they're ready, we all lie down. As soon as I'm on my back, some of the tension leaks out of me; it's a lot easier to imagine we're not on water when I'm not staring straight at it. Agatha is on one side of me and Lileas is on the other. Lileas closes her eyes and pretends to be asleep. I have no idea what she's making of all this. I should have talked to her more, reassured her somehow. I still could. I'll do it in the morning. Everything will be better then.

Agatha is staring at the stars. The shine has been drained out of them. I pull the edges of the blanket over my ears and tight into my sides. My eyelids are so heavy they hurt. For once, the gentle rocking of the boat is a comfort, and before long I am fast asleep.

A CACOPHONY OF CHIMES WAKES ME. I SIT UP, LICKING salt from my dry lips. It is not yet dawn, and a thin mist lies over the sea like a frail blanket. It takes a few moments to remember where I am and why. The chiming is coming from the enclave, which is now much farther away than it was before. We've drifted during the night. Dammit! I forgot to drop the anchor. How could I be so stupid? I glance at the water and immediately regret it. It is so deep. My breathing becomes erratic.

It's okay. I'm okay. I am Clann-a-Tuath. We don't feel fear.

My ears tune back in to the chimes, which remind me that the depth of the water is not my only problem right now.

"Agatha, wake up. Something's happening."

Agatha's eyes spring open.

"That's the Fourth," she says. "Something's—wrong."

She's right—it is the Fourth. It's the one chime we are all taught to listen out for. All of the Fourths—from all around the wall—are being struck over and over again; I've never heard them all ringing at the same time before.

"We need to get back. Help me row," I say.

I pick up a set of oars and hand them to Agatha, but she doesn't take them. She is standing with her mouth open, looking over my shoulder.

"Oh, no . . ." she murmurs.

I turn around and see them at once. Eight longboats, each dominated by the figurehead of an ugly serpent, making straight for the Northern Gate. The enemy raises their weapons, which glint with hostility.

"What's happening?" asks Lileas, standing up beside me.

The words fall from my mouth, and I can scarcely believe that they are true.

"I think we're under attack."

AGATHA

"WE NEED TO BE F-FASTER," I SAY TO JAIME AGAIN. WE ARE rowing fast. I am tired, but we are not going fast enough. We need to get back and we need to help.

"I'm going as fast as I can," says Jaime. "You're not rowing properly. I keep telling you: row in time with me."

"I am. It's you who's not—rowing in time with—me," I say. "Why isn't *she* helping?"

The girl is at the back of the boat doing nothing.

"I can help," she says. She always speaks quiet.

"It's okay," says Jaime. "We only have two sets of oars."

"I want water," I say, and I do not say it nice because I do not like her. She made Jaime marry her even though he didn't want to and now she's not helping. She looks at me like she doesn't understand. "Water," I say to her again.

She brings me some and I drink it quick so I can keep doing the rowing. I do not say thank you because why should I. Milkwort is spinning around in circles in my pocket. He wants me to get him out but I can't. The girl goes back to the end of the boat and is looking through all the things which she shouldn't do because they are not hers. I am watching in case she tries to steal something and I'll know.

We are close to the Western Gate now, but it is closed. Jaime stops rowing and starts waving his hands. "Open the gate!" he says. "Open the gate!"

The gate does not open. There is no one on the wall. Where are all the Hawks? They should be there and they are not.

"What's happening, Jaime?" I ask to him.

"I don't know," he says. "I don't know."

Inside I can hear shouting. We have to get inside. We have to help. "Go next to the g-gate," I say, and I point. There is a secret way and I know it because I am a Hawk. Jaime moves the boat until it is close. I try to find the rock. There is a special one that comes out and I need to find it. Lenox showed it to me before one time. All the Hawks have to know it for the emergencies and this is the emergencies right now.

I find the stone. It comes out and there is a handle and I pull it. It is stiff so I use two hands and pull it hard and harder. It comes down and the metal bars come out of the wall. This is the secret way to get up the wall.

"We can climb—up from here," I say to Jaime.

"Good job, Aggie," he says, which means I was very clever to find the handle and to pull it.

I climb up first. The metal bars are cold but it is easy for me because I am good at climbing. Jaime climbs up second,

"Stay in the boat," he says to the girl. "We'll open the gate from the other side."

I get to the top and look over. No one is on the wall. People in the enclave are running all over and some are still asleep. How can they be asleep when the chimes are clanging so loud in my ears? They need to wake up. What is happening? What—? The Northern Gate is open—it should not be open—and enemy people are coming through. Why is the gate open? Where are all the Hawks? The enemy people are like one hundred ants all bursting out of the ground. They are deamhain, I know it. This is bad bad so bad the worst. I have never seen a deamhan before but I know it because of the red-and-blue tattoos all over their faces. They are the worst ones. They are shouting from their dark blue mouths all horrible horrible sounds and they have axes and swords and they're swinging them and they're shouting and my clan our home my—

I push myself up onto the wall. Jaime grabs me and pulls me down again.

"Let go!" I say. "We have to—help!"

"It's too dangerous," he says.

"We have to do—something!" I say. We need a clever plan but I can't think of one. I look at Jaime to see if he can think of one but he is staring wide eyes. "Jaime!" I say. "Jaime!" He doesn't say anything or even look at me.

People are running all over everywhere. An ax flies through the air and nearly—Two deamhain use their swords and they're hacking at—The goats are running loose and don't know where to—Shouting and screaming and shouting and—The ground is covered and trampled in—All bodies are broken and pleading and—

69

There is an arrow that goes fast from a crossbow. It is Maistreas Eilionoir. She is on the roof of a bothan and she is firing at the deamhain. Yes! You can do it. She hits one and then another one and keeps firing even though it is hard for her to load the arrows because she is old. She is doing good aiming and getting them. Other people have weapons now too. My clan is fighting back and we can do this. We will win because we are Clann-a-Tuath and we are the best.

I can help too. I know a plan. If I go to one of the launchers I can turn it around and use it to fight. I am not afraid. I push myself up on the wall again. I need to help them. I can do it.

"No, Aggie—look," Jaime says.

Everyone has stopped. No one is fighting anymore. Everyone is still and watching.

"Why have they stopped?" I say. Did we win already?

Then I see it. The deamhain have Maighstir Ross. Let him go! They walk with him through the Gathering. It is hard for Maighstir Ross to walk. He is hurt very bad. The largest deamhan is pushing him. He is an ugly deamhan with a scar on his face that goes all through his tattoos from his mouth to his ear. He has an ax and he is holding it at Maighstir Ross's throat. He kicks the back of Maighstir Ross's leg and there is a crack because it breaks. Maighstir Ross does not show that it hurts even though I know it hurts a very lot. He goes down on his knees.

"*Vér as sigrade!*" shouts the deamhan with the scar. It is their language so I do not know what it means. "*Nå ævi ykar fulgja vid Øden.*"

The deamhan lifts the ax above his head.

"Forgive me, old friend," shouts Maistreas Eilionoir from the roof where she is. She fires one more arrow and it hits Maighstir Ross in his heart.

His body falls forward.

We have lost.

AGATHA

JAIME IS PULLING ME. "WE NEED TO GET BACK TO THE boat!" he says.

"No! Let me go!" It is not right what they did. I want to hurt them all.

"There are deamhain coming. They're on the wall."

I look and he's right. There are two deamhain running toward us. I go back over onto the metal bars. I don't think they saw me. Jaime is already going down. I go down too.

"What's happening?" says the girl who is still in the boat.

"We need to get away. Agatha, quickly."

I am trying to be quickly. Climbing down is not as easy as the climbing up. I fall into the boat and Jaime starts rowing again away from the wall. I pick up the other oars and help him. The deamhain are near us now on the wall and they stop. Both of them have axes with the long handles. They have their backs to us so they cannot see us but if they turn around they will see us. Please don't let them turn around and see us. Water from the oars is flying into the boat all around. The deamhain start walking again and go away farther on the wall. They didn't see us and that is the biggest phew ever.

"Where are we going?" I ask to Jaime.

"I don't know," says Jaime, and then he says it again. "I don't know. Away from the wall, away from everything."

We try to get farther away, but we are going around as well because the water makes us and it is pushing us to the Northern Gate. That is bad because that is where the deamhan boats are.

"Row harder," says Jaime. "You need to put both oars in at the same time."

I'm rowing as hard as I can. My hands are all sore and red from as hard as I can. And it is too hard to do both oars at the same time.

"Look," says the girl. "They're leaving."

I turn around and squint and she is right. First one then another of the boats is going away from the gate and is leaving.

"Why? Why are they leaving already?" says Jaime.

"I found this," says the girl. She is holding something and hands it to Jaime. It is a spyglass.

"Good job," he says, which I do not like. He takes it and looks through it for a long time and his head is shaking and then he shouts, "No. No!" and his mouth is open big.

I take the spyglass from him and look into it. I see the boats and I see the deamhain. Closer they are even worse. All of their skin is blue-and-red tattoos, even on their eyes and arms and necks. Their hair is all braided with bits in it and so are their beards. They are pushing people onto the boats and it is my clan. They are all tied together. Flora is there who is my friend and Lenox and other Hawks and everyone. This is bad bad bad.

Then I see who is on the wall. They are not all of them deamhain. Why are they—? The chiefs of Raasay are there—I know them from the Ceremony. They are talking to the deamhain on the wall and watching our clan and they are not stopping it. I turn to Jaime to ask him but he shakes his head and nods at the girl. This means he does not want her to know, but I do not care about that. She is from Raasay so she knows already. She helped them to do it.

"What have you done?" I scream at her. I am all hot inside. I jump over one bench and push past Jaime and then over another bench to reach her. She looks scared but she is pretending and I need to hit her because she did this. It is her fault. I grab her by the hair and I shake her and she screams.

"What have you done?" I say. "You did this. You knew they were coming!"

Jaime is trying to pull me off, but I am too strong and I will not stop until she tells me the truth and I hit her.

"I didn't know, I didn't know anything. I don't know—" she is saying, but it is a lie.

"Let her go; stop it," Jaime says.

I have hurt the girl which is good but I stop because she is crying. Crying is not *dùth*, doesn't she know that? She shouldn't do it. Jaime is holding her and I hate that. The crying makes me think that maybe she didn't know. Otherwise why would she do it? I go back to the front of the boat. I do not say sorry. Jaime tells the girl what we saw.

"I didn't know, I promise. I didn't know," she says.

"I believe you," he says. "But what do you want to do now? Your parents are still on Skye. You could swim back to them if you want to?"

"I'll go wherever you go," says the girl.

Stupid girl. I want her to go away. I look through the spyglass again. Another two boats are leaving.

"We have to—follow them," I say. "We can catch them and get on the boats and help."

"That's a terrible plan, Aggie. How would we get on board? They'd see us before we got close. And there's hundreds of them and only three of us—"

"We h-have to do something! We have to—try."

"Okay, okay. I just need to think. Let me think."

Jaime thinks for a long time and then he says that we can't catch the longboats but we can follow them to see where they go, so that is what we do. All the time I try to think of a plan that is a better one. We pass the Northern Gate from far away. None of the longboats are there now but it is too dangerous to go close because there is still the chiefs of Raasay on the wall. Jaime says the waves will hide us because our boat is small. The gate is still open. Jaime stops rowing. He picks up the spyglass and looks through it at the gate. His breathing starts to get faster and then louder as well. Something is wrong with him. His hands go tight and one of them hits himself in his chest. Then he drops the spyglass and goes down on the floor of the boat and he's making sounds like hurting. The girl moves toward him.

"Stay away!" I say to her. Then I say, "Jaime." And I say it again,

"Jaime. What's wrong?" He can't talk to me. His breathing is so loud and he's sucking in the air like he can't get enough inside.

"He's having an attack," says the girl. "My father gets them. I can help."

I look at her and I don't know if she is a good person or an enemy person. The chiefs of Raasay are an enemy but maybe she is a good person, and Jaime needs help and I don't know what to do.

"Okay," I say, "but if you hurt him I will—hurt you more."

She kneels next to him and puts her hand on his shoulder. Then she picks up one of his hands and puts it on her chest.

"Look at me," she says in a quiet voice, and Jaime looks at her.

She breathes slow and she is squeezing his hand. Jaime tries to copy her breathing and after a while his breathing is slower too like hers. Then he says, "Thank you," which comes out with lots of breath.

"What was it, Jaime? What—happened?"

He points to the gate. It's still hard for him to speak I think.

I pick up the spyglass and look through it. I wish I didn't do that. Inside the gate there are only dead people on the ground. So many of them. Some have tattoo faces and are deamhain. All the other ones are not. All dead people and broken and horrible and blood.

And then I look up and what I see is even worse. Seven faces are above the Northern Gate. The first I see is Maistreas Sorcha, then Maighstir Clyde and Maighstir Ross. It is all of the elders. They do not have bodies anymore. They are heads hanging from chains that are dangling.

All of the elders are dead.

JAIME

I'VE BEEN ROWING FOR SO LONG THE RHYTHM OF THE oars feels like a second heartbeat. Lift, stretch, pull. Lift, stretch, pull. Lift, stretch, pull. I grit my teeth to prevent tiredness from closing my eyes. My pathetic arms feel ready to snap. The repetitive motion has worn away the skin on my fingers, leaving raw patches that throb with every stroke. The pain is good. It helps keep me focused, helps prevent the panic from taking over again. I don't know what happened before, but I can't let it happen again. I have to keep going. I have to be strong.

We're no longer following the boats. They disappeared from the horizon long ago, leaving us deserted on the open sea. Was it yesterday? Or maybe the day before? I've lost track. I don't even know if we're going in the right direction. We could be going around in circles, or heading back toward Skye. And who knows what we'd find back there? The whole of Raasay could have taken over the enclave by now. They betrayed us, that much is clear. They must have made a deal with the deamhain to get us drunk and open our gates. Which means the whole marriage was a sham. All the torment I felt in the weeks leading up to it is almost laughable now. The thought of those spineless *meirlich* living in our enclave, our home . . . If I ever see them again, I'll—Well, I don't know what I'll do. What *can* I do? Nothing. Except row. Endless, endless, pointless rowing.

At least I'm doing something. Unlike before, when we were on the wall, watching it all happen. Agatha was desperate to climb over and help, but I kept stopping her. Was it to protect her? Or was it because I knew that if she went, I would have to go too?

Unwanted images keep swamping my mind: visions from the battle, the grass soaked red, the heads of the elders spinning on their chains, their years of wise counsel reduced to nothing but hollow faces and empty eyes.

And Aileen.

Aileen, who I saw through the spyglass, struggling against a deamhan. He had a tight grip on her upper arm and was forcing her onto a boat. She tried to pull away from him, so he pushed her, hard. She fell backward into the boat. The deamhan laughed.

She's alive. She's alive. I have to keep reminding myself that that is much better than the alternative. And they'll keep her that way. It's what the deamhain do: kill enough people to force a surrender and then take the survivors back to their homeland to use them as slaves. That's where they're taking Aileen and the rest of my clan. That's where we have to go.

I don't know much about Norveg, the country the deamhain come from. All I know is that it's hundreds of miles away to the east, on the other side of Scotia and across the vast North Sea.

They haven't been seen in these waters for as long as anyone can remember.

There's something in the water. I shake my head. Exhaustion is making me see things. It's still there. A broken barrel, maybe, or part of a tree? I stop rowing and put the spyglass to my eye. There's no mistaking: it is a deamhan, bobbing faceup on the surface. Braids float around his head like tentacles. His eyes are closed and he's not moving. He looks dead.

"What is it?" Agatha asks as I lower the spyglass. It is the first time she's spoken all day.

"Something in the water," I say. "Nothing."

"But what is it?" she asks again. She'll keep asking until I tell her the truth.

"A deamhan," I say, "but I think he's dead."

"We should—search him," she says.

"I don't think that's a very good idea."

"He may have a m-map or a—weapon."

"If he's still alive, he'll kill us."

"If he's alive we can make him tell us which way to—go."

"Of course. I'm sure he'll be more than happy to point us in the right direction." The sarcasm comes out thicker than I intend it to.

"You shouldn't be so mean to me. It's a—good plan. I'm not stupid. Everyone thinks I'm stupid, but I'm not—stupid."

"I don't think that, Aggie; I'm just saying it'd be too dangerous to try."

"You're scared. I'm not. I'm brave, and you should be too. We're Clann-a-Tuath and—"

I put my hand up to silence her midsentence. He's gone. I scan the water back and forth, hoping the body is hidden behind a wave, but no: the deamhan is no longer there.

"Where did he g-go?" Agatha asks.

"I don't know." I swallow.

Fear is the greatest weakness. Fear is the greatest weakness.

My stomach feels like it's churning sand.

"Maybe he sank," Agatha says.

"Probably," I say. "We should move on."

No sooner have I spoken than a powerful thrust from underneath the boat rolls my side into the air. As the boat drops back down, a hand reaches up and grabs the top of my arm. There is a flash of angry teeth, and then I'm submerged under the waves. The cold water stabs me all over. I squirm, trying to loosen the deamhan's grip, but his strength is absolute. My head turns thick, and the pressure in my chest gets tighter and tighter. A heavy pulse beats behind my eyes, as if they might burst at any moment. Dark blue blurs my vision, and time slows to nothing. This is it. I am going to die.

Three dull thumps reverberate through the arm that is holding me, muffled by the water. Just as my senses are about to shut down, the vise-like hold disappears, and I propel myself to the surface with desperate kicks. I inhale my first breath with an animal cry. Above me, an oar swings down and strikes the deamhan on the side of his face. Blood races across his neck into the water. I follow the oar back to the person holding it, expecting to see Agatha, but it is Lileas who has come to my rescue.

Now that the deamhan has both hands free, he grabs hold of

the oar and yanks it away from her, nearly pulling her overboard. I splash my way to the other side of the boat and pull myself in.

I stand there dripping, deciding what to do next. The deamhan has disappeared again.

"He went under the water," says Lileas.

Agatha is at the far end of the boat, staring down at the deck.

"Stay away from the sides," I warn them both. Lileas nods; Agatha does not react.

"We need a weapon," says Lileas.

She's right. I rush to the stern and start scrabbling through the supplies, keeping my body low in case the deamhan tips the boat again. I find a length of thick rope and a *corcag*, a small knife used for gutting fish. I hold one in each hand and creep back to the center of the boat. Lileas is next to me, looking up at me with wide eyes.

The thud of my heart echoes in my ears. Far away, a bird screeches out in pain or surprise. I blink back the wind and grip the *corcag* even tighter in my hand. Could I really use it if it came to that? I think I might be sick.

There are bubbles rising to the surface a few yards away. It's him, it has to be. The bubbles get more intense, and then his whole body bursts out of the water as if possessed. He thrashes his arms and howls foreign words. Something is attacking him. He punches beneath the surface with his fists. From behind me, Agatha lets out a gasp.

His struggles move him closer to the boat. Now is my chance. I weigh the rope in one hand against the *corcag* in the other. The knife would be the swifter option, but I can't bring myself to use it. I sling it to the deck and wrap the rope around both my hands, keeping them shoulder-width apart. The deamhan is still fighting to dispel the creature from his legs. He's now so close that his head keeps knocking against the side of the boat. It only takes one attempt to reach down, slip the rope over his head, and loop it around his neck. With all my strength, I pull the two ends of the rope into my chest. Surprise flashes in the man's eyes for the briefest moment, replaced by an intense anger. Two fists fly out of the water, aiming to crush my skull. I whip my head back just in time. The deamhan forgets about the sea creature and focuses all his energy on stopping me. His hands find my wrists, and his thumbs press into my veins. I'm not strong enough for this; he's so much stronger than I am. I tense my jaw in resistance. He flings his head from side to side and pummels my arms. I respond by pulling even tighter. *This is for Clann-a-Tuath,* I think. *For what you did to the elders. For what you tried to do to me.*

His whole body goes slack, the deadweight of it almost dragging me over the side of the boat. I hold on for another couple of beats, then release the pressure on his neck. He doesn't move. I killed him. *Ò daingead.* Did I really just kill him? He tried to do the same to me—he would have done the same to me—but still, still . . . A mouthful of vomit gurgles up into my throat. I stop it before it gets any farther and swallow it back down. Its acidy tang lingers in my mouth.

"Help me p-pull him in," Agatha says. "We need to search his—body." She leans over and grabs him under one arm. At least she's snapped out of her stupor. Lileas follows her lead and holds on to his opposite shoulder. Without really thinking what

I'm doing, I help them haul him up out of the water. It takes all of our combined strength, and we collapse backward as soon as his body tips into the boat. His legs are still dangling over the side, his trousers torn to pieces. Wrapped around his right ankle is the largest jellysquid I've ever seen. It's the first time I've seen one alive. Ripples of orange and yellow flash across its translucent body.

"Don't go near it," I say. They're renowned for being volatile, even out of the water.

The jellysquid slides off the deamhan's foot and drops back into the sea.

"Thank you," says Agatha, waving goodbye to it.

"That thing probably saved our lives," I say.

Agatha nods in agreement.

Our relief is interrupted by a spluttering behind us. The deamhan is on his side, coughing up water. He's still alive. I don't know whether that's a relief or not.

"We need to tie—tie him up," says Agatha.

Shouldn't we just push him back into the water? He's so weak he'd probably just drown. I need to make a decision fast, while he's still slipping in and out of consciousness. Agatha passes me a coil of fishing rope, making the decision for me. I bind his wrists and ankles and then drag him to the prow and tie him to the bowsprit. I was taught how to tie knots by the caiptean himself, so I'm confident they'll hold. Finally, something good has come from being made an Angler.

The deamhan's forehead is hot, as if he is getting a fever. There must have been poison in the jellysquid's sting. Large, blistering welts have appeared on his legs, distorting the tattoos beneath them. There's not much I can do for him, even if I was inclined to. He'll just have to ride it out. He's unconscious again, so I search his pockets but find nothing of any use.

I take a step back and look him up and down. Every visible part of his skin is covered in tattoos—all of them red and dark blue, making it look at first glance as if he's been skinned alive. They contain an intricate latticework of interlocking images: animals, weapons, people, trees, ships . . . The whole world is there, across the curves and slopes of his body. His eyelids, lips, and tongue are also tattooed, midnight blue. He has dark-blond hair—turned darker by salt water and sweat—which is laced with scruffy braids. His braided beard stretches down to his chest.

"What should we do with him?" Agatha asks.

"I don't know," I say. "Maybe what you suggested: make him tell us how to find our clan. It was a good plan."

She beams at the compliment.

"And then we'll kill him," she says as an afterthought.

She's right, of course. It would be far too risky to keep him alive. Yet the thought of it fills me with unease. It is one thing to strangle a man after he has attempted to drown you, but another to slit his throat while he is tied up and defenseless. *No mercy.* That's what Maighstir Ross would have said.

"You need me." The voice is croaky and carries a heavy accent. I didn't think the deamhan would be able to speak our language. I was wrong.

"You're in no position to tell us what we need," I say, trying my best to sound assertive.

To my surprise, he starts laughing. It is an ugly laugh, like a wolf choking on glass.

"Little man," he says to me, "trying to be the tough one. Chasing us in the tiny boat. You have no hope. I am only hope for you."

There is a melodic quality to his voice that is at odds with the halting way he speaks our words.

"What do you mean?"

"You are just a boy. Boy with no plan. What can you do? Little boy with little girl. And this one they should drown at birth."

He nods toward Agatha, who leaps up at the insult, fury in her eyes.

"We stopped you, didn't we?" she yells. "M-maybe you shouldn't be so—so—you don't know anything about me. I could kill you right now." By the look on her face, she certainly could.

He starts to laugh again, but soon collapses into a fit of coughing. Once he has regained control of his breathing, he shakes his head and repeats, "I am only hope for you."

"Why do you keep saying that?" I ask.

"You are lucky. Very lucky." He lifts his head as high as the ropes will allow in an attempt to add more weight to his words. "I am Knútr Grímsson of Sterkr Fjall, son to Konge Grímr, warrior of First Fjóti. I am Norvegian prince."

"A prince? I don't believe you," I say.

"It is Konge Grímr, my father, who takes your people. Return me—his only son—and he will be so happy to free your people. This is why I laugh. You want to kill me, but you must not do it."

This could change everything. If what he is saying is true, we would have something—some*one*—to bargain with.

"Prove it," I say.

He is unfazed by my demand.

"Lift my sleeve now," he says. "On the side of left."

I take a step toward him. It might be a trap.

"Do not be scared; I do not bite," he says, baring his teeth and gnashing them at me.

I use the end of an oar to push back his sleeve up to his elbow. On the underside of his forearm, among all the other tattoos, there is one in the shape of a large medallion. It is a deeper red than the others. There are runes surrounding it that I cannot read.

"This is insignia of prince," he says with pride. "Made with blood of my father, the king. Only royal persons are having the tattoos of blood. So now you know it."

It might be what he claims it to be, but he could just as easily be lying.

"Why were you in the water?" I ask, buying myself time to think. "If you're so important, surely your people would have stopped their boats to search for you?"

"They do not see that I am gone for much time. It is night and we drink lots of *mjǫð* to celebrate our *great* victory." He gives me a cruel smile as he says this. I do not react, so he continues. "I feel I want to see the stars, so I go to top. The stars are very beautiful at sea. I want to be close, so I climb—I do not know word for it. But I climb very high. I have drink too much and when I am at top, there is big wind and I fall down to water. No one sees me fall. I shout, but no one hears. I try to swim, but the boat is fast.

Much time later the boat stops, and they know I am gone. They come back to me and in circles looking, but they are too far away and cannot see me. They think I am dead and leave with the sadness. When they go, I swim far and then I see this boat and think to take it. If not for *dakkar* sting on my legs, I will kill you all and have your boat." He spits to punctuate the end of his story. It lands at my feet.

He closes his eyes, beginning to succumb to the fever that is squirming through his body. Something about his story nags at me, like he's not quite telling the truth.

"Where are your boats headed?"

"To Norveg, of course: the greatest nation. Your people are slaves now. They go to Norveg and are slaves until they die. It is the end of them. Unless you take me back."

"How do we get to Norveg?"

His eyes spring back open; they're bright white against the dark blue of his eyelids. He runs his thick blue tongue behind his lips, weighing whether to tell me.

"North. Around top of Skottland and across Norðsjór, the North Sea."

"And you can show us the way?"

"Of course. But it takes many days, and not good in this boat. Better you take shortcut across Skottland."

"Skottland? You mean Scotia?"

"If that is what you say."

We can't. As much as I want to get out of this boat, there's no way we can cut across the mainland. No one goes near it anymore. It's a wild place now, full of nothing but death and unknown terrors.

"Why we wait?" he says, before closing his eyes again and muttering to himself in his own language.

I turn my back on him and walk to the stern, where the others are waiting. Agatha is staring thunder at the deamhan, and Lileas is crouching in the corner, wanting to be as far away from him as possible.

"What do you think?" I ask them under my breath.

"I—hate him," says Agatha.

"He's not my favorite person either," I say, "but that tattoo does look like it could be genuine."

"So what do we do—now?"

Agatha and Lileas are both looking at me. Why do I have to make all the decisions? The oar that the deamhan snatched from Lileas earlier is still floating on the water. I stretch over the side of the boat and retrieve it.

"We should keep him alive," I say. The oar is ice cold in my hand. "As long as he's tied up, he can't harm us. Let's head toward Scotia. Once we're near, we can follow the coastline north. We'll be safer in shallower water."

"But what about the shadow things?" asks Agatha.

"*Sgàilean* aren't real, Agatha. They were made up to scare little kids."

"You don't know that," she says. "And there's also the—the terror beasts. We shouldn't go near the mainland, Jaime, we—shouldn't."

"We need to be close to the coast so we can follow it north. We'll be safe as long as we stay in the boat. What other choice do we have?" I look from Agatha to Lileas and then back again. "So are we in agreement?"

Lileas gives a tiny nod, and Agatha shrugs.

"Which way to Scotia?" I ask the deamhan.

He looks at the sky—at the sun, perhaps—and then points.

I pick up another oar and start to row in that direction, full of doubt about whether I have made the right decision.

JAIME

"I NEVER THANKED YOU," I SAY.

"Thanked me for what?" asks Lileas.

"For saving my life. When the deamhan attacked." I glance in his direction. He's asleep, his body twisted by the ropes.

"We're clan," she says with a modest smile. "We have to protect each other."

I hadn't considered that before, but she's right. She's one of us now.

A day has passed since the deamhan, Knútr, tried to take our boat. A misty sleet haunted us all morning, but as soon as it cleared, we could make out the Scotian mainland in the distance: a long smear, hostile and uninviting. I rowed toward it until we were about fifty yards away, then turned the boat north. I feel better for having a plan, even if it's vague and not a very good one. If nothing else, it's giving us a direction to travel in. Every now and then, I squint at the mainland, searching for any signs of life. Despite all the horror stories we've been told about it, my heart beats a little slower knowing there is land nearby.

I've managed to get the sail working. Sort of. The wind's a bit unpredictable at times, but at least it makes the rowing easier. While I row, Lileas leans over the side with a crude fishing line she's made. So far this afternoon she's caught and gutted three fish, which are splayed out on the bench beside us. She learned how to fish from her father, who's a sort of Angler. They don't have duties on Raasay—everyone is allowed to choose whatever job they want—but her father goes out on a boat every day and catches fish, just like the Anglers do. Did. *Don't think about that.* The only difference is, he's allowed to keep all the fish he catches. I don't know why anyone would want that many fish. Nothing about the way they live on Raasay makes any sense.

"Why doesn't your clan allow marriage?" Lileas asks me now.

I should have guessed that question was coming. "They used to, a long time ago," I say. "But then the elders realized it only led to jealousy and resentment. We're better off without it."

She looks at me, unconvinced and slightly offended.

"Not us, necessarily," I backtrack, surprised at my own thoughtlessness. "I mean, you're so young, and, I don't know—It's just, I guess we don't have to be—for the alliance, I mean. Safe to say that's dead in the—What I'm trying to say is—" What *am* I trying to say?

"It's okay. I understand," says Lileas. "Marriage isn't always a bad thing, though. My mother married my father when she was my age, and they have been happy together their whole lives." Her face drops, and she shuffles in her seat.

After a few beats, I say, "I'm sure they didn't know what the chiefs were planning."

"What are *your* parents like?" she asks, changing the subject.

"The whole clan is my family," I tell her.

"I mean your mother and father."

"I don't know who they are. No one does. All children are cared for and loved equally, without favoritism."

"You don't know who your parents are?" She scrunches her nose. "Doesn't that make you sad?"

"Why would it make me sad? The ties between us are unbreakable. We are more than content with the way we've chosen to live. Or at least we were."

Lileas blushes. "I'm sorry," she says.

I look out to sea. "You have nothing to apologize for. It's just hard to accept how much has changed."

For a while, the only sound is the creak and splash of the oars as they dip in and out of waves.

"That's pretty," says Lileas, pointing at my bracelet.

"Thank you. My friend, Aileen, made it for me."

"You wish she was here instead of me." It is a statement, not a question, but it contains no hint of resentment. Not for the first time, I am struck by how astute Lileas is for someone so young.

"She's my best friend. Maybe the only close friend I have."

She's the reason I'll never give up.

A gannet swoops down and lands on the side of the boat.

Agatha springs up from where she's been resting and shoos it away with manic arms. "Go away, you. Go away, go!"

The gannet squawks and flies off.

"See a gannet, make it fly, or someone close is sure to die," I say. Lileas frowns. "It's an old saying. People used to believe gannets carried the souls of the dead into the afterlife. They're supposed to be bad luck."

"Don't blame me, I'm just a bird," says Lileas, flapping her arms and croaking her voice like a bird's.

It is so unexpected that I burst out laughing. Lileas joins in, and we sit there laughing in each other's faces until our cheeks ache.

"What are you laughing at?" says Agatha. "It wasn't even a funny—joke."

Lileas falls silent.

"Sometimes it's good to laugh," I say.

"It's my t-turn to row anyway," says Agatha.

"Thanks. I could do with a break." I stand up and roll back my shoulders. Agatha's rowing has improved a little. She's now good enough not to send us wildly off course at least. She sits down. Lileas presses herself against the side of the boat, away from her. The two have not spoken since Agatha hit her.

"Have you seen the fish Lileas caught?" I say.

"Yes, I saw the fish, Jaime," says Agatha with a scowl.

"It's good, isn't it? We've got plenty of food now."

What we don't have is water. Our supply ran out this morning. It's agonizing to be surrounded by so much water and not be able to drink any of it. I haven't decided what to do about that yet.

"I don't like fish," says Agatha. The frown on her face shows no sign of disappearing.

"Lileas just reminded me that she is Clann-a-Tuath now."

"No, she's not."

"She is. We got married. That's how it works. She's one of us, Agatha. She's family."

Agatha doesn't reply.

"Look, we've got enough on our hands with that deamhan over there, so it'd be great if the two of you could try to get along."

"I'd like that," says Lileas.

Agatha presses her teeth into her bottom lip and then says, "Fine. Although I wish you didn't marry Jaime and I—I hate the chiefs of Raasay. And if I see them again I will—kill them."

"If they really did betray your people," says Lileas, "—*our* people—then I'll help you do it." Her words are rendered even more powerful by the meek voice in which she speaks them.

Her promise appeases Agatha, who starts chatting with her as if they've been friends for years. Satisfied, I slip off to have a quick lie-down. It occurs to me that I haven't felt seasick all day. Aileen was right; it does get better with time. I lean my head against a bundle of blankets and force myself to relax.

Rough hands shake me awake. How—? I only just closed my eyes.

"We're sinking," says Agatha. "It wasn't my fault; I d-didn't know."

Knútr is shouting from the other end of the boat.

94

"What should I do?" Agatha says. "T-tell me, Jaime, and I'll—I'll do it."

I pull myself to my knees and spot the leak right away. Lileas is bent over, trying in vain to block it with her hands. Agatha must have rowed over a high rock. I should have known the coast-line would be rocky. This is my fault. We should have stayed in deeper water.

"Jaime, what should we do?" Agatha asks me again.

I don't know. I don't know what to do.

"We have to swim to the shore," says Lileas.

That is not a good idea. Besides, we need the boat. The water is already up to my ankles. There's no way we can save it.

"I can't," Agatha shouts. "I can't do that. I can't do s—I can't do swimming."

"I'll help you," says Lileas. She upends a crate and hands it to Agatha. "When the boat sinks, keep hold of this and kick your legs."

"But the shadow things, Jaime! They'll get us! We can't go there, we can't."

"We don't have a choice," I say, realizing as I say it that it's true. We're going to have to swim. To Scotia. Right now, I'm more concerned with what might be in the water than what we might find on land.

"Take off the rope! Take off the rope!" Knútr hollers. "You need me. I cannot die."

I'd forgotten about him. What do I do with him? If the boat goes down while he's still attached to it, he'll drown. Is that what we want?

No, we need him. He's all we have to bargain with. I have to believe he is who he says he is. I have to keep him alive.

But if I untie him, he'll attack us while we're panicked and disoriented. The water is rising fast. I need to make a decision. *Come on, come on, come on.*

I look to the bowsprit. If I can detach it somehow, maybe I can release Knútr without needing to untie him first. Is that the right thing to do? I don't know. If I don't break it off in time, he'll be dragged down with the boat.

I stumble toward him and then crawl over his body until I am balanced on the wooden spar that extends over the water from the front of the boat. Holding on to it with both hands, I swing down, dangling my feet into the water. I then start to kick the front of the boat, trying to break apart the paneling.

"What do you do?" shouts Knútr. "No, no, no! Take off the rope!"

I ignore him and continue to kick with both feet, swinging out each time to gain more momentum. Agatha is shouting for me. I should be helping her instead. It's too late now. I swing out and kick again. It is having no impact at all. Although the boat is old, it's sturdier than I'd anticipated. My plan is terrible; this is never going to work. I pull myself back up.

"Listen to me," I say to Knútr. "I'm not going to untie you, so if you want to survive, you're going to have to help. I'm trying to break off the part of the boat behind you, so I need you to strike back with all your weight while I kick from the other side. Understand?"

He doesn't reply but lifts himself as far forward as he's able, preparing to do what I said. I slip back down over the water and continue to kick as he thuds from the opposite side. The water is halfway up my thighs. We're running out of time.

"Harder!" I yell. The boat starts to tip; I only have time for one more kick before it goes under. I swing out and slam my feet into the wooden slats as hard as I can. There is a crack, but the bowsprit does not detach. The front of the boat jerks upward and then the whole thing sinks in one fluid motion. Still clutching on, I'm sucked under with it. I hold my breath. *One more kick, one more kick.* Knútr doubles his efforts, and one kick is all it takes. The wood shatters and the front of the boat is torn apart. Knútr propels himself to the surface, dragging me up with him.

"You are crazy boy," he says once we break the surface.

"You're alive, aren't you?"

I look for the others. Agatha is using the crate to keep herself afloat, and Lileas is helping her swim toward land.

"Start kicking," I say to Knútr. "You're a big guy; there's no way I'm hauling you all the way in."

With a grunt, he does as I say. Despite the fact that he's still tied to the remains of the bowsprit, he moves through the water at an impressive speed. I grip the ropes and let him pull me along, desperate to be out of the water.

When we reach land, he tries to bolt, but I still have a hold on the ropes, and one sharp tug is enough to bring him to the ground. I kneel on his back while I remove the shards of broken boat and retie the knots.

"Don't try that again," I say.

His beard is covered in sand. He spits out bits of grit with an angry frown. I grin. The plan worked. I saved him. Only now I'm doubting whether that was the right thing to do. As long as he's tied up, he can't hurt us. Can he?

I hurry to my feet, pulling him up with me, then turn around in a jerky circle, scanning the beach where we've landed. It is sludge gray and spattered with bleak rock pools. It stretches for as far as I can see in both directions, with only a few ugly rocks to break up the monotony. In front of us, a small sandbank leads up to a cluster of wiry trees. There is no sign of life. I push Knútr ahead of me and walk over to Agatha and Lileas.

"I carried as much as I could," says Lileas, shivering from the cold. "Most of the things fell out when we were swimming."

A small pile of supplies lies at her feet: a broken mug, a blanket, and a small package of dried meat. It could be worse. She is also holding the wooden heron I carved for her, which makes me smile even though it's not going to be useful to us in any way.

"You did great," I say. I wring out the blanket as best as I can and stuff the meat into my pocket to share later.

Agatha flicks her head from left to right as if expecting something to jump out at us at any moment. She's right to be nervous. We're on the mainland. The place where no one comes. The place where everyone died.

"What are we—what are we going to do, Jaime?" Agatha asks me.

"I don't—" I take a moment to calm my breath. Then another moment. "Maybe this is a good thing." It's definitely not a good thing. "We can cross Scotia much faster than we could have sailed around it. We might even be able to intercept the deamhain before they cross the North Sea."

"But what about the b-boat?"

"We'll find another one. A better one."

"But how?"

I don't know. I have no idea about anything.

"I know where we find boat," says Knútr.

"Really? Where?" I ask.

"Trust me," he says. His smile is rotten fruit. "Finding boat is good for me, good for you. We find it in harbor by big castle, on coast of east."

"You mean Dunnottar Castle?" I ask. It's where the Scotian king used to live. Maistreas Sorcha told us about it. The whole royal family lived there, but they're all dead now, killed by the plague, along with everyone else.

"I show you the way," says Knútr.

"How do you know where to go?" I ask. "Have you been here before?"

"No, but I see map in my country and I remember. Also, I am very, *very* clever."

Once again, I find myself agreeing to a terrible plan through lack of better alternatives. Trusting Knútr is the last thing I want to do, but I know next to nothing about this land.

"Fine," I say. "The sooner we get there the better."

The trees at the top of the sandbank are spindly and mean. Their shadows writhe in the wind. Could there be shadow things—*sgàilean*—hiding within them, ready to grab us as we pass?

Of course not. *Sgàilean* aren't real. It's impossible to remove someone's shadow, and even if you could, shadows definitely can't sneak around and attack people.

Even still, anything could be waiting for us just beyond the trees.

A sudden sea breeze whips around us, as if urging us to take our first steps.

"Let's go," I say.

We walk up the beach in silence, into the unknown.

PART TWO

SCOTIA

NATHARA

Stay in your room

Stay in your room

Something's happening

Something bad

People are sick

You'll be safe in here

I'm going to lock you in

I'm going to lock the door

But I'll be back

I promise

I'll be back

I love you darling

Darling girl

Precious angel

I love you

I'll be back

I promise

I'll be back

I promise I promise I promise

I'm waiting Daddy

I'm waiting

I didn't mean to be a naughty girl

Stay in your room

Stay in your room

I couldn't

All the food was gone

Please don't be mad Daddy

Please don't shout

The door doesn't open so I broke it

Smashed it

Mummy won't be pleased

All the mess

I was too hungry

If you don't feed the birds the dogs won't catch them

We all need to eat

Except for them

They don't eat

They only kill

It's all they know how to do

AGATHA

WE WON'T BE GOING BACK TO THE ENCLAVE FOR A LONG time. I know it now. We are far away. The only thing I'm glad is I have Milkwort with me. He didn't like it on the boat and he didn't like it even more in the water. He had to go on my head so he didn't get wet. He is happier now. We are in Scotia which is a big place and a bad one. It is dangerous, but I'm not afraid. We haven't seen any shadow things or any terror beasts. All we saw is some birds and a ferret once which isn't scary.

The nasty deamhan goes first. He says he knows which way from the stars but there aren't any stars so I don't know. He says it will take five days or maybe six days to walk to where the harbor is. It's next to the castle and that's where we'll get the boat. When everyone died they left the boats there. We have already been walking a lot. It is tiring to do so much walking. Jaime tells the nasty deamhan to go slower so I can catch up.

A few times we hear a sound that is like an animal or something big. I ask Jaime what it is that makes that sound, but he says he doesn't know. The nasty deamhan says it is probably a moose or a bear but I didn't ask him. I know what a bear is but I don't know what a moose is. Maybe it's a terror beast.

Jaime has tied the deamhan up tight. I hate him. I'm not going to talk to him. Last night I made Jaime tie him up away from me. I talk to Lileas though. She helped me with the swimming. She is not bad like I thought. Earlier she told me something so funny. It was about the sea doing a wee which is funny because the sea can't do that and also seaweed so I laughed so much.

There is a river and we stop to drink some water. I wash my hair in it to make it pretty. It is not nice when it is salty with sea-water. It is hard to get all the salty out.

"That's two boats you've sunk in two weeks," Jaime said to me yesterday when we were walking. "That's pretty impressive."

He was smiling so he wasn't cross. I told him the first one was not my fault because I was only doing my duty and I was clever to use my sock to make the fire, and the second one was also not my fault because I did not know about the rocks and no one said.

My boots are wet which makes my feet sore, but it's okay because we have to keep doing the walking. We are going to find our clan and to save them. It's the most important thing. The ground is hard and stones. I wish it didn't always rain so much. We need to find something to eat because we don't have any food now. And we also need to find somewhere to sleep. Yesterday we ate the meat that Lileas took from the boat but now it's all gone and I'm hungry. I couldn't sleep last night because I was so hungry. When we find somewhere to sleep tonight, Jaime says he will get us some food. I like Jaime. He is my best friend.

After more walking we are in a place where there is more trees and it is colder now and darker. There are sounds around us like I don't know what they are.

"What do you think that is?" I ask Lileas.

"It sounds like a bird," she says. "Maybe an owl. Nothing to worry about." She holds my hand and I like that.

"We have to look out for the—terror beasts," I say.

"What exactly is a terror beast?" says Lileas.

"They're the animals that live here now that everyone is d-dead," I say.

"Oh," she says. "How did everyone die?"

Doesn't she know?

"There was a plague," says Jaime, "the worst that's ever been known. It spread like wildfire, infecting everyone on the mainland: both in Scotia and in Ingland. No one survived."

"And if anyone did survive, the shadow things probably got them," I say.

"What's a shadow thing?" Lileas asks me.

There is lots she doesn't know. "Shadow things are very bad things. They hide in the dark and you can't even see them and they grab you when you aren't looking and rip you all to pieces. They could be hiding in the trees and under rocks or—or—or in your own shadow even."

"Agatha, stop it; you'll scare her," says Jaime.

"Is the shadow thing an animal as well?" asks Lileas.

"No, it's a shadow." I said that already. "The king made them.

But then the p-plague killed him and now the shadow things are free and no one can—stop them. That's why we shouldn't be here, because they'll probably—probably get us too."

"Okay, that's enough," says Jaime, and he looks at me which is to say I shouldn't say any more, but I was only being polite and answering questions.

"How did the king make them?" asks Lileas.

"He used the—blood magic. You shouldn't do that because magic is not *dùth* which is why he is a bad man."

"He didn't make them at all," says Jaime. "It's just a story grown-ups tell to scare little kids. Don't you have that story on Raasay?" Lileas shakes her head to say no. "It's about how King Balfour, the last king of Scotia, and how he cut off people's shadows and turned them into deadly assassins. In the story, he plans to use them against his enemy, King Edmund, the Inglish king, but then the plague kills him and the shadows break free. Adults pretend they're real to scare us into coming inside when it gets too dark, or to make us go to bed sooner, because *sgàilean* only come out at night. When I was young, it definitely worked. I was terrified of them."

Lileas looks scared, I know it.

"Now it's y-you who is scaring her," I say.

"Well, magic isn't real, so *sgàilean* can't be real either," Jaime says. "But if it makes you feel better, we'll make another fire as soon as it starts getting dark."

We find a place in the trees with a falling-down bothan in it that is made of wood. It is old and there is a hole in the roof. Jaime says we should stay here for the night because if it rains we won't get wet. I think if it rains then the rain will come through the hole in the roof, but when I say that to Jaime he ignores me. The blanket is still damp because of all the raining and so it isn't dry. I don't mind if it's cold.

Jaime ties the nasty deamhan to a tree. The nasty deamhan moves about to make it hard for him and even tries to bite Jaime one time and then he laughs. It is not funny so I don't know why he does it. I help Jaime pull the rope tight even though I don't want to go close but because to help.

Afterward, Jaime says, "I'm going to see if I can find us some food."

"I'll come too," I say.

"Uh . . ." Jaime says, which means he doesn't want me to go with him. "It'd be better if you stay here. I need you to watch Knútr."

"Is that an important job?" I ask.

"Very important," Jaime says.

"Then I will do it," I say.

"I'll be as quick as I can."

He goes so it is just me and Lileas and Milkwort and the deamhan. I take Milkwort out and say sorry I don't have any food for him still. He is good at finding food on his own so I put him down and he runs away to find something to eat. He will come back to me soon.

"Be careful of the terror beasts" is what I warn him. He is only small so they will not find him.

Lileas goes into the place that is like a bothan and uses a branch to get out some of the dirty bits. Then she starts collecting sticks for a fire. I watch the deamhan like Jaime says.

"You like me a lot, yes?" he says. I do not answer him because I don't want to talk to him. "You stare at me so I think you like me a lot." I still do not say anything. He is wrong. I do not like him at all. "It is hard for you, to be like that. You are lucky not to be born in Norveg. You want to know for why? If you are they will kill you already."

"Shut up," I say.

"They kill you when you are born. It is the right thing to do. You can do nothing. It is sad for you to be alive."

"Shut up!" I say again. He is trying to make me angry, I know it. Also it is working. He stops talking and is whistling. I want to tell him to stop the whistling but I don't because it is better than the talking. He stops it by himself.

"What was that sound?" he says. I didn't hear anything. "Did you not hear? A cry. Maybe it was your friend. There is animals worse than bears in Scotia. Animals worse than moose. The boy is not safe to be alone."

I don't say anything.

"Will you not help him?" he says. "Oh, I forget: your brain is broken. You cannot think right."

"Yes, I can," I say. He does not know it. "I'm very—clever."

"Then why do you not help your friend?"

"He told me to watch you. It is an—it is an important job."

He laughs. "No it is n-not." He says it like me to be mean. "I am tied to the tree and cannot move. Why does someone need to watch me? The boy tells you to watch me because he does not want you with him, because you always do wrong. And now you do wrong again because you do not help him when he needs you.

I wonder. . . . What will you do when he does not come back?"

What does he mean Jaime's not coming back? He will come back.

I hear something far away that maybe is a shout. Was it Jaime? I don't know. There is another one. I stand up and, keeping looking at the deamhan, I call for Lileas.

"Did you hear the shout?" I ask her.

"No," she says.

"I think Jaime might be in—in trouble. I have to help him."

"Okay," she says. "What should I do?"

"You wait here and watch the deamhan. You do the important job and I'll—I'll do the—more important job."

I try to think which way Jaime went when he left. I think it was this way so I go. I push the branches away and they scratch me. When I find Jaime and save him he will be so happy that he will hug me like he hugged Lileas on the boat and it will be nice. I shout his name so he will hear me. I say don't worry because I'm coming to save you.

The trees are thicker and I think maybe I have gone the wrong way. It is so dark in the trees now. I shout Jaime's name again two times. Still I can't see him. I listen to hear if he shouts again but he doesn't. What if the moose already got him or something worse and is eating him and he is dead? I turn around in the circles. I don't know which way to go anymore. A branch brushes my head and I scream because I did not know there was a branch there.

"Agatha?"

I am surprised and nearly hit him.

"Jaime!" I say.

"What are you doing here?"

"I came to save you because you shouted."

"No, I didn't."

"There are worse things than m-mooses and I thought—I thought they got you."

"I'm fine. I've just been looking for food. I found these mushrooms, but I'm not sure if they're edible. You were supposed to stay and watch Knútr. Where's Lileas?"

There is a scream and it is a loud one.

Jaime doesn't say anything. He drops the mushrooms and starts running fast. I try to keep up but it is hard because of the branches and the scratching.

"Wait—wait for me, J-Jaime," I say, but he keeps on fast.

I get back just after him. I see him first and his face is bad. Then I see the deamhan who is Knútr and I see Lileas. The deamhan is not tied up anymore. He is holding Lileas with one hand over her mouth. The other hand is holding the *corcag* knife and the blade is on her neck.

"What do you want?" Jaime says. "Don't do this. We're taking you back, remember. Just say what you want. You need us as much as we need you. We're going to help each other. That was the deal."

The deamhan laughs. His face is all creases.

"There is no deal," he says. "I need no help."

The deamhan's hands are holding tight. The blade is on her and her eyes are so big. I do not know what to do I do not know I do not know. Lileas looks at Jaime and then at me and then at Jaime. I have to help her but I do not know how and I cannot think.

"Just let her go," Jaime says. "Please. Don't do this."

"You will not find your people," says the deamhan. "And I will never be your prisoner."

He is laughing when he kills her. Everywhere is blood.

The deamhan roars and then he is gone.

NATHARA

It is sad when something dies

But only if you like that thing

I was sad when they killed the bird because I liked it

It used to sing to me and I called it Grizel like my mummy

I've told them before not to kill the birds

Why don't they ever listen

They get fidgety when there is nothing they can get

I still ate it

No point in it going to waste

I thought about it singing when I was eating it

Ha ha ha

It's not singing anymore

I pulled off its legs and threw them out the window

Stupid bird got caught

Should have flown away

If I had wings that's what I would do

Fly away

Away from them and the smell of dead
I'd fly so high they'd never catch me
I know they'd try
If I was a bird they'd try and kill me for sure
They want to kill me now but they know they can't
They can try they can try
I'll never let them

JAIME

WE BURIED LILEAS THIS MORNING. I USED MY HANDS TO dig the grave. Agatha decorated the top with stones and a few flowers, and I placed the wooden heron among them. We stood on either side of it in silence. I wanted to say how brave Lileas was, how funny and kind, but when I tried to speak, nothing came out.

I repeat the moment over and over again in my head.

It all happened so quick; there was no time to think. I should have said more, I should have done something differently. I could have changed his mind.

I keep seeing her face just before. The pleading in her eyes, the terror.

We should never have brought Knútr with us. I should have killed him when I had the chance, or left him to drown when the boat went under. And why did I leave Agatha on her own with him? What was I thinking? Every decision I've made has been wrong.

Knútr must have gotten hold of the *corcag* when the boat was sinking and then hidden it somehow, which means he had it on him for two days before he used it. Two days! He could have easily killed us in our sleep, but no: he wanted to see the looks on our faces when we realized he'd outsmarted us. He wanted us to feel responsible.

I put one foot in front of the other in a monotonous plod. My legs are heavy, as if they've been filled with lead. Agatha follows a few paces behind. She tried to speak to me this morning, but I didn't reply. She blames herself for what happened, and I can't bring myself to convince her otherwise.

I push on, just to keep moving. All that matters now is finding our clan. Every day that passes, they get farther and farther away. All I can do is keep walking east. There might not be any boats there; it could be another of Knútr's lies. But if we stop, it means we've given up, and then what would we do?

The trees have fallen away and we are back out in the open. Scotia is even more mountainous than Skye. The sun is bright, drying our throats and mocking our grief. All I've eaten in the past two days are some wild nettles and a handful of berries, but I'm not even slightly hungry. Perhaps I am walking to my death. It certainly feels that way.

Knútr is out there somewhere. I keep thinking I see him at the edge of my vision, but when I look again, there is never anyone there. What is his plan? Has he gone on to Dunnottar harbor to take a boat for himself? More likely he is still nearby, stalking us, preparing to kill us when we least expect it. We wouldn't stand a chance.

By late afternoon, I am drenched in sweat, and the fading heat is a welcome relief. The sun begins to set, smearing rusted tears across the sky. If last night was anything to go by, the temperature is about to drop dramatically.

There is a heavy thud behind me, and I turn to see Agatha on the ground some distance away.

"Agatha!" I run back to her.

"I'm fine," she says, wiping off mud as she climbs to her feet. "I tripped—I—I tripped o-over, that's all."

Her face looks like scrunched-up leaves. I've been so selfish, marching on without giving her a second thought. I take her arm and put it around my neck.

"Lean on me. I'll get you to some water. I saw a stream not far away."

The stream turns out to be a river, fast running and wide. I prop Agatha against a tree and then use my hands to scoop up as much water as I can. Before it drips through, I rush it to her mouth. She drinks through cracked lips. I leave for more water, and keep bringing it to her until she signals that she's had enough. Then I scoop some up for myself, gulping it down.

"I'm sorry for ignoring you all day," I say, sitting down next to her. "It's been hard."

"It wasn't my—it wasn't my fault," she says.

"No, it wasn't."

"Do you h-hate me?"

"Of course not. It's just you and me now. We have to stick together."

I put my arm around her. She smiles that broad, affectionate smile of hers, then leans her head against my shoulder and gives me a big hug.

THE ANIMALS ARE UPON US BEFORE WE KNOW WHAT'S happening, the sound of their approach masked by the roar of the river. They tower above us, one on each side. We are pinned against the river, so there is no way for us to escape. Long, matted hair covers their eyes, and enormous horns protrude from either side of their heads.

"Terror beasts! It's the terror beasts!" Agatha screams as I pull her to her feet. I back up to the river, shielding Agatha behind me, which is when I notice the riders. Sitting atop each of the two animals is a person, one male, one female. People. Alive on the mainland. They're both young, maybe a few years older than I am. The boy has the most piercing green eyes. The girl has fair hair, cut short, and wears a brown cloak that falls over her bare arms. Her mouth is pursed, her forehead frowning. Both riders are holding spears, which are pointed at our chests.

"Who are you?" says the boy. His voice is deep and strong. "Speak."

My throat is in knots. Agatha comes to my rescue.

"I'm Agatha-Cabhar and this is J-Jaime-Iasgair, both of—of Clann-a-Tuath. Who are *you*?"

"You need to come with us," says the girl. Despite her surliness, it is easy to tell how attractive she is. They both are.

"We're not your—prisoners," says Agatha.

"Not yet," says the boy. "It's dangerous to be out on the plains at night. We're a better option than what might come next."

"We thought everyone on the mainland was dead," I say. Some of the words slip out high-pitched, bringing a flush of heat to my cheeks.

"You thought wrong," says the boy.

"What are they?" Agatha asks, indicating the animals.

"Highland bulls."

I've heard of cows and bulls but never seen one before. These are completely different from how they were described to me. They're as tall as I am and covered in thick orange-brown hair that falls in shaggy locks almost to the ground. By far their most striking feature is their horns, which twist out of their heads like giant thorns.

"Where will you take us?" I ask.

"Enough questions," says the girl. "Get on."

"But—"

The girl cuts me off by raising her spear in line with my throat. The boy holds his hand out to Agatha. She looks at me. I don't know what to say. She takes hold of the boy's hand and lets him pull her up, onto his bull. The bull makes no sign of discomfort at having two people on its back.

I let the girl pull me onto hers. I sit behind her, my arms hanging limp at my sides. Despite its thick hair, the bull's back is bony and uncomfortable.

"We need to go east," I say.

"You'll go where you're taken," says the girl. "Hold on."

I grab fistfuls of the bull's hair. The girl snorts. "Not to him, to me." She reaches back and pulls my arms around her waist. Before I can protest, she kicks the bull with her heels and we gallop upstream, with Agatha and the other bull following close behind.

JAIME

THE HIGHLAND BULLS MOVE SURPRISINGLY FAST FOR such large, inelegant creatures. As we bound along, every bump and groove reverberates through my backside. Agatha squeals with delight behind me. The boy laughs at her, then tells her off for being so loud.

Night creeps up on us like a predator hunting prey, and I soon lose sense of where we are going. Warmth from the girl's back seeps into my chest. I try to keep my distance, but the motion of the bull keeps forcing us together. She smells of earth, just after it's rained, or maybe that's the bull. Who are these people? And where are they taking us?

After a while, smoke tendrils appear in the distance, spiraling up in an idle plume. We make our way toward them, and thirty or more tents come into view. They are set up around a communal cooking fire, which is the source of the smoke. People are milling in and out of the tents. As we approach, they stop what they are doing and stare at us. Their clothing is crude, made out of animal hide and fur. Many of the women have their hair cut short, and some of the men wear theirs long. Although there are other fires dotted about, people move freely in and out of the darkness, which is all the proof I need that *sgàilean* definitely don't exist. I knew it, but it still comes as a relief.

The girl pulls up on the bull's horns, bringing the animal to a halt. "Get off," she says, swinging down. I try to copy her, but my descent is, at best, a controlled fall.

"Where are we?" I ask, massaging my thumbs into my lower back.

The girl ignores me.

Agatha plops down beside me.

"That was—the best!" she says. "I hope we can do that again." She pats her bull on its head, and it licks her hand with a thick, slobbery tongue.

People start moving toward us from all directions, with spears in their hands. Agatha is too distracted to notice. Within moments, we're surrounded.

"Wait. What's going on?" I say.

The spears rise as one, cutting off any chance of escape.

"You need to come with me. Try to flee and we will kill you," says a gruff older man. He grips my shoulder and shoves me in the direction of one of the tents. Agatha shouts in protest as I am led away. I struggle, looking around for the boy and girl who brought us here. They can explain. Surely this is some kind of mistake? I catch a glimpse of the boy. He raises his eyebrows and says nothing. The hand guiding me lowers my head through a tent flap and pushes me inside. The flap closes and I am on my own.

There is nothing in the tent except for spindling shadows cast from a lantern high above my head. Wooden poles run up the tent sides, meeting in a crisscross at its peak. The walls are a patchwork of material, sewn together with thick stitching. I reach out and run my fingertips down the side nearest to me. It is coarse and smells of sour meat. I pull my hand away. It's skin. The walls are made of skin. I swallow. Is that what they plan to do to us — use our skin to make their tents?

The entrance flaps in the wind like a caught bird trying to escape. Through the gap, I can see the boots of two guards. I have to get out of here. My clan needs me — Aileen needs me — and we're wasting time. I run my hands along the base of the tent, trying to find a loose peg that I can dislodge, but from inside it's impossible to get the right angle. I scratch at the skin walls, trying to make a tear. One of my nails snags on the stitching, and the top of the nail rips off. I shout through gritted teeth and start kicking the walls. The kicks rebound off the taut skin, barely even causing a shudder. It's hopeless. I'm never going to get out of here. I can't do anything. I sit down on the ground. Its dampness bleeds into me.

The entranceway opens and a tall woman enters. She stares down at me over an angular nose. "Don't stand up," she says. Something tells me it would be wise to obey her.

"Why are you here?" she says. Her dark hair is shot with a streak of gray.

"I was brought here. There was a boy and a girl. They made us come."

"But why are you this far north? Where have you come from? What do you want?"

For every question I answer, she asks me three more. I explain as best as I can about the wedding, the attack, our journey to Scotia, the fight with Knútr. When it comes to recounting what happened to Lileas, my body starts to shake. Tears leak out of my eyes and run down my face. I wipe them away, but more replace them. I can't. I mustn't. *Stop it. Stop crying. Stop crying!* I press the palms of my hands into my eyes, willing the tears to stop, but still they spill out. My chest cramps, and my shoulders start to tremble. My body is no longer under my control. Something opens up inside me, and I'm wailing and gasping and these sounds are coming out of me and I know she's watching, but I can't stop any of it. I can't.

We have to protect each other. That is what Lileas said to me. I was supposed to protect her and I failed.

The woman does not try to comfort me. She stands looking at me for a few moments, then leaves. I lie on the floor with my arms wrapped around my sides and sob myself to sleep.

WHEN I WAKE UP, THE AIR IN THE TENT TASTES STALE. I stretch my arms and rub my jaw, which aches from sleeping on it at an awkward angle. The lantern has gone out, but sunlight shines through the translucent skin walls. Someone has left a bowl of oats by my feet. I spoon some into my mouth without tasting anything. Just as I am finishing, a girl walks in. It is the one who brought me here yesterday.

"Good, you're awake. The contest is about to start," she says.

"What contest?" I ask.

"He thought you might like to watch."

"Who? Watch what?"

"Cray. He wants to show off, I expect."

She turns and exits the tent. I step out after her and notice there is no longer anyone guarding the entrance. Am I a prisoner here or not? Why is no one telling me what's going on?

I follow the girl to a large, open space a short walk from the tents. The grassy area is cordoned off with ropes and wooden poles to form a huge rectangular arena. People are standing all the way around—the whole clan by the looks of it. I search among their faces for Agatha, but there's no sign of her.

Six highland bulls stomp into the arena, each with a rider sitting upon its back. The crowd cheers as they circle the space.

"There's Cray," says the girl with a yawn, pointing to the boy who rode with Agatha yesterday.

"And what's your name?" I ask.

"Mór," she tells me, as if insulted. That's the end of that conversation.

Each of the riders is holding a different weapon. Cray has a short wooden pole that he spins above his head as he smiles at the spectators. His top is sleeveless, showing off his toned arms. After a short parade, the riders settle their bulls around the edges of the arena, so they are an equal distance apart. A hush settles over the crowd. The bulls' feet shuffle in anticipation, and a lone fly buzzes around our heads. Then a horn blast breaks the stillness and all six riders kick their bulls into action. Three of them run headlong into a collision at the center, while the other three play it safe on the outskirts.

"What are they doing?" I ask Mór.

"Last one to fall," she says, without taking her eyes off the action.

A bald man is the first to go down, taken off guard by an attack from a woman with studded gloves. Another woman tries to trap Cray with a net, but he ducks out of the way, flicking his stick into her chest. The impact sends her tumbling off her bull in a backward somersault. As she goes down, Cray snatches the net from her hands and tucks it into his trousers. One by one the other riders topple, until only Cray and the gloved woman remain. They separate to opposite sides of the arena, squaring up to each other. Silence unfurls across the field. Then both riders kick simultaneously, and the bulls hurtle forward. They are going to collide head-on. Surely that could kill them?

At the last moment, the bulls swerve, but their mighty horns still crack together as they pass. Cray strikes at the exact moment the horns hit. The woman predicts his move and beats his stick away with her fist. With her other hand, she pummels Cray on his jaw. In the time it takes him to regain his composure, the woman circles around so the two are side by side, both still galloping forward at top speed. The woman tries to push Cray off. He crouches low and holds on tight. Steering with just one hand, he stretches over and tickles the other bull's nose with his stick. It shakes its head in agitation, and the movement reverberates through its entire body. The woman struggles to keep her balance. Cray is focusing all his attention on the bull, so he doesn't notice that the woman is pulling one of her gloves off with her teeth. She flings it at Cray's outstretched hand. It takes him by surprise, and he drops the stick. The woman smiles, sensing victory now that

Cray's lost his weapon. She rounds on him and punches him on the shoulder. He cannot dodge the strike. He loses his balance and falls. The competition is over.

The woman raises her arms in the air and calls out in victory. The crowd, however, does not join in, for they have seen something that she has not: Cray has slipped down to the underside of his bull, where he is clinging on with both hands. He only pretended to fall! His bull approaches the woman from behind, as if it knows where to go without being told. The woman realizes too late what is happening, turning to see Cray swing up from beneath his animal, launching the net he picked up earlier. It sails over the woman's head and ensnares her. Its ends are weighted and it falls around her body, holding her tight. Cray slips a corner of it over one of his bull's horns. His bull breaks away and the net is pulled taut. The woman is dragged from her mount and crashes to the ground, taking the net with her.

She stands, still tangled in the net. Her defeat is not elegant, but she takes it graciously and acknowledges Cray as the victor. He, in turn, bows to the roaring crowd and takes his bull on a victory lap.

Two men jog into the arena, carrying something between them. Cray returns to the middle and they pass it up to him. It is a spear, the longest I have ever seen. Four interlocking triangles come together to make its point. The crowd rumbles. Something else is about to take place.

"What's happening?" I ask Mór.

"He claims his prize for winning," she replies.

"What's the prize?"

"He gets to kill the prisoner."

The prisoner? My heart misses a beat. Does she mean me? No, that can't be right. No one is paying me any attention. Not Agatha?

A hooded body is dragged into the arena. The shape of it looks oddly familiar. Then they remove the hood. It can't be— My knees buckle.

The prisoner is Knútr. And now Cray is going to kill him.

NATHARA

Where are all the horses

I know we used to have some

I helped look after them when I was a little girl

Big things they were with hairy nostrils and yellow spit

They should be in the stables but they're not there

They'd better not have taken them

Perhaps they went for a walk or ate each other

No that's not right

Horses don't eat horses

We used to feed them carrots

There was a shadow in the stables with blood on its hands

It didn't bring me food so it wasn't from an animal

Someone must have come too close

It slipped away and I haven't seen it since

Slippery slippery like soap and mud

I knew a song about that once

Mummy used to sing it to me

She'll be coming home soon

Mummy and Daddy and Calum

They made a promise and promises can never be broken

You'll be safe in here Daddy said

So where are the horses

I'm worried they're lost

If they went for a walk they should be back by now

It's past their bedtime and the bugs will bite

Stupid horses deserve what's coming to them

Hope they die

Even if they do come back I won't let them in

Or I'll give them to the shadows

Ha ha ha

That'll teach them a lesson

That will be the end of them

AGATHA

IT IS THE BEST THING I EVER SAW. THE BIG BULLS ALL running and crashing and the people pushing all the other ones off. And best of all is the man who is called Crayton which I know it is his name because I asked the woman and she told me. I don't like that woman. I was in a tent that smelled all horrible and I didn't like it so I shouted a lot and then the woman came who was tall. She kept asking me questions. Some were easy questions like what is your name and some were hard ones like why were you spying which I didn't know why because we weren't.

I asked her lots of questions too. She didn't like it when I did that. She kept saying, "I'm asking the questions," and I said, "Yes, you are. And so am I." She wouldn't answer them though. She said that I had to stay in the tent until they decided what to do with me. Then she told me the man's name was Crayton because that's the question I kept asking all the time because I wanted to know it because he is the most handsome one. I was holding on to him on the bull and I liked it.

When the woman left I tried to go out too but the rude man wouldn't let me. He's the one that stood outside. He told me I had to stay inside. I told him I was not a prisoner and I can do what I want. I tried to push past but he stopped me and called me a "good-for-nothing menace" so I spat in his face hard. Then he was really mad. Other people came in and tied up my arms and I shouted more so they tied up my mouth as well so I couldn't do it. I was kicking and kicking because they were holding me and I hated it so I was more angry. Then I thought about Maistreas Eilionoir. She would be cross if she knew I got angry and tried to hurt the man. Also, I was worried they might hurt Milkwort, who was in my pocket. I stopped kicking. The hot inside went away and then the people let me go and they left. They should not do that holding me and tying up.

I checked on Milkwort when they were gone and lucky he wasn't hurt.

Then I had a clever plan which was for Milkwort to chew through the rope on my wrists and the cloth in my mouth. It was easy for him and we were both happier after that. I stroked him behind his ears to say thank you and he liked it.

I wanted to sleep then because I was so tired from so much walking, but my head was all whirring and thinking and I couldn't stop it. I was thinking all about the rude man and about Crayton and about our clan and how we have to rescue them, but the most I was thinking about was Lileas. I liked her so much because she was my friend and now she is dead. It's not fair that she is dead. Jaime says it wasn't my fault and I know that it wasn't my fault but also I keep thinking that maybe it was my fault.

This morning the rude man came back in and he was surprised I wasn't tied up anymore. He gave me food that wasn't nice. After I ate it, he tied my wrists and my mouth again and I couldn't stop it.

He took me outside to the place I am now which is where all the people are. I like being here because Crayton is here on his bull and he is so handsome and strong. It is so nice to look at him. And he was so clever to trick the woman with the gloves and he won and I knew he would.

Now he is holding up a spear and he spins it above his head so fast.

"Bring out the prisoner!" someone shouts.

Two men with spears drag in a body and then pull it to its feet. That is who is the prisoner. Oh, good. I was worried it might be me. They take the hood off the prisoner but he has his back to me so I cannot see him. Then he turns around and I know him.

It is the deamhan who is Knútr.

Why is he here? All I can think in my head is Lileas and the knife and her eyes and the blood, and my legs do not keep straight and I think I will fall over.

"That spear is going right through his heart. Which is what will happen to you if you spit at me again," says the rude man.

The nasty deamhan is going to be killed. That is what is right. But if he is dead we don't have a plan for when we get to Norveg or know how to get there. Jaime pretends we have a plan but we don't have a good one. The nasty deamhan has to be our plan. The men push him on his knees. Crayton goes on the bull to the faraway side of the field. He holds up the spear and starts the bull running.

The bull will run past and he will stab the deamhan, I know it.

I do not think. I go under the rope and run for the deamhan. It is hard because my hands are tied and so is my mouth. The rude man shouts behind me but I do not listen. Crayton and the bull are running straight at me. He has not seen me and I will be trampled. I cannot shout because the cloth is in my mouth. There is only one choice I make.

I throw myself into the deamhan which knocks him over. Crayton on the bull is raising the spear and it is coming toward me and it will kill me. I shut my eyes and wait for it to happen. It doesn't happen. The bull runs past me. A different person grabs my arm and I open my eyes. It is a man I don't know. I shrug him so he isn't holding me because I don't like it.

"What on earth?" he says.

Crayton has gone to the side. He did not kill me because he likes me. He is off the bull and is running over now.

"What are you playing at? You could have been killed," he says.

I try to speak to tell him, but I cannot do it with the cloth in my mouth.

"Come here." It is the rude man who has come to get me and grabs my arm too hard. I try to shake him off too but he squeezes more.

"She's trying to tell us something," says Crayton. He reaches out and pulls the cloth from my mouth and I am happy.

"You can't—k-kill him," I say.

"Why not?" he asks.

"We need—we need—for the plan. C-clan for our clan—with the N-Norveg." It's not coming out right.

More people have run in. The nasty deamhan looks at me and grins. I kick him hard on his leg. The rude man pulls me more tight.

"Take her away," says a fat man with a gray beard. "Let's get this over with, Cray."

Crayton walks toward his bull.

"No, wait. You can't." My head is going fast for a clever plan and then I think of one. "I—ch-challenge you," I say.

Crayton stops. The man pulling me stops as well. Crayton looks at me. His face is puzzle and a little smile.

"You challenge me?" he says.

"I want to do the—the competition on the bull and push you off."

Crayton laughs. "Why?"

"I want to be the one to—to kill him."

"I thought you just said you needed him alive?"

That is true so I don't know what to say to that.

"No, this is ridiculous." The rude man starts to pull me away again.

The crowd is shouting something. It gets louder and it is "Do it! Do it! Do it!"

Crayton walks over to me until he is close. He is a nice smell. "Now you've put me in a very difficult position," he says. He is smiling and I like it. "It's not in our custom to turn down a challenge. Besides, I've got to give the crowd what they want."

This means he says yes.

"We have a new challenger," shouts the man with the gray beard. He is scratching his head when he says it. "Remove the

138

prisoner and prepare the battlefield. Untie this girl and fetch her a *bó*."

The rude man doesn't want to untie me but he has to. Someone comes in with a bull. It is even bigger than Cray's one. It is hard for me to climb on. I keep trying but I cannot do it and everyone laughs.

"You can do it, Aggie!" is a shout and I look and it is Jaime. I didn't see him before and he is watching and I wave at him and I smile. The next time I try I do it and I pull myself up. The bull stamps its feet and is not happy. I hold on to its hair which is thick.

"Choose your weapon," says a boy holding up a box with all things in.

"I don't want one," I say, and then I say, "Thank you," because it is manners. I only have two hands and I need them for holding.

"Let's see what you've got," says Crayton with a wink that is for me. It makes my heart wibble. He gets on his bull and rides it to the other side.

Everyone is quiet. They are all looking at me which I don't like. The ground is a long way down to fall so it will hurt. Now I am not sure that it is a good plan. I didn't think about this part. Crayton is the best one. I cannot beat him.

A horn goes. Crayton kicks his bull and it comes charging straight toward me.

JAIME

I HAVE NO IDEA WHAT SHE'S DOING. I DOUBT SHE THOUGHT that far ahead. Her hands are clasped around the hair at the base of the bull's neck, and her head is shaking a little from side to side. She's going to end up hurting herself. Or worse. She looks like she might fall off before the contest even begins. Her feet dangle far from the ground.

The starting signal blares, and Cray's bull runs at Agatha's. There are maybe fifty yards between them, and Cray is closing the gap fast. Agatha does nothing, staring at Cray's bull, probably regretting her bravery now that the situation has spun out of her control.

Cray is not riding full speed; he's going easy on her. When he is within reach, he taps her bull on its rear with his stick, sending it trotting across the arena in the opposite direction. There is laughter from the crowd, and Cray smiles, soaking up the adoration. Agatha's bull comes to a standstill in the center of the arena. Cray catches up with her and starts riding around her in circles. She sits with her head bowed, waiting for the inevitable.

"Well, this has been fun," says Cray, raising his voice so everyone can hear him, "but I'm afraid there can be only one *bó* champion."

He raises his stick, ready to deliver the final blow.

"You're right," says Agatha, lifting her head for the first time. "There can only be one ch-champion. And that is—that is me because now you're going to f-fall off, Crayton."

Cray smiles, charmed. The smile does not last long, though, for at that moment his bull breaks away from Agatha's and starts bucking wildly. Cray holds on, leaning forward to whisper into his bull's ear. Its kicks get more turbulent, and even from a distance I can tell that Cray is spooked. Agatha's bull remains still, more than content to let her sit and watch the action from its back. The crowd does not know whether to cheer or be concerned.

Cray lasts an impressive amount of time, given the violence with which his bull is trying to hurl him off. Finally, it is one kick too many, and he flies into the air, landing on his side with a thud. It must hurt, but he hides it well. He jumps to his feet, sweeping his hair from his eyes, and looks up at Agatha in bewilderment.

Agatha does not celebrate or gloat. She topples down from her bull, stumbles over to Cray, and shakes his hand.

"I t-told you you would fall," she says, loud enough for the whole crowd to hear.

No one knows how to react. For a couple of moments there is silence, then a huge cheer erupts and everyone starts chanting, "Champion! Champion!"

Cray stares at Agatha, a questioning frown in the middle of his forehead. Then he grabs her hand and raises it into the air.

The crowd cheers once again. Agatha's smile is the biggest I have ever seen it.

❧

THERE ARE FIVE PEOPLE INSIDE THE TENT: THE WOMAN with the white streak in her hair who questioned me yesterday—whose name is Murdina—a round, weathered man called Hendry, Cray, Agatha, and me.

After Agatha was named the winner of the contest, people flocked around her, asking her how she'd done it. Claims that it was a fluke were bandied about, and a few other people were more concerned about whether Knútr's execution would still take place. The term *teanga-bèist* was mentioned, spoken with an equal mix of excitement and trepidation.

All the people crowding in made Agatha twitchy. I steered her away from the throng before she lost control and lashed out at whoever was nearest. A few people started to protest, and one woman even went to grab Agatha's wrist. Agatha yanked her hand away with a threatening scowl.

"Enough!" I shouted as loud as I could. "You want answers and we want to give them to you. But not like this. Take us somewhere quiet with whoever your leaders are, and we'll tell you the truth."

Cray watched me from the edge of the crowd, his intense eyes filled with curiosity. Murdina stepped forward and apologized for the raucous behavior. She agreed to my request and led us to the tent we're in now.

"We're not getting anywhere," says Hendry, resting his hands on his belly. "Why won't she talk?"

Agatha hasn't said a word since we left the arena. Her shoulders are slumped and she is staring at the floor.

"I don't know," I say, although I could make a good guess. Agatha is proud and loves getting attention; admitting that she had nothing to do with Cray falling would be a big blow to her ego.

"Why don't you tell us what happened from your perspective?" Murdina says to Cray.

"There's not much to tell, really," he says. "Bras has never acted that way before. It all happened so fast. I didn't feel like he was angry or in pain. More that he was playing a trick on me, that he threw me off because he wanted to."

"That would fit," says Hendry. He rakes his fingers through the gray bristles of his beard.

"Fit with what?" I ask.

Hendry and Murdina exchange glances.

"You don't really think—?" says Cray.

Hendry's eyes open wide, but he doesn't say anything.

"I don't know how much you know about us Bó Riders," Murdina says to me.

"I don't know anything at all," I admit. "We thought the mainland was deserted."

"The vast majority of it is. But we survived. Our tribe has lived in the Highlands of Scotia for hundreds of years, living off the land, traveling from place to place, side by side with the Highland cows. When a child turns five, he or she is paired with a newborn bull, and the two grow up together, spending their lives as one.

"What Hendry was alluding to is a skill possessed by the very first Bó Rider, a man named Tòmas. It is said he was a *teanga-bèist* — someone with the ability to enter the mind of an animal and request it to do their bidding. It was Tòmas who established the relationship between our two species, by proposing a way of living that would be beneficial to us both. The herd agreed, and we have lived in harmony ever since.

"There has not been a *teanga-bèist* heard of since Tòmas, and many refuse to believe such a thing is possible. Today, they may have been proved wrong."

I laugh, although it comes out more like a splutter. "What, you think Agatha controlled that other bull with her mind?"

"We would know more if she would speak to us," says Hendry, pressing his thick forehead with three of his fingers.

They're playing a joke on me. They must be. Yet their faces are stern and humorless.

"Maybe I should talk to her in private?" I say.

"That might be best," says Murdina, getting up to leave. The others follow her.

Once they're gone, I turn to Agatha. Her eyelids are heavy and her cheeks are sallow.

"Hey, Aggie," I say. "It's just me and you now."

"Hello, Jaime," she slurs, sounding a little drunk. She wrinkles up her nose and then smiles as if nothing out of the ordinary has happened today.

"So, what happened out there?"

Her smile fades. "I'm not—not—not supposed to say," she whispers.

"Says who?"

"M-Maistreas Eilionoir."

Maistreas Eilionoir? What does she have to do with anything?

"Well, she's not here anymore," I say. The memory of what happened to her sends a pang through my chest. "And we're a long way from home."

She pauses for a long time and then, with a tight jaw, she says, "I can do it, J-Jaime. I can do—I can do what they say."

I sigh. She so desperately wants it to be true.

"How?" I ask, pretending I believe her.

"I ask them in my head," she says. "And try to remember manners." Her voice is like dandelion seeds, floating away. "The jellysquid . . . But it is not *dùth*. Don't tell—I'm so sleepy now. Don't tell. Can I sleep now, Jaime?"

She doesn't wait for my reply. She faints into my lap, her hair spilling across my knees. I lower her onto the floor, cover her with a blanket, and step out of the tent.

Cray is outside, leaning on a tent rope, waiting for me. Something about him irritates me. Maybe it's the way he looks down on me, as if I will never be as good as he is, with his perfect body and his perfect face.

"Where are the others?" I ask.

"They wanted to give you some privacy. They'll be back soon."

"We need to leave. Are we free to leave?"

Cray shrugs. "Are you hungry?"

"A little."

He reaches into a pouch and offers me a handful of cobnuts.

"Thanks," I say.

"What about her?" he asks, indicating inside the tent.

"She's asleep. The contest exhausted her."

"She's a funny one. I like her."

"Me too."

I fill the silence by eating some of the nuts. The crunch they make is uncomfortably loud, so I swallow them half chewed.

Could there be any truth to Agatha's claim? And why did she mention the jellysquid? Could that have been her as well? It did come out of nowhere right when we needed it, and Agatha was behaving strangely at the time. I've never heard of anyone being able to speak to animals before, but the Bó Riders seem to believe that it's possible.

"You don't say much, do you?" says Cray.

"I don't know what to say."

"Did she speak to you?"

I chew on nothing. The cobnuts have left a dryness on the roof of my mouth. Agatha told me not to tell anyone what she said, but only because magic is not *dùth*. She's right that if the elders had discovered she could do something like that, there would have been serious repercussions. Although what did Agatha say about Maistreas Eilionoir? That she knew and told her to keep it a secret? Why would Maistreas Eilionoir break her elder oath to protect Agatha?

The Bó Riders think differently from our clan. They speak of the ability with great reverence, as if it ought to be treasured and encouraged. I can't believe I'm seriously considering the possibility that it might be true.

Cray places his hand on the side of my arm and stares at me. Something about him makes it impossible not to tell him the truth.

"She says she can do it," I say.

He whistles. "Ò *ioc*. I knew it. I could feel it. Incredible."

"But it's not possible."

"What do you mean?" He is grinning, barely listening to me.

"I don't believe in magic."

"It's not magic; it's communication," he says. "We're all animals, after all. Why shouldn't it be possible for one species to communicate with another?"

I hadn't thought of it like that.

"So, what now?"

Cray doesn't answer. He shakes his head in disbelief and then jogs away without saying another word.

NATHARA

Where did everybody go

Are you hiding

I'll come and find you

I'll count to ten

Ready or not I'll either find you or you'll rot

Where could you be

Not in that room

Not in that room

Don't look in there

Daddy says

We're not allowed in that room

Daddy will shout and shout and shout

I've come here before

I come here all the time

It doesn't smell nice

Calum showed me

Naughty Calum

I can go wherever I like

My daddy is the king you know

It's the room with all the bones in it

Little ones and big ones

Hands and legs and heads in a jumble

Silly head's lost its body

You can't walk if you don't have any legs

And you can't talk if you don't have a mouth

Talk to me talk to me

What did you say

You can't talk stupid head

Stupid bones

Stupid heads all dead

Why did everybody die

Don't go in there again

It smells disgusting

Mummy will be cross with all the mess

Someone needs to clean it up before she gets back

I'm not going to do it

Sorry Mummy not my fault

I only wanted a look

Just a little peeky peek

Everyone is bones now

No one wants to play with me anymore

AGATHA

I THINK I HAVE BEEN ASLEEP A LONG TIME. I NEED SOME water. It hurts in my head that is a really bad headache. It is in the place where I talked to the bull. It never hurts when I talk to Milkwort and it was sore only a little bit with the jellysquid. I think it is because the bull is a big animal so it was harder. I am in the tent where everyone was, but they are not here now. Only Jaime is here and I can see him.

"You're awake," he says.

"It is—rude to watch someone when they are—sleeping," I tell him. I rub my eyes and stroke my hair to make it nice.

"Sorry. I was just waiting for you to wake up."

"I'm awake now," I say.

"How are you feeling?" he says.

"Like my head hurts and I want water," I say, and he gives me some. It is nice in my throat when it goes down.

Jaime doesn't say anything and then he says, "They want to see what you can do."

I don't like that and I am panic. He was not supposed to say.

"No, they will hurt me. It's supposed to be a s-secret. I told you not to t-tell," I say, and the angry is coming.

"I'm sorry; you're right. I shouldn't have said anything without asking you first." Jaime sits next to me. "But it's okay, I promise. They think differently from us. They believe you have a great gift. If you really can do it?"

Someone comes in and it is Murdina. She is the tall one and the bossy one that I don't like.

"Good, you're awake," she says.

"I am," I say. "I woke up."

"We are excited by your claim," she says. She does not look excited. "If proved right, you will authenticate all of the tales of our forefather Tòmas."

The round beardy man who is Hendry comes in. He is holding a box and it is resting on his tummy because it is a big one. He hands the box to me. It is pretty and also heavy too.

"What is this? She's only just woken up," says Jaime.

Murdina doesn't say an answer to him. "In that box is a viper," she says to me. I do not know what is a viper. "I want you to open the box and take it out. Be warned, though, if you can't stop it, it will probably bite you and kill you. So I'd advise you not to open the box unless what you have claimed is true."

"Wait! This is crazy," shouts Jaime, and he stands up.

"Silence," says Murdina. She stares at him and he doesn't speak. "We need proof" is what she says then.

Everyone is looking at me. I'm still sleepy from before. It makes me tired when I do it. "Okay, I will try," I say.

I try to do it, to talk to it in my head like I do with Milkwort. It is easy with him. The jellysquid was easy too because it liked to do what I wanted. The bull was the hardest. He wasn't sure so I had to make him like me. Then he agreed it would be funny to play the trick on Crayton.

The one in the box isn't talking. I think it is because I do not know what it looks like so I can't see it in my head. I will have to open the box first. I hope it won't bite me and I die. I put my hand on the lid.

"You don't have to do this, Aggie," says Jaime.

I'm happy that he does not want me to be dead.

I open the box.

It is a snake that is a viper. It is brown and green but mostly brown. Now that I can see it I think I can talk to it, but it is too quick and it comes out of the box and hisses and it has the fangs which I do not want to bite me.

"Don't you bite me," I say aloud even though I can say it in my head for it to hear me. The viper snake doesn't answer and slides onto me and up my body and on my arm. "Oh, no, no, no," I say. I have not touched a snake before and I do not like it. Now it is going across my neck and it goes around it so it is harder for me to breathe and I do not like it at all. I close my eyes.

"Somebody do something; it's going to kill her!" Jaime shouts.

I try to talk to it but it doesn't want to listen. I close my eyes tighter. *Get off me* is what I say to it. It tightens around my neck. It is even harder than the bull and I am still tired and my head hurts. Something is strange though because it is not mean. It is scared, I think. *What do you want?* I ask it, and I know in my head that it does not like the box and the people and the tent. *Okay,* I say, *let go of my neck and do not bite me and I will take you away from here and the box.* It still squeezes me tighter and I think maybe it wants to kill me anyway. It is thinking and while it thinks I cannot breathe. My eyes are hurting and please get off me now.

It goes looser on my neck and then it goes off. I can breathe again and it didn't kill me. Now it is wrapped around my arm. It is heavy and feels wet but it isn't.

I open my eyes and stand up. Everyone is still looking at me and staring.

"It wants to be outside," I say, showing that I am brave and I go.

I walk past the tents to the edge of the trees. Some people are looking at me and pointing and it is rude to point so they shouldn't do it. I say goodbye to the snake and it drops off my arm and goes away in the grass. When I turn around there is Murdina and other people and also Jaime but not Crayton.

"Remarkable," says Murdina.

"Are you crazy?" says Jaime. "You could have killed her!" He is shouting when he says it. He is being cross because he likes me, I know it.

"Calm down," says Murdina. "A bite from that snake would not have been fatal. I just needed her to think that it would be, to test how much she believed in her own abilities."

This means she lied to me. It is not nice to make someone

think that maybe they will die when they won't die. It makes me not like Murdina even more.

Hendry walks to me and holds my hand and shakes it which I do not like. He is smiling. I do not smile back. I want to tell him not to hold my hand.

"As a sign of our respect, you may take whatever food and supplies you need before you leave," Murdina says.

"What about Knútr?" asks Jaime. "We need to take him too."

"The deamhan?" says Murdina. "Absolutely not. His crimes against us are too great. He killed and ate one of our own."

"Knútr *ate* a person?" says Jaime.

"Not a person, a cow," says Murdina. "The herd are part of our tribe—both the cows and the bulls. They are our equals, so the crime is viewed with the same severity. The girl has earned the right to kill him, which she may do before you leave. Either that or we will kill him ourselves. Those are the only options."

Murdina goes and then everyone else goes and it is just me and Jaime.

"Let's walk over to the field," Jaime says.

We walk together away from the tents to the place where the arena was. It is not there now. Some flies go around us and I shake my head so they don't go on my hair. My head is hurting again because of the snake that was called a viper.

"We need to leave," Jaime says. "We've already wasted too much time here. But we can't go without Knútr. Without him to bargain with, it'll be the two of us against the whole deamhan army. What do you think we should do? We have to smuggle him out somehow so we can take him with us."

He is looking at me and I think he wants me to say the plan, but I do not know what the plan is or can't even think of one.

"Do you hate me?" I say.

"Why would I hate you?" he says.

"It's not *d-dùth* to speak to animals in your—head."

"I think it's amazing what you can do. . . . Maybe some things that are not *dùth* aren't as bad as we've been told they are."

I can't say anything to that because it is a bad thing that he has said. If the elders say it is a bad thing of course it is a bad thing. It is quiet in the field.

"Can you talk to more than one animal at once?" Jaime asks me next.

"I don't know," I say, because I don't.

"Could you try?" he says.

"W-why?" I say. I am thinking it will make my head hurt a very lot.

"What if you made all of their bulls run around at the same time? Maybe it would cause a big enough distraction for us to escape with Knútr."

It is quite a clever plan although I do not know if I can do it and I don't want my head to hurt more. I will try it though because you have to try, don't you?

"I will try it, Jaime," I say, and he smiles.

"Okay, first we need to—" but he doesn't finish what he was saying because he hears the barking. I hear it too. It is far away but I can hear it because my ears are good and I am good at hearing. It sounds like a lot of animals barking a lot.

Jaime is looking all around to see it. I see them first.

"Look, Jaime, there," I say, and I point. They are far away and dark shapes and moving fast. There are so many of them and they're running toward us. I know what they are. I know it this time.

It's the terror beasts.

JAIME

WE'RE RUNNING. AGATHA IS IN FRONT OF ME, EVEN though I'm usually much faster than her. I can't stop looking at the animals. They're running toward the camp from all directions, racing down hillsides and bounding through the grass. I don't know what they are; they're barking, but they're too big to be dogs, too big to be wolves. There are so many of them. Hundreds.

A horn blasts, then another. People are running, pulling out weapons, jumping onto bulls.

"Terror beasts. Terror beasts. Terror beasts," Agatha pants as she runs, the words tumbling out every time she exhales.

I think she's right.

They're close enough now that I can make out the power in their hind legs, the sharpness of their teeth, the determination in their eyes. They're closing in on the camp. We won't make it back before they get there. They're going to kill us. They're going to kill us and they're going to eat us.

I freeze.

"Agatha," I say, but it is no more than a whisper. She doesn't hear me. She keeps running. I'm finding it hard to breathe.

What do I do? What do I do? My heart is pounding so hard it feels like it might explode.

"Agatha," I call out again, a little louder this time, but she is too far away.

I should have kept running. I'm exposed, out in the open like this. Now I don't know where to go. The creatures are closing in on the Bó Riders and all I can do is stare.

Some of the beasts have noticed that I've stopped. They change their course, accelerating toward me. I might still be able to out-run them, to reach the camp before they cut me off, but it would mean running at them almost head-on. There's no way I can do that. I turn and flee.

That wasn't the right decision, I know it wasn't. It's too late now.

I need somewhere to hide, but I'm surrounded by nothing but open grassland.

A large rock. To my right, a short sprint away. I can't tell how big it is or how easy it'll be to climb, but it's my best chance. I speed toward it.

The animals chase me. Five, ten, twenty of them. Their barks get louder; they're closing in. They are much faster than I am. Their breath warms the backs of my legs. Any moment, one of them is going to jump up and push me over, and there's nothing I can do to stop it.

I'm nearly at the rock. It's bigger than I thought, its sides steep.

A little farther, a little farther.

I launch myself at the rock, ignoring the pain that hammers my elbows and scrapes across my knees as I frantically search for something to grip on to. My fingers find a crack and I start to pull myself up. The animals crash into the rock, snapping their jaws at my feet. I kick back and keep climbing. My ears throb with their deafening barks. I haul my body over a ridge, onto the small flat area at the top. Below me, the beasts jump against the rock, their claws scrabbling at its sides. They yelp in frustration as they try again and again to scale it. They look like wolves, but they're much larger, with bright yellow eyes and long black tails. Their fur is dark gray, streaked with patches of white. Although they're big, they're also skinny, their rib cages visible beneath their mangy fur.

Their barking attracts the attention of others, until there must be more than thirty of them circling and jostling at the base of the rock. I'm trapped, and too far from the camp to call for help. Besides, the camp is already overrun with beasts; the Bó Riders are charging around on their bulls, trying to fend them off with their spears.

Where is Agatha? Did she make it back?

The barks beneath me quiet. The beasts are trying something new. The ones at the front hunch forward, allowing others to climb onto their backs. More join from behind, and then more again. I can't believe what I'm seeing. Their bodies shift and falter as the ones above step on those beneath them. They're gaining height; the ones on top are no more than a couple of feet away now. Their teeth are stained yellow, and foamy spittle sprays out when they bark. I shuffle backward to the very tip of the rock.

One of them strains forward and tries to bite my ankle. I kick it as hard as I can on the side of its jaw. There is a sickening crack and it falls off to the side. Another one has already replaced it. I kick again and again, but there are too many of them and they are too quick for me.

The highest beast crouches back onto its hind legs and then springs toward me. I half shout, half scream, raising my arms to protect my head. Something wet splashes across my face. I open my eyes. It's blood, but it isn't mine. The beast is on the ground with a spear through its side. The other beasts are on it at once, tearing it apart, fighting over its flesh and lapping up its blood. They're barking and squealing in equal measure.

"Quick, while they're distracted."

I turn around. Cray is there, mounted on his bull. He's holding out his hand to me. "You're going to have to jump."

I look down and shake my head. The gap is too wide. I'll never make it.

"I can't," I say.

"Quick. We don't have much time."

I stand on the edge of the rock. If I don't jump far enough, the beasts will be on me the moment I hit the ground. My whole body is shaking. The beasts have finished eating and turn their bloody snouts in my direction. They snarl when they see Cray. They're going to attack him. Even on his bull he is no match for that many of them. They'd easily pull him down.

"Jump!" shouts Cray.

"I can't! I can't!"

He's too far away.

I'm going to fall. I'm going to die.

"Now!"

I close my eyes and leap forward.

AGATHA

TERROR BEASTS. TERROR BEASTS. TERROR BEASTS.

They're going to get me. I have to do good running. They're going to get me. I'm not good at running.

Faster faster faster faster.

Nearly there. The terror beasts are too. I do not want to look where they are. They are the most worst things I ever saw and I know they want to get me and eat me. Their barking is the loudest ever. It hurts in my ears and I do not like it.

My breath is coming out loud and it's hard to breathe. I need to stop but I can't. I look behind me to see where Jaime is. He isn't there. No, no, the terror beasts didn't get him, did they?

The bull people are on their bulls now and they charge into the terror beasts. The ground is shaking. There is a big and horrible hit of teeth and legs and bones when all the animals crunch together. More terror beasts run down from the hills. I do not know where to go. There is too many of them and too many bulls all running all different ways around me.

"Agatha, up!" someone shouts who is Murdina. She is on her bull and she pulls me up.

"Jaime!" I say.

"Where?" Murdina asks.

"I don't know. He was over there." I say it, and I point.

"I'll go," says Crayton, who is on his bull too and I didn't even know he was there. He kicks his bull and goes to Jaime. Please find him. Murdina kicks her bull too and it runs toward where a big group of terror beasts are. Already lots of terror beasts are on the ground and they have been trampled. I do not like seeing it. The terror beasts are trying to bite the legs of the bulls when they run. The bull people are using their spears to try and get them off and hurt them. One of the bull people nearly falls off when his spear is caught in a terror beast's mouth. On the other side, a terror beast jumps at a bull and bites it with its teeth. The bull puts its head down and then trips over and crashes on its side. The man who was on it is on the ground and the terror beasts jump on him. I do not want to see it. There is too much for my eyes.

Murdina moves her bull away from a big group of terror beasts that is coming toward us. The one at the front jumps, so she gets it with her spear. The sound is crunching. I think I will be sick. Murdina shakes the terror beast off so she can use the spear again. We keep on going faster.

"We need to draw them away from the children's tent," Murdina shouts to two other bull people. "Circle around and spread the word. On my signal, we move as one to the southeastern peak." They nod their heads and go.

"Look!" I say. The girl from yesterday is on the ground next to her bull. She can't get back on because the terror beasts keep coming at her. Her name is Mór because Jaime told it to me. She is using her spear to keep the terror beasts away, and the bull is using its horns but there are too many terror beasts and they can't get them all.

Murdina steers her bull straight at them so so fast. We trample over one and Murdina uses her spear to get two more of them at the same time. Mór swipes at the others and they go away enough to let her get back on her bull.

"We're heading to the southeastern peak," Murdina says to Mór. "From there we'll coordinate a stampede. It's our only hope." She takes a horn from her belt and blows it. It is a long sound and a deep one. We turn away from the camp and other bulls come too and we all go as fast as fast as we can. The terror beasts are following. Barking and barking. We are going up the slope, a big one.

When we are halfway up, Murdina shouts to all the bull people, "On my count, we turn and stampede. Pull in tight. Three, two—" But she doesn't finish because there is more barking and it is above us, not below. More terror beasts. They were waiting at the top of the hill like they knew we were coming. Now they are running down and the other ones are running up and we are trapped in the middle and where can we go?

Murdina swears. Bull people and bulls go in every direction all splitting up which was not the plan.

"Anything you can do to help would be greatly appreciated!" shouts Murdina in front of me.

What can I do? My head is all heavy which makes it too hard

to think. I can only watch it happening. All around is nothing but terror beasts. There is more than one hundred or one thousand of them. They are ripping and tearing and biting and howling. It is the worst thing ever. I do not like it and it is horrible. I close my eyes and scream as loud as I can.

"Agatha! That's really not helping," says Murdina. It is hard to hear her because I am screaming. "Stop screaming!" she shouts.

But I can't stop. It is too bad and horrible and I hate it I hate it all.

"If the wildwolves don't kill us your bloody screaming will," says Murdina.

I stop screaming. I think something. I do not know if it is a clever plan but it is the only one I have. I have to get down. I cannot do it on the bull. It will be dangerous but I do not mind dangerous. I am brave. I put my leg over the bull's back and fall off it to the ground. It is a long way down and it bangs on my knees which hurts.

"What are you doing?" says Murdina, but I don't answer. I get up and start to run. There is a tree ahead of me which is where I am running. It is the fastest I have ever run. All around me is a mess with terror beasts and bulls and bull people. I try not to look at them. I only look at the tree. Run run run run run run run.

I trip over something and the ground is dizzy. I sit up. A terror beast runs at me and jumps. I use my elbow to hit it in its mouth and some of its teeth break. It hurts my elbow a very lot. The terror beast gets back on its feet. I crawl away from it. Blood is coming out of its mouth where I hit it.

"Stay where you are," I say out loud and tell it in my head.

It stops and its nose does twitching. It is looking in my eyes and its eyes are horrible yellow like bad things.

If you try to get me I will hurt you again, I say.

It wants to know how I am in its head. It does not like it.

You need to go, I say to it. *You all need to go and stop all the killing.*

It tells me that's impossible. They are gathered for the great feed. It has been promised to them. It is their last hope.

I know it in my head that it is very hungry. It has not eaten for a long time. It makes me sad a bit about that. It comes one step toward me.

Don't come closer, I say. *I don't want to hurt you.*

The terror beast does not reply. It shakes its head. It does not want me to be inside its head anymore. It runs toward me.

I need to stop it. Near me is what I tripped over. I reach my hand toward it. It is a horn like the one Murdina had to blow in. I try to grab it. I can't reach it. The terror beast jumps on my chest and pushes me backward. It is on top of me. Blood is coming out of its mouth onto my neck and its breath is all hot. Its tongue is out of its mouth and is so long. My fingers are reaching reaching for the horn. It is too far away.

The terror beast is in my head again. It says that they will eat and we cannot stop them.

My fingers find the horn and I grab it. *I'm sorry. I tried to warn you,* I say and I hit the horn into its side as hard as I can. It howls because it is hurt and it falls down on top of me. I am sad that it is hurt or maybe dead but I have an important job to do so I cannot think about it. I push it off me which is hard because it is heavy and so much blood is on me and then I run the last bit to the tree. When I am there I climb it which I am good at climbing. I go all the way to the top and then I can see everything around which is what I wanted. I want all of the terror beasts to hear me.

Then I do the screaming. I scream as loud as I can, in all of their heads.

I know they hear me because they all stop and are turning around and looking for what the sound is. Some of them shake their heads or hit them on the ground. They snap at each other and bite their own tails. I keep screaming louder and louder. Their howls and their pain is all full inside me. It mixes with the screaming and I do not know which is them and what is me. My head is so full it is going to burst. Something breaks inside. My eyes flip over and I cannot hold on. I fall out of the tree, down to where the terror beasts are hungry waiting.

NATHARA

I'm hungry

They haven't brought me anything in days

Naughty shadows

Straight to bed for you

And don't come out until you're ready to say sorry

We used to eat all the food

Cow cheese and porridge and biscuits and honey

Yummy yummy honey in my tummy

I told them bring me some

I don't want dead animal

Too gristly

Gets stuck in my teeth

Why can't you bring me honey for a change

When Mummy and Daddy and Calum come back we'll eat it
every day

I'll make sure of it

I'll eat it from the jar with my hands until I'm sick

No more dead meat for me

AGATHA

"IT WAS YOU, WASN'T IT?"

"Agatha? Are you okay?"

"Stay where you are. Don't stand up."

"How did you do it?"

"Give her some space."

Too many people are talking and I can't see any of them. My head hurts the worst ever. That is the only thing I know. I am sitting but I don't remember sitting. I blink a lot to see more and the blurry goes. There is a not-nice smell.

"Are you okay?" someone asks, and I blink again and it is Jaime. The terror beasts didn't get him! That is the best news.

"Where did you g-go?" I ask him.

"I got stuck on a rock," he says, and his face goes red. "There were wildwolves all around, but Cray helped me escape. By the time we got back, the wildwolves were all running away."

Standing near me is Mór as well and someone else who I don't know who it is. Crayton is not here which is the big shame. What about Milkwort? I put my hand into my pocket and he licks my fingers. He did not get squashed and dead. That is a big phew.

"My head—hurts," I say.

"Here, drink this, it'll help," says the person who I don't know who it is, and he gives me a mug with something in it that is brown.

"Who are you?" I say, and he laughs but it wasn't funny.

"I'm Finn," he says. "That really will help." He means the drink in the mug. Finn has big arms and his face is nice. His hair is dark like the same color as mine. He smiles at me and I like it, but Crayton is still my favorite.

I drink the drink and it tastes disgusting.

"That was—disgusting," I say, and Finn laughs again. I don't know why he's always laughing.

"I didn't say it would taste nice," he says. That is true.

"What happened?" I ask. "The—the terror beasts?"

"You mean the wildwolves?" says Mór. "Something spooked them and they all bolted. The scouts followed them, and they just kept going south. It was you, wasn't it? You made them go?"

The tent opens which is when I realize I am in a tent. It is Murdina who walks in.

"I thought I heard you," she says. "How are you feeling?" She does not smile.

"My head hurts," I say and, "I drank a drink and it was disgusting."

"You should be feeling better soon. You're lucky to be alive, and not to have broken any bones. You fell a long way." She pauses and then says, "Do you know why the wildwolves left?"

Of course I know. I'm the one who did it.

"I screamed," I say.

"You screamed?"

"In their—heads. They didn't—didn't like it," I say.

"I knew it was you," says Mór, and she looks happy.

"That was clever," says Murdina.

I smile the biggest ever. No one has called me clever before.

"Thanks to you, the number of deaths was kept to a minimum," Murdina says as well. "Many people were injured, but we lost few lives. It could have been a lot worse. It *would* have been a lot worse without your help."

"We can't believe how many of them there were," says Mór. "Wildwolves usually only hunt in packs of about ten, and they never used to come near the bulls. We've never seen anything like the number there was today. We were lucky you were here."

"The Bó Riders will forever be indebted to you," says Murdina. "As a sign of our gratitude, we will escort you to your destination in the east. And you may have your deamhan prisoner."

That is very good news. That is what we wanted.

"It's too late for us to leave tonight," Jaime says to me, "so we'll go first thing in the morning."

"Are you hungry?" Finn asks me. "We saved you some food."

I nod my head because yes I am hungry.

"Follow me," says Finn.

I stand up and blackness rushes behind my eyes and my knees go floppy.

"Whoa!" Finn catches me and helps me stand back up.

"What happened?" says Jaime. "Is she all right?" It is because he cares.

"She's fine," says Finn. "Just a little weak. Food ought to sort her out."

He helps me walk out of the tent. I like him holding me and I hug him a little bit. It is dark outside because it is nighttime. It is cold which makes my head nicer. Some of the tents are broken from the terror beasts but the other ones are fixed. All the bull people are sitting around a big fire, like when we do the meeting circle. When they see me, they clap their hands together and are cheering and I know they are doing it for me and they are smiling and I am smiling too.

"Good to see you awake," says Hendry. He stands up and holds my hand, which is what I wish he didn't do so I pull it away. He is nodding his head with a smile and makes his beard wobble wobble.

Someone gives me a bowl with food in it and Hendry shows me where to sit. I sit down and Jaime sits next to me. Crayton is on the other side of the fire. I wave to him and he waves back at me and it makes me warm inside and the best. I eat the food. I am very hungry and I eat a lot. It has meat in it and it tastes good. When I am finished eating I look up and lots of people are looking at me still.

"You don't have to all l-look at me, you know," I say. "It is rude to do it."

Some people laugh and I don't know why.

"Forgive them," says Hendry. "They are simply eager to hear what happened. Our tribe is going to be talking about you for many generations to come. You are a great *teanga-bèist,* just like Tòmas, the first Bó Rider. As you can imagine, we are all fascinated by what you can do."

"Oh," I say. "Okay."

They want to know about the terror beasts that are called wild-wolves and what happened so I tell them about being on the bull with Murdina and how I had the plan so I got down and did the running and then about the terror beast with the broken mouth who tried to hurt me so I hit it with a horn and it died I think. I tell them I was sad to do it because it was only hungry. Then I say about my plan and how I climbed the tree and did the screaming. There is lots of cheering when I say that and I am happy again.

After I have eaten there is singing. Singing is not *dùth* so it is a big surprise to hear it. I have never heard people doing it together before. It is a nice thing to hear. I want to join in and do the sing-ing too. I look at Jaime and he shrugs. I do some of the singing. It is fun. I like the bull people a lot and they like me too.

After the singing is finished I say to Jaime, "Do you want to see s-something?" I think it will be okay now.

"Sure," says Jaime.

I reach into my pocket and take out Milkwort.

"This is Milkwort," I say, and I hold him on my hand. "He is a vole and my friend."

"Hello, Milkwort," says Jaime, and he looks at him. "Wait, did you bring him all the way from Skye?" he asks me. I nod yes. "Wow, he's had quite an adventure. Can you talk to him as well?"

"Of course," I say.

"Amazing." He puts his hand in his pocket and takes out some nuts. "Ask him if he wants a cobnut," he says.

"I don't need to ask him that—he always wants food!"

Jaime gives him the nut and Milkwort eats it and he's happy.

"I'm sleepy now," I say to Jaime. "I want to go to s-sleep."

"Of course," he says.

He stands up and so do I. The black rushes up me again and this time I can't stop from falling. Jaime tries to catch me but he doesn't. I hit the ground. All people are talking around me. I can't hear them. I can't move. All I can see is the fire. It's the wrong way. Inside my head is wrong too. This is bad bad bad.

NATHARA

Daddy made the shadows

Mummy wasn't happy

It's okay Mummy they won't hurt us.

Daddy said so

The magic man made sure of it

He doesn't have a name

Badhbh Badhbh Badhbh Badhbh Badhbh

That's not a real name

It's a stupid name is what it is

Where are you now Badhbh man

Did you go away with everyone else

Or did the shadows pull out your eyes

Ha ha ha

Serves you right

Mummy told you not to make them

No no they can't hurt us

Daddy promised

They'll only kill the other people

Far away in Ingland

And the wicked man King Edmund

He wants to hurt us but we're not going to let him

If you're the first to throw the dirt you'll only end up getting hurt

Goodbye people

The shadows are going to get you

The shadows are going to kill you all

JAIME

I WALK AROUND THE OUTSIDE OF THE TENT SHE'S IN, three times one way, three times the other way, over and over again. Finn is in there with her, trying to find out what's wrong. I stayed with her all night, watching her fall in and out of fitful dreams. As soon as she woke up, Finn asked me to wait outside. The sun is up; we're supposed to be leaving. What if she's too ill to travel? What if the sickness doesn't go away? What if she gets worse and worse until—

"You're going to make yourself dizzy."

Cray. I pause for a moment, then keep walking. He falls into step beside me.

"She's going to be all right," he says.

"You don't know that," I reply.

"She's a fighter. I can tell."

We walk in silence for a bit. Why is he here? I should have thanked him for rescuing me from the rock yesterday, but I haven't. I don't know why.

"I came to tell you I'm ready to leave when you are. I'm not sure if anyone's told you, but it's me who'll be taking the two of you east." Great. "You don't look very happy about that." He laughs.

"Sorry, no, I'm grateful," I say. "I'm just worried about Agatha. And my clan. We've been here too long. We have to leave. We have to get Knútr to them before they get hurt."

I stop walking, struck by a new wave of futility. I squat by the entrance to the tent. Cray sits down next to me.

"I was going to ask about that. So your plan is to drag that deamhan all the way to Norveg, and then hope his people free your clan in exchange for his life. Is that right?" He raises his eyebrows, making me feel like a naive child. I could really do without him picking holes in my plan. I found out he's sixteen—only a year and a bit older than I am—but his self-assurance makes him seem much older.

"He's a prince," I say, tugging up blades of grass from the ground. "They need him to continue their bloodline. At least, that's what he told us."

"He was telling the truth. We examined his blood tattoo—it's an authentic insignia."

Relief floods through me. At least there's one thing I can cross off my current list of worries. It's still a very long list.

"Good," I say.

"Even so . . . Have you considered handing him over to his enemies instead? And asking them to help rescue your clan in return? That might be a better plan."

"Who are his enemies?"

"No idea. But everyone has enemies. It's the way the world works. Always has been. People want more than they have: more land, more possessions, more power. And in trying to obtain those things, they make enemies. We're an inherently greedy race. That's the reason your clan was taken away in the first place, I'm guessing."

"What about your people?"

"What about them?"

"Do they want more than they have?"

"You're astute; I like that." I can't tell if he's mocking me. "Not to the same extent. We pride ourselves on only taking as much from the land as we need, but that's not to say there aren't days when we struggle against our own beliefs. And we still have enemies, like everyone else."

"The wildwolves?"

"Since everyone else in the country died, they're the main ones, yes."

A large cow lumbers past us without a care in the world.

"Why are you alive?" I ask.

"Now, there's a question!" He does that annoying side smile of his.

"No, I mean your tribe. How did they survive the plague when everyone else died?"

"We were lucky. Or, I should say, *they* were lucky. It was before I was born, of course. Once a year our tribe travels to the northernmost tip of Scotia. It's a sort of pilgrimage. We have a ceremony there on the first day of spring to welcome in the new year. That's where my tribe was when the plague struck. They realized something bad was happening when they saw huge fires in the distance. The fires burned for many months, filling the sky with thick red smoke. They stayed north for over a year, until the sky returned to normal. When they came back down, everyone was dead. Can you imagine?"

"No one else survived?"

"There are pockets of people here and there. And a few settlers have come over from the islands in the years since, but our paths rarely cross. That's why it was such a surprise when we stumbled across the two of you."

The tent flap opens and Finn comes out. I spring to my feet. Apparently, he's the best healer they have, even though he looks quite young, maybe early twenties. His broad smile offsets his dark features and his messy black hair.

"She's doing well," he says. He crosses his arms, which makes his muscles look huge. "I think she must have hit her head when she fell out of the tree, which is what's causing the dizziness and the fainting, but I've done lots of checks and I can't see there being any long-term effects."

"Thank goodness."

"However," Finn continues, "she needs rest. The time immediately following an injury such as this is when we need to be most cautious. We can't risk her doing anything active—including traveling—for at least a day or two."

"What? But we need to leave now. We've already been here too long. Can I speak to her?"

Finn holds up his hand. "She's asleep again, and I'd rather you didn't wake her. She needs time to heal."

Cray sees my face. "The two of us could leave now," he says. "We could scout ahead and then Finn can bring Agatha once she's feeling better?"

Leave Agatha behind? I can't. She needs me. And I need her. But every day our clan is slipping farther away, and so is my feeble plan to rescue them. I don't even know if the boat we need is where Knútr said it would be. If I go ahead, it could save us time. And from what I saw of Agatha last night, she really is too ill to travel.

"Wait, you're not planning on keeping her because she's a *teanga-bèist*, are you?" I ask.

Cray laughs. "She'd turn our bulls against us if we tried. Don't worry; we made a promise to take you both east, and the Bó Riders always keep their promises."

I ROCK FORWARD AND BACKWARD IN RHYTHM WITH THE bull's gait. Cray sits in front of me, his legs occasionally knocking into mine. My legs are so weedy compared to his. Knútr is tied to a cow, which lopes along on one side of us. It's not attached to us in any way, yet it stays close at all times. Every now and then, it breaks the calm with big, wet sneezes.

"Enjoying the ride?" asks Cray. He half-turns his head to speak to me, making our faces very close. It's strange talking to someone you're pressed so tightly against.

"Not particularly," I say. I've decided Highland bulls are my least favorite way to travel. Perhaps second least favorite, after boats.

"Well, the good news is you have at least another two days of this. Let's hope Dunnottar lives up to your expectations."

Knútr sniggers. He has been staring at me all day, mocking me with his presence. On the one occasion I made the mistake of looking over at him, he flashed me a carnivorous grin. Thoughts of Lileas came flooding back. I bit the inside of my cheek and turned away.

A flock of geese flies above us in the shape of an arrowhead, honking as they pass.

"You are not afraid of the killing shadows?" Knútr calls across to me.

"Ignore him," says Cray. "He's just trying to scare you."

"People say there is killing shadows at Dunnottar," says Knútr.

"Be quiet," says Cray.

"He's talking about *sgàilean*?" I ask.

"You've heard of them?" says Cray.

"Yes, but they're not real, are they?"

"I don't know. It is true that King Balfour was obsessed with the idea of making them. And Dunnottar Castle was where he carried out his experiments."

A familiar feeling creeps over me. I try to swallow the fear, but it won't go away. *Fear is weakness. Clann-a-Tuath does not feel fear.* Although I'd rather not admit it, a part of me is glad that Cray is with me.

"We only need the harbor," I say. "We'll stay well clear of the castle."

I look out to the left, at the wide expanse of the sea. We've been following the same coastal path for ages. From this distance, the waves lose all of their brutality. They're actually quite beautiful. They toy with the light, throwing it this way and that.

We've made good progress so far, according to Cray. We traveled southeast this morning, over misshapen hills and around soulless lochs. Around midafternoon we rode through the ruins of a town called Inbherness. What a grim place that was. There were hundreds of bothans there, all crammed together. They gaped at us with their empty windows and broken doors. The clan that used to live there must have been massive. It's given me a whole new perspective on just how many people died during the plague. Gnawed bones littered the streets, and rats ran across our path without the slightest hint of fear. The town belongs to them now.

By the time we stop for the day, my backside, back, and jaw are all throbbing. Even my arms ache from holding on to Cray for so long. We are in a place called Lossiemouth, a small coastal settlement due east of Inbherness. I don't know how Cray knows the names of all these places. Perhaps his tribe has been this way before. There is only a smattering of bothans here, but it has the same ugly feeling of desertion as everywhere else we've passed.

After leaving the animals to graze, Cray chooses a bothan for us to sleep in. I am expecting the ceiling to be really high because it is such a tall building, but it's not. Cray explains that there is a second floor above us. I have no idea what keeps it from falling on our heads. He goes up the steps—which he tells me are called "stairs" or a "staircase" when they're inside—to check there are no animals hiding there. While he's gone, I wander around the main room, tracing my fingertips over all the unfamiliar objects: things made out of twisted metal, large pots full of dry earth, woven items hanging on the walls.

"All clear," says Cray as he comes back down. He takes Knútr into the connecting room and starts tying him to a metal grid that's attached to a fireplace.

"Shouldn't we keep him where we can see him?" I ask.

"He's not going anywhere," says Cray.

I relent, grateful that he can no longer stare at me.

In the center of the main room is a hearth with a large cooking pot sitting askew in its ashes. Cray starts a fire and, after giving the pot a quick rinse, uses it to make a stew. I didn't expect him to know how to cook.

"What's the meat?" I ask when I see him adding some to the pot.

"Wildwolf," he replies.

"Oh."

"From the battle. No use in it going to waste."

It makes sense, I suppose.

When it's ready, he spoons a large portion into a wooden bowl and hands it to me. It's still bubbling. I wrap my hands around the bowl and let the steam warm my face.

"How did you enjoy your first day as a Bó Rider?" Cray asks.

"Every single part of me aches. Even parts of me I didn't know *could* ache. I don't know how you ride those things every day."

"*Highland bulls*, Jaime. Don't call them 'things' to their face. They'll get very upset."

He's joking. I think.

"What's the plan for tomorrow?"

"We'll set off at first light. Not far from here is an overgrown road that leads almost all the way to the harbor."

Cray raises his bowl to his lips and slurps down a big mouthful of stew.

"Is it dangerous?"

"Is what dangerous?"

"The route we're taking."

"Shouldn't be. Besides, you lucked out: you got me as your protector." He winks, with an unattractive mix of pride and patronization.

"What do I need protecting from?"

A shadow from the fire passes over his face, wiping away his cocksure smile.

"You think he did it, don't you? King Balfour. You think he managed to create a *sgàil*?"

Cray puts down his bowl and stares at me. It's the most serious I've ever seen him. He drums one of his knuckles against his teeth. "When I was a child, I was taken on a hunting trip not far from Dunnottar. Bras was only young then and not as fast as the other bulls. Everyone else shot off in pursuit of a roebuck, and we got left behind. We were following their tracks when the worst smell you can imagine hit us. I can't tell you how bad it was, but I was intrigued. I had to find out where it was coming from. We circled around until I found this ditch. I knew right away it was the source of the smell. I also knew I would regret looking, but I looked in all the same. The body must have been there for days. I couldn't tell if it was a man or a woman. Half its face had been pulled off, including one eye. It was missing a leg and both of its arms. From the mess that remained, it looked like the limbs had been clean ripped from its body. I only glanced at it for a moment, but the image has stayed with me ever since." He looks down at his feet. "I've never told anyone that before."

"You think the person was attacked by a *sgàil*?"

"I don't know. It could have been a mountain cat or a pack of wildwolves, I suppose. There was just something about the way the limbs had been removed that looked more like they'd been *pulled* off than bitten or chewed. I was young; that's probably why it left such an impression on me."

A sea wind sneaks through the cracks in the door frame and plays havoc with the fire. I finish the last of my stew. The empty bowl turns cold in my hands.

"Tell me about the girl," says Cray after a while. "If you want to."

"Which girl?" My throat clenches.

"The one who died. I heard the deamhan killed a girl who was traveling with you."

I don't want to talk about it. Least of all to Cray. Just because he opened up to me doesn't mean I have to do the same.

When I don't respond, Cray continues, "I can tell how difficult it is for you to be around him. I respect you for fighting to keep him alive, even though I'm sure that's the last thing you want to do. I'm not sure I'd have that much willpower."

His compliment derails me.

"She was my wife." I say.

He doesn't hide his surprise.

"I'm so sorry. I had no idea. You marry young in your tribe."

"We hadn't been married long. It's complicated." I look away to make it clear I have no intention of saying anything else.

The fire crackles and spits between us.

"I know what it's like to lose someone you care about," he says. The faintest glimmer mists his eyes. Now it is my turn to be surprised.

"What happened?" I ask.

"Another wildwolf attack. About three months ago. There were only ten or so of them, but they took us by surprise. We lost two cows and one of our people."

A lazy tear drifts down his cheek. He does nothing to hide it.

"I'm so sorry," I say. "Was the person a friend of yours?"

"More than a friend. He was my . . . partner."

"You mean your bull-riding partner?"

"No, Jaime. My *partner*."

I must have misunderstood. "But you just said—?"

Cray looks at me, his expression blank.

"Oh. Oh, okay. Okay. You—Okay."

"*Is* it okay?" he asks.

I honestly don't know. I've heard about people like that, but I also know it's not right. The elders were very clear on the subject. I breathe in too deeply, and smoke claws my chest. All the air has been sucked out of the room.

"I need to go outside," I say, making my way toward the door.

Cray lets me leave.

As soon as I open the door, the wind bites my face. I walk toward the sea, letting the breeze tousle my hair and pummel my eyes. The moon glows between the clouds, like a neat circle of spilled milk.

Why does it bother me so much who Cray is attracted to? It's none of my business. Yet I'm now forced to reassess everything I thought I knew about him, as if he's been lying to me this whole time. I've had my arms around him all day. I feel hot. Itchy.

I slip down onto a boulder. My hand finds a stone lying next to me. I pick it up and throw it toward the endless black of the sea.

Tears streak down my face, and I have no idea why. There are too many reasons. Everything is wrong. Everything in the whole world is wrong.

What am I even doing? I know nothing about Norveg. Nothing. Ever since the attack, I've been stumbling forward without any real sense of where I'm going or how I'll get there. It's too dangerous. First Knútr, then the wildwolves, now possibly even *sgàilean*. I can't do this. I'm not the leader my clan needs me to be.

Fear is the greatest weakness.

It's true, and I am afraid. I am weak.

The first spots of rain land on the nape of my neck. I lean back and let them tickle my face. It starts to fall more heavily, but I stay where I am. The boulder feels reassuringly solid beneath my palms. Only once the rain becomes torrential and the sky starts to rumble do I pick myself up and walk back to the bothan. I stand outside, underneath a small roof that juts out above its door. I'm soaking wet, shivering. Lightning streaks through the clouds, and the rain intensifies to a deafening roar. The sound of it fills my ears and drowns everything else away.

The door opens.

"Are you all right?" Cray asks.

"I'm fine," I say without looking at him.

"Are you coming back in?"

"In a bit."

He closes the door, leaving me alone.

When I was young, one of my favorite *òrain* was about the two clouds, Tàirneach and Dealanach. They'd been enemies since the dawn of time and would frequently fight. Dealanach had a magical sword that could shoot out deadly flashes of light, and Tàirneach possessed a large bronze shield capable of rebounding light in any direction. Sometimes their battles would last all night, filling the sky with dazzling flashes and unearthly bellows. If they fought long enough, it was said, they would eventually tire and drop their weapons on the earth below for one lucky person to find.

Once, when I was very young—long before the elders gave me my age—Aileen woke me up in the middle of the night. Her face lit up in a sudden flash of lightning from outside.

"They're fighting!" she said. "Quick, let's go."

She whipped back my bedcovers, and the two of us sneaked outside. We'd made a secret plan to watch a whole fight from below so we'd be first to see where their weapons fell. Hand in hand we ran around the enclave, our necks craned to the sky, whooping and howling at the wonder of it all. We got into a lot of trouble when the elders found us, but it remains one of my favorite memories.

While there is a chance that Aileen is alive, I will keep fighting. I will find a boat, I'll make Knútr lead us to Norveg, and I will demand my people's release. It is as simple as that. It has to be.

NATHARA

It's raining

I like it when it rains

They don't like it though

They sulk

They don't like the rain and they don't like the sun

There's no pleasing some people

They're not people

Not anymore

Raindrops on my fingers raindrops on my toes

I don't remember the rest of it

They're whispering

More than usual

Outside in the courtyard and up on the roof

All around the castle walls

Stupid shadows

They know something but they won't tell me what it is

Whispering whispering always whispering

Stop it will you I can't hear myself think

If you don't stop soon I'm going to get really mad

I'll trap you inside

Don't think I won't do it

I know how

Daddy showed me

You have to do everything I say or I'll trap you forever

Then you'll be sorry

JAIME

CRAY IS CAUTIOUS AROUND ME WHEN HE FIRST WAKES up. I got up early and prepared our morning meal, which I present as a sort of peace offering. He takes it from me with a nod. My clan would not approve of him, but he's not a bad person. Annoying, maybe, but not bad. We won't talk about it again and everything will be fine.

We eat the meal in silence. Once Cray has finished, he wipes his mouth and leaves to check on the cows. I busy myself by packing up our few possessions and then take some food and water in to Knútr. His snores sound like he's swallowing gravel. It takes three shouts to wake him. He licks the sleep from his lips with a fat tongue. I scoop some lukewarm oats onto a spoon. My hand trembles a little as I hold it toward him. I squeeze the spoon tighter to keep my arm steady.

"You scared I bite off your fingers?" he says.

I shove the spoon against his lips, and he opens his mouth. I keep my eyes locked on his the whole time I am feeding him.

Afterward, I put a water flask to his mouth, and he takes a long swig. As I lower the flask, he spits the water back out into my face. It takes all my willpower not to react.

"If you're not thirsty, you should have just said," I say. I walk out, taking the flask with me.

As soon as I am out of the room, I wipe away the water with the back of my sleeve. As much as I scrub, I can still feel his spit on my face.

"Are you ready to go?" Cray asks from the doorway.

I nod. Cray fetches Knútr while I take out the sidebags and attach them to the cow. Last night's storm has left a freshness in the air that I can almost taste.

Once Cray has secured Knútr, he pulls himself onto Bras and then reaches his hand out to me. I hesitate. If I sit behind him, I will have to hold on to him all day. The space between us becomes heavy.

"It's okay, I'll walk today," I say.

The way Cray looks at me rips up my insides. "Fine," he says.

"Lovers' argument?" Knútr taunts.

It is too much. I turn around and shove Knútr off his cow. He thumps to the ground like a sack of turnips. I am not finished with him yet. I stride around to where he has landed and kick him as hard as I can.

"Take that back," I shout, kicking him again. "You take that back!"

Blood erupts from his burst nose and pools onto the sandy ground. I kick him again; I cannot stop. My teeth are clenched so tight they may crack.

"Take that back!"

Cray jumps down and grabs me from behind.

"That's enough," he says, pulling me away.

He is strong and I don't resist. He walks me a few paces, and then I shrug him off. He turns me toward him and puts his hands on my shoulders.

"It's okay," he tells me, holding me at arm's length.

My breathing is short and irregular.

"I don't know why I did that," I say. "That's not like me at all."

"You've been through a lot."

I stare at the ground. Cray's hands are still on my shoulders. I wish he'd take them off.

"You ride Bras," he says. "I'll walk."

I don't argue. I walk over to the bull and drag myself up.

Progress is slow with Cray walking, and the silence is torturous. Knútr's face is covered in thick, crusted blood, and beneath his tattoos, both his eyes are starting to bruise. He is full of rage, which makes him even more dangerous. Still, I am glad to have finally wiped the constant smirk from his face.

CRAY WASN'T EXAGGERATING WHEN HE SAID THE ROAD to Dunnottar was overgrown. Great twisting brambles snake in from both sides, and we have to keep stopping to cut our way through. Around midday, I dismount to help Cray hack at another tight knot. Knútr is slumped forward on his cow, asleep. That man can sleep anywhere.

Cray attacks the branches with fierce stabs. I only have a small knife, so the work makes my skinny arms ache.

"I'm sorry if I upset you earlier," I say. "And I really am sorry about what happened to your friend."

Cray doesn't reply. He continues to thrash at the brambles in front of him and I keep cutting too, ignoring the thorns that nip at my wrists.

"Did everyone in your tribe know about your relationship?" I ask.

"Yes," he replies.

"And they didn't mind?"

Cray stops and looks at me. His forehead and chest are covered in a thin layer of sweat. "Why would they mind?"

I pause, not wanting to offend him further. "My clan would never accept it," I say. "It's not *dùth*."

"What does that mean, '*dùth*'?"

"It means what's honorable, what's proper and right."

"Right according to who?"

"Um . . . Well, the clan elders, I guess."

"And why did they decide two people can't be happy?"

"I don't know," I say. I have no answer for that.

Cray starts cutting again, and the conversation is over.

Once we've cleared enough for the animals to get through, I slip the knife back into my belt and then say, "If you'd rather not walk, I don't mind."

"You walk slower than I do," he replies. "It'd take us even longer."

"No, I mean we can ride together again. If you want to?"

"How very noble of you," he says, before swinging up onto Bras. He then gives me a flicker of a smile and offers me his hand.

This time I accept, and he pulls me up. I try not to tense as I put my arms around his waist.

The rest of the day is uneventful. I think about Agatha a lot. I hope she's feeling better, and that they're on their way. I miss her already.

Once the sun goes down, we set up camp under a temporary shelter, which Cray erects by tying a large covering to three inter-secting trees. It is made from pieces of sewn-together skin, just like the tents at the Bó Riders' camp.

"A mixture of wildwolf, sheep, and elk hide," Cray says when he sees me looking at it.

"Oh, good," I say.

"Why? What did you think it was?"

I shrug.

"After a successful hunt, we use every conceivable part of the animal's body. You shouldn't take anything nature gives you for granted. All life is precious, after all."

"Is it the same with your bulls?" I ask.

"What? Do we use bull skin?" His face crumples, as if my question is absurd. "Of course not. Would you skin a member of *your* tribe?"

"Oh, right," I say. "Sorry."

I glance at the bull and the cow, who are lying down next to us. They really are beautiful animals. So majestic. Cray settles down to sleep next to Bras, nuzzling into his long hair for warmth. He suggests I do the same with the cow, who he tells me is called Sruth. Her body is warm and smells of dust and mud.

I try to sleep, but the few snatches I manage are haunted by dreams of Knútr, hunting me through a dark wood with a serrated knife. More than once, I sit up to check that he is still tied up where we left him. The morning light is a welcome relief.

❧

LATE IN THE AFTERNOON ON THE FOLLOWING DAY, THE road ends, forcing us to cut across open fields. The grass is dense and pocked with ditches and marshy bogs. It must rain here a lot. There are odd patches of trees, scattered about as if lost.

A castle comes into view, a small blot in the far distance. Dunnottar. The harbor should be right next to it.

"Time to light the torches," says Cray, "before it gets dark."

Knútr laughs. "The big man is scared of the story for little girls," he says.

Cray dismounts and pulls two torches from one of the sidebags. When he strikes his flint, the material at the top ignites almost at once. He passes one to me and then walks in a circle around Bras to check the reach of the light.

"Hold it high to make sure it doesn't cast any shadows," he says. Then, when he sees the look on my face, he adds, "They're just a precaution."

"You are really so stupid?" says Knútr. "Stupid and scared. It is not a true story."

"No one asked for your opinion," Cray says.

"They make it up so no one attacks the castle. Everyone knows this. Only a fool thinks it is real."

"Please keep talking," says Cray, "and give me a reason to gag your mouth."

Knútr snorts. Cray waves the second torch in front of Knútr's face. "I'm going to attach this to the cow. Try anything funny and you'll regret it."

He ties the torch to Sruth's right horn. She swishes her head from side to side, trying to shake it off.

"It's okay, Sruth," Cray says. "This is for your protection too." He then turns to Knútr and adds, "You'll need to lie forward so the light spreads behind you."

"So stupid," Knútr mutters, but he does as he's told, and we continue toward the castle.

As the sunlight fades, my unease starts to grow. Shadows from nearby trees twist and stretch, and I imagine other, more sinister shadows moving between them. The tips of all my fingers start to feel numb. I focus on my breathing; it takes all of my concentration to keep it under control.

The castle looms ahead of us, dark stone erupting from the ground. Is that where the *sgàilean* are hiding? I count the castle's windows; there must be at least five different floors. That's when I see it. In one of the highest windows. The outline of a person, I'm sure of it. Not a shadow, an actual person. A blink later, it is gone.

"Did you see that?" I ask Cray.

"See what?" he replies.

"The person. In the castle. I swear I just saw someone in one of the top windows."

"No, it's been abandoned for years. No one lives this far east anymore."

"Oh."

"Knútr, lie down."

Knútr is sitting up on his cow, causing a shadow to drop down his back all the way to the ground.

"It is not comfortable for me," he says. "I do not need fire. I sit and you see I am right."

"Lie down or I will tie you down," says Cray.

He does not get the chance to carry out his threat. The world around us suddenly becomes much darker, as if all the light has been drained away. I shiver, even though it's not cold. Something is coming. A cruel whisper rustles toward us, then Knútr is somersaulted backward from his cow and dragged away by invisible hands. The cow bolts in the opposite direction.

"*Daingead ort!*" swears Cray, leaping down in pursuit of Knútr's retreating body. The grass swishes as Knútr slides through it into a wooded area nearby.

"What should I do?" I shout after Cray.

"Stay in the light," he calls, and then he's gone.

I jump down to follow them but stop in my tracks. I can't leave Bras alone in the dark. I grab hold of his right horn and try to steer him toward the trees. He stamps his feet and refuses to move. Bloody stubborn animal. Now what do I do? Indecision gnaws at me. Cray wouldn't want me to leave Bras unprotected, which means I'm stuck here. I hold the torch above my head and look around for—what? I didn't see what took Knútr. I didn't see anything at all. It was a *sgàil*; it had to be.

A sound, behind me. I freeze, my ears pricked. The wind is carrying whispers again: an onslaught of voices, twisting over one another. I can't make out what any of them are saying. If it's more *sgàilean,* it sounds like there are an awful lot of them. My head starts pounding, and bile rises into my throat. I move the torch from side to side. Next to me, Bras snorts, releasing a small puff of steam.

"Nothing to be afraid of," I say, wishing it were true.

A light in the foliage catches my eye. It's the other torch, the one tied to Sruth. But something's not right. I blink, finding it hard to focus. The torch is getting bigger. Then I understand: the woodland is on fire, and the fire is spreading.

Smoke engulfs the sky. Below it, the blaze jumps from tree to tree. *Come on, Cray. Where are you?* So much fire. He's going to be burned alive.

Something moves on my right. It is too dark to see what it is. I draw the knife from my belt. Not that it will do any good; *sgàilean* can't be killed with a knife. A shape bursts out of the undergrowth and charges toward me. It is much bigger than I expected and traveling fast. I crouch, holding the knife out in front of me, my eyes practically shut. It runs straight at me, wild and unpredictable. I brace myself for impact. At the very last moment, I jump out of the way.

"You stupid cow," I say.

The torch is still tied to Sruth's horn, but its flame has gone out. She stops when she reaches Bras, and the two of them touch noses. Her long hair is singed down one side. The breath I have been holding in falls out of me.

"What happened?" I say, stroking her flank.

"She saved my life, that's what happened."

I turn and Cray is there, covered in mud, with Knútr slung

over one shoulder. I almost run to him in relief. He dumps Knútr's body on the ground. He looks dead.

Cray whistles, and both Bras and Sruth walk toward him. "Come over here, where there's more light," he says to me.

"Is he—?" I ask, indicating Knútr.

"He's unconscious. Something had a good go at him, though."

A deep gash runs all the way down Knútr's left thigh, and his right arm lies at an impossible angle. He's had a rough couple of days.

"A sgàil?" I say.

"I couldn't see anything, so I'm guessing so. It was almost invisible."

Cray wrenches Knútr's dislocated arm until it clicks back into place. "That's going to hurt in the morning," he says. He then takes some bandages from one of the sidebags and wraps them around Knútr's leg.

All I can think is: Sgàilean *are real. They're real.* And the one that just took Knútr could come back at any time. I stare into the darkness, fixating on every slight movement.

"What happened to him?" I ask, indicating Knútr.

"It's hard to say. I caught up with him and grabbed one of his legs. I swear, the sgàil nearly ripped him in two, it was so strong. Then I felt something cold wash over me, like being submerged in water. I think there was more than one of them. It sounded like there were lots. Knútr was torn from my arms and dragged out of sight. That was when Sruth came crashing through with the torch still tied to her head. The fire spread, which must have forced the sgàilean to flee. That whispering noise stopped soon after. Knútr was halfway up a burning tree, unconscious. I only just got him down in time."

"Are you sure we're safe here?"

"They'll stay away as long as there's fire."

There is a screech from within the burning trees; an animal that didn't make it out in time.

"I suggest we stay here until morning," says Cray. "The grass is too wet for the fire to spread, but the trees will burn through the night and offer us protection. As soon as the sun is up, we'll head for the harbor."

Even with the fire, there is no way I am going to be able to sleep. I offer to take first watch, and Cray accepts, resting his head on Bras's side.

By moonlight the castle is even more imposing, a dent against the starry sky. Its windows hint at the secrets it's hiding. I stare at them, searching for any signs of movement, but there are none. All the same, I can't shake the feeling that there's someone inside, watching us. Waiting.

AGATHA

WE ARE GOING TO FIND JAIME. I HAD TO WAIT TWO DAYS first. I didn't want to because our clan needs us and we have to be quick, but Finn said I could hurt myself a very lot if I went so I said okay. I am not dizzy now and the black isn't coming anymore so Finn says I have done a speedy recovery. That is the good news and now we are going. We'll find Jaime and Cray and the boat in the harbor. Then we can sail it to rescue our clan. That is the most important thing.

When Murdina said who I wanted to come with me I said Mór because she is nice now and Finn because he helped me to feel better and I like him as well. I did not say Hendry because I didn't like it when he held my hand and I did not say Murdina because she is rude and doesn't smile. When I said goodbye to everyone I waved and they all waved back to me.

I ride on a bull with Mór and Finn comes too on his bull. Milkwort is not a secret now so he doesn't have to stay in my pocket. He sits on my shoulder. I said to him to be careful you don't blow away. He didn't answer to me. I think he is sad because I didn't talk to him the last few days. It was only because of the dizzy. He will talk to me again soon. When he is hungry he runs down to the bag on the side and eats some of the food without even asking. He is cheeky like that sometimes.

It is a long day of riding all day which is fun because we go fast and I like it but also it hurts on my bottom and is more boring. Sometimes we sing because I like it so I say can we sing again. I shouldn't do it but there is no one to tell me off. When I am with the bull people I can do what they do and when I am with my clan I will not do singing anymore.

After a while, Mór says that is enough singing now, so we don't do it anymore.

I don't have anything to do but look at things. There are some mountains bigger than any I ever saw with white at the top which is the snow I think. There are lochs too which are big ones and black. Then it starts raining and I cannot see anything. The rain makes the bulls smell funny and I am wet.

When it starts to get dark we stop by the water. Finn makes a tent for us to sleep in and Mór makes a fire to keep us warm and cook the food. I stroke the bulls' hair to make them happy.

While we're eating evening meal, Finn asks me what it's like when I talk to an animal. I don't know what he means what's it like.

"Sometimes it makes my h-head—hurt," I tell him.

"Yes, I know. But what I meant was, what does it *sound* like?"

"I like talking to Milkwort," I say, and I stroke him. "It's easy to talk with him and it doesn't hurt. The w-wildwolf didn't want me talking to it."

"So you could hear a wildwolf's voice in your head?" Finn asks.

"It's not the s-ame as talking to—people," I say. "I don't hear it. I just know in my head what—what it says."

Finn eats some of his food and then he says, "Do you think you could you talk to Gailleann for me?"

"Who's G-Gailleann?" I ask.

"My bull. We've been together since I was a child. I would love to know what he's thinking."

I don't want to do it. It will make my head hurt again and it only just stopped. But also I like Finn. I want him to like me too and so I say okay I will do it. Only just a little bit.

The bulls are lying down on the grass.

"Wake up, lazybones," says Finn, which is a funny thing to say. He shakes his bull who is called Gailleann and it opens its eyes. Finn rubs the hair on top of its head and it licks its nose. Its tongue is so long and pink.

"What do you want me to say?" I ask to Finn.

"I don't know. . . . The number of times I wished I could talk to him. Now I can't think of a single thing to say. Maybe ask him what his earliest memory of us is?"

"Okay," I say.

I ask Gailleann it in my head like I always do. He doesn't reply. I ask him again, but he's not there.

"He won't answer," I say.

"Why not?" asks Finn.

"I don't know," I say.

"Maybe he doesn't understand the question? Animals' memories probably work differently from ours," says Mór.

"Good point," says Finn. "Try something really simple. Like, ask him if he's sleepy. He's always sleepy."

Are you sleepy, Gailleann? I ask him in my head. He doesn't answer me again and something is wrong. It feels all different in my head. He can't hear me and I can't do it.

"I need to try with your one," I say to Mór.

"Sure," says Mór.

Her bull is awake and next to Gailleann. I say hello and can you hear me and then I say it again and I even say it out loud as well. It doesn't do an answer. It is not working. Why won't it work?

"I can't do it. It's not working," I say, and the panic is coming. My cheeks are going hot and my eyes are loud.

"You're probably just tired," says Mór. She puts her hand on my arm and I shake it off because I don't want it.

"Talking to all those wildwolves at once must have taken it out of you," says Finn. "You just need a bit more time to rest."

"Yes. Yes," I say, and I am nodding my head. But they are wrong. Something has happened and it's different now. I can feel it in my head. That's why Milkwort wasn't talking to me. He can't hear me anymore.

No, no, it's not true. I can still do it with Milkwort. Please, I can still do it with Milkwort. I take him out from my pocket and hold him close to my face. *You can still hear me, can't you?* I am breathing even louder now and I am sweating too. *Milkwort? Milkwort?*

I cannot hear him. He looks at me and he runs down my arm and down my leg and onto the grass.

Where are you going? "Where are you going?" I say, but he

cannot hear me and I cannot hear him. I run after him but I don't know where he is going and he runs away.

No no no no no, Milkwort, come back. Why is he leaving me?

My heart inside is hurting. I fall on the grass and grip my hands in the mud and I scream at the sky. I cannot stop the tears.

Everything is different in my head and I know it. What I could do is gone and it is not coming back.

JAIME

"CAN'T SLEEP?"

"Nope." I tried, but it was never going to happen.

Cray is staring at the burning trees. The flames dance in his eyes.

I sit next to him, leaning against Bras's side. The fire has lost some of its ferocity but it's still mesmerizing. There is a piece of charred branch by my feet. I pick it up and start slicing off the bark with my knife.

"I was worried it might have been the end of you earlier," I say.

"It'll take more than a *sgàil* to get rid of me." He sits up straight and puffs out his chest. "I'm a hero."

"Don't you get bored of always being so modest?"

"Ha!" Even though I am not looking at him, I know that he's smiling that teasing side smile he does. "I took on the *sgàilean* and won! They'll sing songs about me for years to come."

"Unlikely. Unless the song is about your arrogance."

"As long as they're singing about me, that's all I care about."

"They should be singing about Sruth, anyway. She did all the hard work."

"What? All she did was run around and accidentally set fire to some trees. I was the one who dived courageously into the unknown, battling an invisible foe to save a man we don't even like. Fearless, that's what I am."

"Reckless is what you are."

He laughs.

A large branch topples from a tree, sending a shower of sparks up into the sky.

"So you weren't scared?" I ask.

He shrugs. "I didn't really have time to be scared, to be honest."

"What about now?"

"A little. You?"

"No," I lie. "Clann-a-Tuath doesn't feel fear."

"Wolfcrap. Everyone feels fear."

"Really?"

"Of course. It's in our nature, in our blood. It drives our instincts and keeps us alive. We'd be lost without it."

"That's not what I've been told."

"Trust me. Fear should be acknowledged, accepted. Embraced, even. Otherwise it'll always control you." Cray turns his head toward me. "It's nothing to be ashamed of."

"I shouldn't have asked."

What he's saying isn't true.

"You're stronger than you realize," says Cray, as if reading my mind.

I look down at my bracelet and trace the strands of metal with the tip of my knife. The metal catches the firelight and warms my wrist.

"You play with that a lot, you know," says Cray. "Where's it from?"

"Someone gave it to me."

"Your wife?"

"No, someone else. Someone from my clan. A friend."

"This friend means a lot to you."

"We spent our whole lives together. I'd do anything for her. I miss her."

"She sounds special," says Cray. "How come you married the other girl and not her?"

"It's not like that with Aileen." I press my lips together. "Besides, I was forced to marry Lileas. Our wedding day was the first time we'd ever met."

Cray whistles. "An arranged marriage? I didn't realize people still did that kind of thing."

"It was supposed to create better ties with Raasay, the island next to ours. Turns out, it did the opposite. The whole thing was a lie. Raasay set it up so they could betray us to the deamhain. In exchange for their own protection, I suspect. It was the first marriage our clan had allowed in more than a hundred years."

"What? You don't have marriage?"

"None of the clans on Skye do." I put down the knife. "Does your tribe?"

"Of course. We always have."

"Oh. We believe it's not worth the struggle."

"It's the struggle that makes it worthwhile. Marriage is the ultimate commitment of love. It's a beautiful thing."

"My clan doesn't think so."

"Your clan sounds kind of messed up, no offense."

"None taken." Actually, no. He has no right to speak about my clan like that. "You don't know them. Not like I do. Everything they do, all of their rules, they're there for a reason: to protect us and make our lives better. My clan has always been there for me. They've taken care of me and given me everything I've ever needed. And now they need me, and I won't let them down. No matter the cost."

Cray's eyes widen, but he doesn't say anything. I inhale charred grass and burning wood. It scorches my throat. The taste is not unpleasant.

"Why don't you go back to sleep?" I say. "There's no point in both of us being awake." I don't want to talk to him anymore. We may think differently from his tribe, but that doesn't make us wrong.

"I'm all right," he says, but a short while later he closes his eyes. Good.

It's been at least nine days since the invasion. *Nine days*. How many of my clan have the deamhain killed since then?

An image flashes through my mind. I am in the clearing in the woods and Knútr holds the *corcag* to a girl's throat, but it is Aileen—not Lileas—he is about to kill.

Then an even darker thought replaces it. One that's been niggling away at me for days, demanding to be acknowledged. I never wanted to marry Lileas. She was a burden, a cause of shame. Now that she's dead, that burden has been lifted.

The thought makes me sick, but that doesn't stop it from being true.

I pick up the tree branch I was carving. A half-finished heron stares back at me, its eyes hollow, its feet burned. I fling it into the flames and they swallow it up.

The fire roars with self-assurance as it turns the world to ash.

KNÚTR REGAINS CONSCIOUSNESS AS THE SUN RISES. HE struggles to sit up. I stretch my arms as wide as they will go.

"Still think the *sgàilean* is a story for little girls?" I ask him.

He grunts in response.

"I make that the fourth time someone's had to save your life in a week."

"Untie me and I save myself next time," he says.

"Next time, do what you're told."

Cray wakes up and rides back to the bramble path to leave a warning about the *sgàilean* for whoever accompanies Agatha.

What happens if she doesn't turn up? What do I do then? Or what if she started getting worse instead of better? If that's the case, I should be there with her. She needs me. *Stop it*. She's fine. She'll be fine. She'll come.

The flames are getting weary, the trees reduced to thin, sooty poles.

Once Cray returns, we light the torches and then set off toward the harbor. Cray doesn't think we'll need the torches now that it's daytime, but after last night, we're not taking any chances. Sruth doesn't protest about having one tied to her this time. Cray makes an additional torch from a fallen branch, which he holds on to so that we have one each.

We approach the castle at a cautious pace. It's built on a rocky peninsula that juts out into the sea, with sheer cliff edges surrounding it on all sides, making it almost impossible to attack. Waves crash on the eastern cliffs like ancient clans colliding in battle.

When we reach the lip of the western cliff, the harbor opens out below us. The remains of the docks stretch across the entire breadth of the cove's calm waters. People in the castle would have been able to look down and observe every ship sailing in and out. It must have looked breathtaking in its heyday, but now the docks are rotten, and large parts of them have been reclaimed by the sea. There are still a few boats dotted around, though, which is a great relief.

"Let's head down and look at your options," says Cray. "I know almost nothing about boats, though. Do you?"

"A little," I say. My days as an Angler feel like a lifetime ago.

We leave Bras and Sruth at the top of the cliff and walk down the steps to the harbor. Knútr goes first, with Cray keeping a tight grip on the ropes that bind him. The deamhan keeps stumbling on the steep, uneven stone.

When we reach the bottom, Cray ties Knútr to a post, and then we walk up the gangway that leads to the tethered vessels. It's slippery underfoot; a thick layer of seaweed smothers what's left of the wooden walkways. I place my feet with care, navigating the many cracks and holes.

The boats are a lot bigger up close than they looked from above. I guess they're ships rather than boats. Cray says that's probably a good thing, that we'll need something big to make it across the North Sea, but I'm worried I won't know how to sail it. I struggled enough with the rowing boat, and that only had one small sail.

The most stable-looking ship—which I thought at first would be our best option—has a massive breach in its hull. There's no way we'll be able to fix it. Most of the other ships are in a similar state. The only one that looks remotely functional is a lot older than the others. It has gold-and-purple trim, although the colors have almost completely faded. The word *Plathag* is written down its side in peeling paint.

"What does that mean?" I ask Cray.

"No idea," he replies without even looking.

We climb aboard and have a look around. Several of the deck planks have come loose, and the sails are torn and will need replacing. Other than that, it's in relatively good condition. Belowdecks, there is a strong smell of mold, but it is dry and there are no obvious signs of damage.

"I think this is the one," I say to Cray.

"It's the best of a bad lot," he agrees.

"I can take the sails and whatever else I need from one of the other ships, but before I can start, I'm going to need some tools."

We both know where our best chance of finding tools will be: inside the castle. Cray says I need to embrace my fear. Right now, it's telling me that going into the castle is a very bad idea.

It's started to rain, making the climb back up the cliff steps a miserable slog. Drizzle swarms around us from all angles, and by the time we reach the top, we are all out of breath. The only way to approach the castle is via a narrow path that snakes around the cliff edge. We walk in single file, and more than once the animals lose their footing, causing small stones to break off and fall into the sea far below. Cray assures me they're more sure-footed than they look.

Once we've navigated the path, we are given an uninterrupted view of the castle. It towers above us, scornful and obtrusive. One of its turrets has crumpled in on itself as if in a drunken stupor. Vines stretch out of the earth like fleshless arms and clamber up its sides. There is an almighty door—bigger even than the gates of the enclave—that hangs askew. There is a second, more regular-size door to its right. Cray tries the handle. It opens.

"Let's see what we can find," he says, and disappears inside.

A short passageway opens onto a large courtyard. Like most of the places we've passed through, it stinks of abandonment. No one has lived here for a very long time.

"Hello?" shouts Cray. His voice echoes across the stone walls. "I guess if anyone was living here, the *sgàilean* would have made short work of them. Let's split up. It'll be quicker that way." Splitting up is the last thing I want to do, but I agree rather than admit that to Cray. "You head for the main tower," he says. "I'll tie Knútr up in that stable and then search the buildings connected to the courtyard so I can keep an eye on him at the same time. It'll probably be dark inside, so keep your torch high and stay away from any shadows."

That's one thing I don't need reminding about.

The main tower is at the opposite end of the courtyard. Looking up at it makes me giddy. At ground level, the double doors are slightly ajar. I slip inside and daylight vanishes. As my eyes adjust, a long room opens up before me. There are windows, but they are slim and the stone walls are thick, making it hard for any light to squeeze through. My torch casts dark shapes over the ceiling and walls. So much for staying out of the shadows. Thoughts of dark hands reaching out to grab me assault my mind. I look behind me at the brightness of the courtyard, just beyond the doors. It is not too late to turn back. I press on, putting my trust in the light from the torch.

The room is largely empty and smells of must. Pictures of morose people in strange clothes hang on the walls. They're all so lifelike. I take another few steps forward. There is a stain on the floor beneath my feet: a dark-brown smear that leads all the way from the doors to the wide staircase at the far end of the room. I kneel and hold my torch to it. My heart thuds heavy against my rib cage. It looks like dried blood, as if something—or some-one—has been dragged across the entire length of the room and up the steps. As if this place wasn't creepy enough already. *Keep going. Keep going.* I can do this.

On either side of the staircase is a door. I try the one on the right, and as soon as it opens, I'm consumed by the smell of death. I hold my breath long enough to peer inside.

I've only seen a skeleton once before. About five years ago, we had the worst winter on Skye that anyone could remember. It snowed without stopping for weeks on end, and the Northern and Western Gates froze shut, making it impossible for the Anglers to leave. Even if they could, the ice gales would have made it too dangerous to fish. Our food supplies dwindled, and two people passed away in their sleep from the cold.

Having run out of other options, the elders turned to the Forgotten Gods. No one actually thought it would help, but the elders were desperate and had to be seen to be doing something. They decreed that our last remaining goat be hanged, an ancient custom that was once believed to reduce widespread suffering by inflicting it instead upon a single animal. Something to do with balancing the universe.

The entire clan, wrapped in as many clothes and blankets as they could find, gathered around the tallest tree in the enclave and watched as Maighstir Clyde and Maistreas Sorcha tied a noose around the goat's neck. It was then hoisted up, its legs scrabbling as it desperately sought ground. When it finally stopped shaking, we all returned to our bothans, pretending not to feel ashamed. Over the days that followed, we watched with morbid fascination as the goat was pecked apart by birds. Some children threw stones, aiming for the empty eye sockets.

The snow melted soon afterward, and spring broke through. The goat's body stayed hanging from the tree; no one wanted to risk taking it down, just in case. After a few weeks, it had been so ravaged by the scavenger birds that only its skeleton remained, hollow and insignificant. It was hard to accept that, under our skin, that's all we are: a collection of dull bones, hanging together.

That same hollow feeling returns to me now, as I look into the room. It contains the skeletal remains of more people than I can count. At the far end of the room, the bodies have been laid out in neat lines. Toward the middle and closer to the door, there is no such order; the bones are a ramshackle heap, as if the later bodies were slung in with total disregard for the people they had once been. Bent hands reach out from the pile. Skulls mock me with garish smiles. I'm not going to find any tools in there.

I shut the door and press my back against it. Once my breathing's settled, I cross over to the second door. It's locked. After the shock of the first room, I'm relieved. Although now the only other option is the staircase. I hesitate and then make my way up, avoiding the trail of dry blood in the center. My footsteps are much louder than I want them to be.

At the top, a corridor curves away in both directions. The path of blood veers off to the left before disappearing underneath a door a couple of paces away. That makes the decision of which way to go a whole lot easier. I turn right and follow the passage past a couple of doors. I stop outside the third. The frame of this one is engraved with elegant symbols that make it stand out from all the others. The handle is metal and cold. I ease the door open and peer inside.

The room is dominated by a wooden bed three times larger than any I've seen before. It's surrounded by moth-eaten material that drapes down from the ceiling like the sails of a ship. I wonder if they could be of any use to us. Next to the bed is a small table with a hairbrush on it. There is still hair tangled in its bristles.

In the far corner is a large clothes chest. I open it to see if there's anything inside that would be suitable for Knútr; the clothes he's wearing are ripped to pieces and reek of stale sweat. The box does have clothes in it, but none that I could convince Knútr to wear. I smile, imagining Knútr dressed in one of the flowery robes in front of me.

"You shouldn't be in here. Mummy wouldn't like it."

I whip my head around and come face-to-face with a gaunt specter. I yell, and the figure starts screaming back at me. I hold the torch in front of me as a weapon.

Someone comes rushing up the stairs, then Cray bursts in.

"What is it?"

He stops when he sees the woman. She is wearing a long, decomposing dress. Her teeth are black and skewed and her tangled hair almost reaches the floor.

"Are you okay?" Cray asks.

"I'm fine; she just surprised me, that's all. She appeared out of nowhere."

The woman doesn't move. Her eyes are fixed on me.

"Hello," Cray says, keeping his distance. "I'm Cray, and this is Jaime. What's your name?"

She doesn't turn toward him or reply. She tilts her head to one side, then cackles, loud and fast, making me flinch.

"You shouldn't be here. They'll tear you up for this," she says.

She is still staring at me. The left side of her top lip twitches up and down.

"We don't mean any harm," says Cray.

"Did you bring the honey?" the woman asks, talking in a slow, calculated manner.

"Honey? I'm sorry, no—I—"

"Why not, naughty boy!" She is cross, and for a moment, I think she might hit me. Then her eyes soften and she smiles. "I'm glad you've come back. Shall we feed the horses?"

JAIME

"SO YOU MEET THE MAD QUEEN," SAYS KNÚTR.

"You knew she was here?" I say.

We're back in the courtyard, sheltering from the rain inside the stable. After surprising us in the upstairs room, the woman fled, and we soon lost her in the tower's maze of passageways.

Knútr shrugs.

"What does that mean?"

"I hear of her. And I see her yesterday in the window."

"Why didn't you say anything?"

"Why I have to say? I am not your friend."

He's right about that.

"What do you know about her?" I ask.

"Nothing."

"You're lying. Tell me."

"You have nothing I want."

"We have your life," says Cray, who's leaning against the broken door frame. "You want to keep that, don't you?"

"I tell you so many times: you need me. You will not kill me."

"Who said anything about killing?" says Cray. "Just because we can't kill you doesn't mean we can't hurt you."

"It is a coward way to hurt me while I am like this. Untie the rope and fight like man, and I will kill you both so quick."

"How about you just tell us what you know?"

"*Gå til Helr!*" Knútr spits.

"Okay, here's the thing," says Cray, taking three steps toward him. "Your body is in tatters. Between the welts on your leg, your nose—which is clearly broken—and the gashes from the *sgàil*, you're in a pretty rough way. And you know it. Your leg is infected; if you don't get treatment soon, it'll become septic. The pain will be unbearable. I don't care what a tough-guy deamhan you think you are, it's going to hurt like hell. Best-case scenario: your leg is amputated and you never walk again. Worst-case scenario: a drawn-out and very painful death. Either of those sound appealing to you?" Knútr does not reply. Cray continues, "Lucky for you, I know of a poultice that can heal the infection. Even luckier for you, I happened to bring some with me. Unlucky for you, there's no way I'm going to give it to you while you keep on being an annoying pain in my *màs*."

I have so much admiration for Cray right now.

Knútr exhales through his nose and shuffles his swollen leg. "Fine," he says at last, "but I do not know lots."

"Start talking."

"Make loose the rope on my hands first."

"This isn't a negotiation. Start. Talking."

Knútr's nostrils flare. He glances at his leg again, then begins to speak. "Long time ago, when everyone is dying, the king and queen keep the princess in the tower so she does not die. They lock her with the key. Then they die. Everyone dies. But she is not die. When she breaks out of tower everyone is dead. She lives here with no one and she is mad. That is all I know. *The Mad Queen.* That is what they call her."

"What who calls her?"

Knútr keeps his mouth shut.

"What who calls her?" Cray asks again.

Knútr's lip curls. "You think you are so clever, but you know nothing."

"Nothing about what? Tell us."

When Knútr speaks next, he is less reluctant, as if delighting in our ignorance. "In the south. You think everyone is dead, but you are wrong. In the south, nobody is dead."

"You mean in Ingland? Some of the Inglish are still alive?" says Cray.

Knútr laughs, his battered face smug once again. "You see how stupid you are. You think the plague kills everyone, but in Ingland it kills *no one.* Because that is where they make it."

It takes a moment for what he is claiming to sink in.

"The plague was *made*?" I say. "How? By who?"

"King Edmund . . ." says Cray.

"Finally he uses his brain," says Knútr. "Yes, King Edmund."

"Why?" I ask.

"Why you think? Always is the same. Ingland and Scotia fight the war for many years. They want to kill each other forever. King Balfour thinks to make the *sgàilean,* but King Edmund in

224

Ingland is more clever. He digs a ditch. A long ditch all way across between Ingland and Scotia. Then he makes an *ilr-mein*—a 'plague' is how you say it, yes? He takes many rats and puts the plague inside them, and then he sends them to Scotia. In the ditch he makes the fire so the rats cannot go back. Plague goes from rats to people, from people to more people, and then everyone is dead."

"If that's true, why didn't King Edmund come north afterward to claim the land?" I ask.

"How do I know?" says Knútr. "Maybe he is afraid of plague. . . . Maybe he hears of killing shadows and is afraid of them too."

"Who's their leader now?" Cray asks Knútr. "Who inherited the throne when King Edmund died?"

"Who says he dies?" replies Knútr.

"He's still alive? But he'd be nearly a hundred by now."

"More than one hundred."

"How do you know all this?" Cray asks.

"You still cannot work it out. So stupid. We Norsk travel far. We trade with King Edmund and Inglish people for many years. People talk and we listen. That is all. I say everything I know. Now heal my leg."

"I'll heal it when I'm good and ready," says Cray. He steps out of the stable and beckons me to follow.

"Do you believe him?" he asks once we're outside. It's still raining, so we huddle under the overhang of the roof.

"I don't trust him at all, but what would he gain from lying to us about this?"

"King Balfour did have a daughter. Princess Nathara. It's

always been presumed she died along with everyone else. It is possible that she survived and grew up here on her own."

"A lifetime of solitude would be enough to turn you crazy, and
the woman we met inside definitely didn't come across as particularly sane."

Cray rubs at the light stubble on his cheeks.

"If it is Nathara, wouldn't that make her your queen?" I ask.

"I guess so. Wouldn't it make her yours as well?"

I shrug. "Even before the plague, the Skye clans didn't really
have much to do with the royal family. We should try to find her,
though, see if we can get her to talk."

"Good idea. You stay with Knútr; I'll see if I can track her
down."

He grabs a torch and starts to cross the courtyard.

"Cray," I call out. He stops. The rain threatens to put out the
torch. "Be careful, okay?"

"Always!" He winks, then jogs over to the tower and disappears
inside.

I head back into the stable. Knútr looks at me, smug-
ness plastered all over his face. There are many things I'd like
to ask him—about the south, about the plague, about King
Edmund—but I refrain. Whenever he answers one of our questions, he views it as a victory against us, as further proof of our
ignorance. I won't give him that satisfaction.

I keep myself busy by attending to Sruth. Cray made up a balm
this morning to help her singed hair grow back. I smear it on her
skin and massage it in.

"He's a naughty boy is what he is!" The voice makes me jump.

"You'll stay there until you've finished your supper."

"The Mad Queen" is standing in the entrance, shaking her head at Knútr. I wish she'd stop creeping up on us like that.

"Hello again," I say. She snaps her head toward me. I scan the stable for anything I can use as a weapon, should it come to that. There's a rusty spade leaning against the far wall, but it's too far to reach without making it obvious what I'm doing.

"You found the horses," she says. "They got all hairy. Stupid horses."

"She is more crazy than I think," says Knútr.

I ignore him, as does the woman. "Would you like to stroke them?" I ask her.

She stays where she is, eyeing the cows, her brow wrinkled. Her body language is not aggressive, but she's already proved how unpredictable she can be.

"Someone stuck them with horns. Who was it? Was it you?"

"They grew them themselves," I say. She stares at me again, unblinking. "You're Princess Nathara, is that right?"

"I knew it was you!" She runs and grabs me before I can stop her. It's a tight embrace, but an affectionate one. The smell of her breath hits me like a tidal wave of vinegar and decay. I try to peel myself away, but she only holds me tighter.

"You're a good boy, Calum, not like the other one. And you grew so tall!"

"Who's Calum?" I ask, straining my head away from her.

She releases her grip and then bursts into wild laughter. "You're funny! You can't trick me, you know."

"Are you hungry?" I ask.

"Maybe there'll be a feast. That's what Mummy says."

I reach into one of the sidebags and take out two apples. I hand one to her. She takes it from me and sniffs it with a frown. I take a bite out of mine to show her it's safe to eat. She pokes at hers with her tongue, testing its surface.

"It's good," I say, taking another bite.

She bites into hers, then spits the mouthful back out.

"You don't like apples, then?" I wonder what she eats, how she stays alive.

Rather than throw the apple away or hand it back, she keeps hold of it, nursing it as if it were a treasured object. She is not as old as I first thought, maybe late forties, which means she would have been about five or six when the plague swept through the castle and her parents locked her away. Her sunken eyes make her look older. Her hair looks like it has never been cut.

"Does anyone else live here with you, Nathara?"

She crunches her teeth together for a long time before replying.

"Mummy and Daddy live here, but they went away with you. Now you've come back and they'll be home for supper. Is there going to be milk?"

"I mean is there anyone else here now? In the castle?"

"She is mad. You waste your breath," says Knútr.

"That's not helpful," I say. "Is there anyone else in the tower?" I ask Nathara again.

"They're coming back, I know they are." She is nodding now, a vigorous bob of her head to affirm her conviction. I try a different question.

"What about the *sgàilean*?"

She stops nodding and furrows her brow, as if trying to place a distant memory.

"You know that word, yes? The shadows?"

Her eyes widen in recognition.

"They're my friends. They're not my friends."

"So they're here? There's more than one of them?"

"They'll tear you up. They always do that. Don't mind them."

"One of them attacked us last night."

"They do. Don't let them eat the pretty horses, though." She stretches out an arm as if to stroke the cows, even though they are far out of her reach.

"The *sgàilean* would eat the horses?"

"No!" She sniggers. "Only for me. But not until it's dark."

"You mean nighttime? The shadows only come out at night? Is that what you mean? Do they come inside the tower? How do you stop them from attacking you?" I'm bombarding her with too many questions.

"*Fuil*," she says, which doesn't answer any of them. "Don't worry, my precious daughter, they won't get you. They are so fussy fussing, always fussing. But they know your *fuil*."

"Full of what?" It's so hard to keep track of the conversation. I'm not even sure if it's still me she's talking to.

"I told them to bring me some honey, but they didn't do it." She turns angry and throws the apple onto the ground. She crushes it with her bare foot, stamping again and again. The pieces are smashed to a pulp beneath her heel. Just as quickly as she starts, she stops.

"I'll hide first and you can find me." Her smile reveals bright-red gums. They remind me of a freshly skinned rabbit. She grabs my hand and leads me out of the stable.

"Wait—I—" She's not having any of it. I grab one of the torches on the way out. She takes me across the courtyard and back into the tower. Her hand is coarse, its grip firm. When I try to wriggle free, she squeezes with surprising strength.

As we walk through the large room, she points to one of the paintings and says, "Daddy's always grumpy." A somber face peers down at us through the gloom. She makes a high-pitched squeal, which could be either a laugh or a cry. "Was it you that made him cross when you burned down all the trees?" she asks. "I saw it. Don't think I didn't see it."

"I don't think so. . . ." I say. We're walking straight over the crusted blood. My heart starts beating a little faster. "Where are we going?"

"Are you hungry?" she asks, using the same intonation that I used when I offered her the apple. "Maybe there'll be a feast. That's what Mummy says."

"Why don't we wait here for my friend to come?"

I try to pull my hand away, and this time she lets me. Then she drops onto all fours and scurries up the staircase like a long-limbed animal.

"Wait!" I run after her.

She stops when she reaches the top step, turns back to me, giggles, then bounds off out of sight. When I turn the corner at the top of the stairs, I find her waiting for me outside a door, sitting on her haunches. It is the door I saw earlier: the one with the trail of blood leading into it. She curls her fingers around the door handle and pulls it down. The door creaks open like a dying bird. She gallops inside. I should go. I should leave. Why am I not leaving?

I edge forward and hover in the doorway, where I am met with an overpowering smell of rotting flesh. I rub my eyes to make them focus. There's some sort of body splayed in the center of the room, its limbs protruding at broken angles. Nathara is crouched over it with her back to me, pulling at it with her hands. I consider shouting for Cray but don't want to provoke her. I place my hand on the door handle so I can shut her in if I have to.

"Pick, pick, pick, pick," she is murmuring under her breath.

When she turns to me, there is something in her hand. Something she has ripped from the dead body. She holds it up in front of her. It is sinewy and dripping. She stands up, and my grip on the door handle tightens. Once she is upright, I get a clearer view of the body. It is some sort of animal, perhaps a roe or a small horse. It's so decimated, it's impossible to tell. She must hunt, and then drag whatever she catches up here to eat.

"Are you hungry?" She offers me the strip of flesh.

After a moment's hesitation I take it, not wanting to offend her. She stares at me with her drooping eyes. The meat is rubbery and wet in my hand; it reminds me of the hare's heart I was made to swallow during the wedding ceremony. What I am holding now is much colder. The animal has been dead a long time.

Nathara is still watching me. A glint of impatience flickers in her eyes. I don't want to upset her, but the rotten meat would poison me for sure.

I have an idea. I take a bite. A bitter tang fills my mouth. I spit the mouthful back out, replicating Nathara's reaction to the apple. She watches me, expressionless. I throw the remaining meat onto the ground and start stamping on it with my heel. She smiles.

"You don't like *fiadh*, then?" she says, imitating me once again. She wipes her bloody hands on her dress and walks past me, out of the room. She is walking upright again now. After a few paces, she glances back to check that I am following. I close the door on the feeding room and catch up with her, feeling like I have passed some sort of test.

At the end of the corridor we bump into Cray, coming down one of the many spiral staircases.

"You found her," he says. "I thought I heard voices." The flames from his torch highlight the strong line of his jaw.

"Who are you? Why are you in the tower? Mummy will be cross."

Nathara shows no sign of recognizing Cray from before. She sits on the floor with her knees pulled up to her chest and starts picking at her toenails.

"She kind of found me," I say.

"I feel like I should bow or something. I've never met a queen before."

"She's not your average queen."

"Where's Knútr?"

"He's still in the stable. She dragged me in. I couldn't really stop her."

"I'll go back down, if you're all right with her on your own?"

"I'm fine. I think she's mistaken me for someone else. Someone called Calum?"

"That was her brother, the prince."

"Oh." I don't know what to make of that. "I'm trying to get her to talk, but it's hard to understand a lot of what she says."

"Keep trying. Find out as much as you can." He holds up a small leather satchel that clunks as he shakes it. "I found you some tools. They're a bit rusty, but they should do the job. I'll take them down and set up camp in the main entrance. Shout if you need me."

Nathara stands up as soon as he's gone. "Come on, then. Don't be lazy or the spiders will crawl into your ears and eat your brain."

For the rest of the morning, she leads me around the tower, showing me the rooms she frequents the most, the things she likes doing, the objects she treasures. We go up and down so many different staircases that I lose track of how many floors there are. Without her as a guide, I would definitely get lost.

One of the rooms she shows me contains hundreds of books. I have never seen so many. I run my hand along a shelf and pick a book at random.

"Don't touch that!" Nathara says as I am sliding it out. "Daddy says don't touch the books. There'll be no eggs for you."

I leave the book where it is.

I wander over to a table at the far side of the room. Nathara is busying herself behind me, counting books for no obvious reason. On the table, there is a collection of papers, bound together in a moss-green cover. It is the only item not on one of the shelves. I flip through the pages. It's some sort of diary. On one of the pages, the word *sgàilean* catches my eye. I start to read from the beginning of the entry:

> There are no prisoners left. The last one died during
> this evening's attempt. My frustration is immeasurable.

We cannot stop now, not now that we're so close.
There's too much at stake. I spoke to the King and
convinced him to send men to Aberdon in search of
drunkards and waifs. They will better serve their King
and country in our hands. Besides, if we fail, it could
be the end for us all . . .

"Twenty-seven. Thirty-seven. Forty-seven. What comes next?"

Nathara's question is not aimed at me, but it reminds me that she's in the room. I slip the diary into my pocket to read later.

"Time to go," says Nathara, and she skips out of the room.

The whole time she's leading me around, I try to figure out what she's thinking. At times, she behaves like a young child, excited to have a visitor to entertain. At other times, she appears old and worn and desperately sad.

At the very top of the tower, there is a room with a battered-down door. Its windows are larger than most of the others, so the air is fresher. A huge pile of blankets lies crumpled in one corner. The walls are covered in childish scribbles. That, and scratch marks. It pulls at my heart to imagine the child she once was, alone and afraid, waiting for a family that would never return. We don't stay in that room for long.

By the time we arrive back in the main hall, it is awash with light. Cray has made a large fire in the hearth and lit hundreds of candles, which hang from the ceiling on three equally spaced metal structures. Bras, Sruth, and Knútr are all inside now too.

"It's pretty like before!" Nathara shouts, and she starts skipping around the room. She is drawn to the main fire and wiggles her fingers in front of it.

"This should be enough light to keep the *sgàilean* away, right?" says Cray.

"It's beautiful," I say, looking up at the hanging candles.

"They're called chandeliers. I found a stack of candles in one of the storerooms—enough to last at least a week."

"Nathara likes your fire."

"It doesn't look like she's used to it. I wonder how she protects herself from the *sgàilean* without it."

"I asked her that. She said something about being full?"

"Full?"

"Yes. That they know she's full or something."

Cray furrows his brow. "Could she have said *fuil*?"

"I guess. What does that mean?"

"Blood," he says.

Nathara appears beside us without either of us noticing her approach. It's a very unnerving talent she possesses.

"Don't be naughty or I'll tell them to gobble you up," she says in Cray's ear, before bursting into squeals of laughter.

"Don't worry, I'll behave," Cray says.

"I won't let them get *you*, though, Calum," she says to me.

"That's kind of you," I say.

"They do what I tell them, but not about the honey." She tilts her head to the ceiling and becomes distracted by the lights. "The room is filled with pretty stars just for me. It's because we're having a party."

She weaves her long hair between her fingers and drifts away.

"I see what you mean about her not really talking much sense," says Cray.

"Did she just say the *sgàilean* do what she says?"

"It would explain how she's survived so long."

"This might provide us with a few more answers." I hand him the diary. "It was on a table upstairs."

"What is it?"

"A diary of some sort, by someone called the Badhbh."

"Sounds creepy."

"I think he's the one who helped the king make the *sgàilean*. Perhaps you could read it while I'm gone?"

"Oh. . . . I can't read words."

"Oh." I'm embarrassed for him; I don't know why.

"We don't write things down very often," he says, "and when we do, we use more pictures than words."

"Okay." I can't believe there's something I can do that Cray can't. "Well, hold on to it and I'll have a look when I get back. Don't let Nathara see it, though; I don't think she'll be happy I took it."

"Understood."

"I'm going to make a start on the boat while there's still light. If I'm not back by dusk . . . Well, let's just hope I am."

"Take this," he says, handing me a short sword in a weathered scabbard. "Just in case."

"I don't know how to use a sword," I say.

"Then let's hope you won't have to. You'll feel safer wearing it, though."

I take the scabbard and tie it around my waist, then sling the satchel of tools over my shoulder.

"Wish me luck," I say.

"You'll be fine."

The rain has stopped, but the sky is still a tragic gray. As I am picking my way around the mud puddles in front of the castle, there is a shout behind me and then something hard hits me on the shoulder. I turn, and a second rock comes hurtling past my left ear. Nathara gawks at me from the top of the battlement.

"Why are you going? You're not allowed to leave," she says.

"I'm not leaving. I'm just going to the harbor. To fix a ship. I'll come back, I promise."

Her frown is so deep, her face looks like it's about to cave in on itself.

"You can come with me if you want?" I could really do without that, but I feel like I have to offer. She's been alone her whole life, and she's worried we're already about to abandon her.

She disappears from the top of the wall and reappears a few moments later at the door below. She hesitates. I take a few paces back toward her.

"Are you coming?" I ask.

"We'll come back for you I promise we'll come back for you I promise," she says.

"Yes, I promise. I'll be back before sundown."

But she's not talking to me.

"Something dangerous is happening it's not safe stay in here my darling my precious daughter you'll be safe in here don't open the door everything's going to be okay stay in here you'll be safe in here don't open the door we'll be back soon it's not safe it's not safe it's not safe—"

The words pour out of her like an incantation. She stares at the ground with empty eyes.

"Nathara. Nathara, are you okay?"

She keeps mumbling under her breath and does not respond. I place my hand on her shoulder. She stops talking and her eyes come back into focus.

"I'm going down to the harbor," I say again. "Would you like to come with me?"

"No!" she says. She backs away from the door frame and slams the door.

So much for trying to be friendly. There was no mistaking the look on her face: she's too scared to leave the castle.

My fingertips linger on the hilt of my sword as I back away. I turn from the castle and start trudging through the wet grass. All the while, Nathara's warning echoes in my ears.

It's not safe. It's not safe. It's not safe.

AGATHA

I WAS SAD ALL DAY YESTERDAY AND I AM STILL SAD TODAY. Milkwort didn't come back and now he is gone. I tried looking for him and so did Finn and Mór, but he wasn't anywhere and if he can't hear me how can I call to him? I think he went to find food which is why he went and I couldn't tell him it wasn't time to do that. I wanted to stay until we found him, but we have to keep going. We couldn't look for him anymore and we had to leave him behind. It is the most sad I have ever been.

All we did again today is ride all day. I don't like it anymore. I tried talking to the bulls again, but I can't, even now my head isn't hurting. I tried talking to a bird I saw as well that was only a small one but I still couldn't do it. The falling out of the tree broke me inside, I know it. Milkwort is gone and I can't do the talking anymore and now no one will like me.

I don't want to sing. Mór was singing and said for me to join in but I said I didn't want to and I didn't.

We're nearly there now which is the only good thing. I want to see Jaime again and Crayton. I think that Crayton will be happy to see me and maybe hug me. But if he finds out my head is broken maybe he won't like me as much after that.

Finn is ahead and stops.

"What is it?" asks Mór.

"There's something on the track," he says.

We've been going the same way Jaime and Crayton came. We know it because of the feet prints their cows made. That is what Finn told me.

Finn gets down from his bull who is Gailleann and pats him on his head two times. I can see what it is on the ground now. It is a big arrow that someone has scraped on the ground to make one. Mór gets down too so I get down too. The arrow is pointing to a tree where there is hair from a bull tied around a big stone.

"Cray," says Mór.

Finn picks up the stone. There are scratches on it but I can't see what and Finn doesn't show me.

"You think this means they're real?" Finn asks. He looks serious when he says it. He is not smiling and he passes the stone to Mór, who is also not smiling. She looks at it but she doesn't show it to me either and she throws the stone away.

"What do we do?" Mór asks Finn.

"Spend the night here, I guess," says Finn.

"Are we sure we're safe here?" says Mór.

"If we build a big enough fire, we'll be fine," says Finn. "Let's get started."

I don't understand at all what they are saying.

"Why do we need a big fire?" I ask, and, "What did Crayton scratch on the stone?" I want to know. It's not fair that they don't tell me.

Mór looks at Finn first and then she says, "Cray was warning us about an animal they saw near the castle. He said we shouldn't travel at night, so we're going to wait here until morning and then go on, okay?"

"But we have to get there soon," I say.

"We will," says Mór. "In the morning."

"Why does it have to be a big fire?" I ask.

"Animals don't like fires," says Finn.

"What kind of animal is it?"

"It didn't say. But don't worry; we'll be safe here."

So we stop even though we are nearly there which makes me cross because Jaime is waiting for me and we have to go on the boat now. That is the most important thing. I'm not scared of one animal. We have bulls as well that are big and can get it. Or I could have talked to it in my head, but I can't do that now which makes me even more sadder.

Finn and Mór make a fire at the end of the track which is next to a big field. The one they make is even bigger than the one in the meeting circle. They keep adding more. It will be warm to sleep.

They give me a job that is cutting up the vegetables which they say is an important one because we all need to eat don't we. After we have eaten the food it is time to go to sleep. Mór says she will watch for the animal first. I say I can do it even though I am tired because I want to do it to take turns. Mór says she'll wake me up later and then I can have my turn so I say okay that is fair and I go to sleep.

When I wake up it is the morning. Mór is asleep and Finn is awake and watching for the animal.

I am cross and I say to Finn, "Why didn't you wake me? It was my—turn to w-watch."

"You were sleeping really deeply. I didn't want to disturb you," says Finn.

It is not true. It's because they do not think I can do it right.

"I can do it!" I shout. "I can watch and I wouldn't f-fall asleep and I would see the animal when it came."

Mór is awake now.

"Hey, what's all the shouting for?" she asks.

"You were supposed to wake me and you didn't—wake me," I say, and I am still shouting.

"We needed you to rest," says Mór. "So you're fully recovered. In case we see the animal today. So you can talk to it and help us again."

"I told you already I can't do it!" I scream, and I pick up a pot that is close and throw it at the fire and I kick all the other things and when Mór tries to stop me I push her and then I run and I don't care where I'm running I just do it.

The grass is long and wet and it makes me wet too. I can hear gallops coming and then Finn is in front of me on Gailleann the bull. I try to go past him and push the bull but he won't let me and blocks me.

"Get out of my way!" I shout, but he doesn't so I grab at the grass and tear it up and throw it at him again and again and rip it more and throw again and scream.

It makes me tired to do it and then I can't do it anymore and I sit down and put my head in my hands but I don't cry because I won't.

Mór is there and she puts a hand on my shoulder and I let her.

"It's all right," she says.

"I'm sorry, okay," I say, and my head is still in my hands.

"You don't need to apologize," says Mór.

"I'm not supposed to d-do it," I say.

"Do what?" asks Mór.

"Get angry and do—bad things," I tell her. "Maistreas Eilionoir said I have to c-control it. But sometimes it just—happens."

"Hey, don't be so hard on yourself. We all get angry. You've had a tough few weeks."

Then I say, "I could do it. I could watch for the animal. I wouldn't fall asleep. I could do it. Why does everyone think I can't—do things?"

"You're right. It was wrong of us not to wake you." It is Finn who says this. He is not on Gailleann now. He has gotten off and is next to me like Mór. "You can have first watch tonight; how about that?"

I nod. I feel better that they will let me. I am not angry anymore.

"Let's get to Dunnottar, shall we? It won't take us long now," says Finn.

I nod and we walk back to where our things are. I am very wet and now it is cold so I stand by the fire while we eat to make me dry. The fire is smaller now so it only dries me a bit. Then Mór stamps on the fire to put it out and we go.

It is not long and then we see the castle. Finn sees it first and he whistles and moves his head to show me to look at it. It is small only because it is a bit far away still. I know that.

The bulls have to walk. They can't run because the grass is thick which means it takes more time. We go past some trees that are all black and fallen down. Maybe that is where the animal lives. I look for it but I can't see it.

The castle gets bigger and bigger and when we are close it is so big I can't even believe it. I don't even know how they made it so big. We're supposed to be going to the harbor, but Finn says the feet prints go to the castle so he thinks that is where Jaime and Crayton are. The path is small to get to it so we have to get off and walk. The sea is a long way down below but it is okay. I am a Hawk so I am not scared. I am good at walking high with the sea below.

We go into the castle through a door but we are still outside like it is a small enclave. Then Jaime comes running out from the tall part and says, "You made it!" He runs all the way to me and when he gets close he stops and asks, "Can I hug you?" and I say, "Yes," and I give him one of my biggest hugs. Afterward he says, "I'm so sorry I left without you. Finn explained why I had to, right? How are you feeling?"

"It's okay you had to leave, J-Jaime," I say, and also I say, "My head is—better now," which is a bit true because it doesn't hurt anymore and a bit not true because it is broken inside. I don't tell him that part.

He says hello to Finn and Mór and we all go into the tall place. Inside is a big room and it's bright from all the candles in the air. It is pretty to look at it. Knútr is tied up in the corner. Crayton who is my favorite is there too. He comes over and I want him to hug me like Jaime did but he doesn't. He touches his forehead with Mór and Finn because that is what they do. Then he says, "Hello, Agatha, nice to see you again." And I reply, "You can touch my head as well, you know."

He smiles and says, "Sure," and touches my head to his head and it is very wonderful and I smile.

"I'm going to do the first watch tonight," I tell him.

"Are you?" he says. "That's great."

Everyone is happy and talking and then a woman runs down the stairs who I don't know. She stops at the bottom and says, "All the people came and the feast isn't ready yet," and then she runs at us so I scream which makes her stop and then she screams too and then I stop and then she stops and she is looking at me.

"Agatha, this is Nathara, Queen of Scotia," says Jaime, which is introducing.

I know what a queen is. It's like an elder but for all the people and an important one. She does not look like a queen. She is dirty and some of her teeth aren't there and her hair is long but it isn't pretty like mine. If Jaime says she is a queen I should be nice to her. I do a bow which is when you bend your body in the middle. Maistreas Sorcha showed me how to do it.

The queen walks toward me and is always looking at me. She looks at my face very close and I don't know why.

"Why do you look like that? Did it get you? You should have waited in the room like Daddy said," she says.

"I don't mean to be rude, but I never even m-met you before," I say.

She laughs very loud then, so I laugh too. Then she sees the bulls that are Finn's and Mór's and shouts, "More horses!" and goes to them, but they're not horses so she's wrong.

Jaime is next to me and leads me over to where there are some big chairs for us to sit on. "We've got a lot to catch up on," he says. "Are you hungry?"

"Yes," I say, because I am.

He gives me an apple from a bag next to him and I start to eat it. Then he whispers to me, "Queen Nathara can act a bit strange sometimes, but she's a nice person. Don't let anything she says make you angry."

"Okay," I tell him, "I won't."

Jaime tells me about the ship he has found and that he has been fixing it for two days and now it is nearly ready. Crayton and Mór and Finn come over to where we are.

"Did you really see a *sgàil*?" Mór asks Crayton.

"I wouldn't exactly say we *saw* it, but it was there, yes," says Crayton. "It was quite insistent on pulling off Knútr's limbs."

The shadow things are real! I said to Jaime they were.

"Thanks for the warning," says Mór.

I think she means the stone. But the shadow things are not an animal.

"So King Balfour succeeded?" asks Finn.

"Yes," says Crayton. He holds up all papers in a book with

green covers and hits it with his hand. "Jaime found this. It's the diary of a man called the Badhbh. Jaime, why don't you tell them what it says?"

"Um . . . well, the Badhbh was the man who helped King Balfour with his experiments," says Jaime. "It says they managed to create a whole army of shadows. They were made to target anyone without Scotian blood. He was going to send them into Ingland, but before he had a chance—"

"King Edmund sent a surprise of his own," says Crayton. "A huge mischief of rats, infected with a plague designed to kill us all."

"Wait—the plague was made by the Inglish?" says Mór.

"That's right," says Crayton. "According to Knútr, everyone in Ingland is still alive. Including King Edmund."

"No!" says Mór. "That can't be true?" Her mouth is a circle.

"So the sgàilean—you're saying they're all around the castle, right now?" asks Finn.

"Thousands of them," says Crayton. "They were made to serve the royal family, so they stay here because of Nathara. We heard her talking to them last night. They've been her only company for the past forty years."

"If they don't attack people with Scotian blood, does that mean they can't harm us?" asks Mór.

"I presume so, although I'm not in any rush to test that theory. When we first approached the castle, they attacked Knútr but didn't hurt me. That could have been a coincidence, though. What we know for sure is that they stay away from light, so we're safe during the day and should stay in this room at night."

No one is talking then and there is so much that Crayton has said that my head is too full with it all and I can't think about any one thing because there are too many. What I do know is the shadow things are real and they are here.

"Luckily, we won't have to worry about them for long," Jaime says to me. "The ship will be ready by the end of today. First thing tomorrow, we're leaving for Norveg."

JAIME

NATHARA WANTS TO COME WITH US. I DON'T KNOW IF I should let her. I must be crazy for even considering it. She can't fight, she's unpredictable, she'd be one more person to worry about. . . . All the same, I can't bear the thought of abandoning her here.

I told her last night that we would be leaving soon, on a ship to find my clan. She furrowed her brow at the word *clan,* so I tried *family* instead. She immediately became animated, thinking we were setting out to find *her* family, and insisted on joining us. I tried to explain that that wasn't the case, but she wouldn't hear it. She hasn't stopped talking about it since.

Cray, on the other hand, is not coming. It was foolish of me to think that he might. I suppose I hoped that he'd want to help with the rescue as well. He told me he wanted to, but he'd never leave Bras, and the bull can't travel on the ship. He also needs to go back to his people in case the wildwolves return.

"All done," says Cray as he helps me attach the final sail.

I jump onto the deck and look up at my work. "You think it's seaworthy?" I ask.

"No idea. I told you, I know nothing about boats. But it looks good to me. As far as I can tell, you've done a great job."

My heart swells with pride. It's taken three days of intense physical labor, but the finished result does look impressive. Even I have to admit that.

"Thanks," I say.

"I don't do compliments often," he says, punching me on the top of my arm, "so don't expect another one any time soon."

"Don't worry, I won't."

I wonder if I'll ever see him again after we set sail. I've been trying not to admit it to myself, but I know, deep down, that my plan is a hopeless one. Even if we somehow make it to Norveg, the deamhain there will be just as untrustworthy as Knútr. What hope do we have that they'll honor any sort of an exchange?

The sun is hovering on the horizon, ready to drop. "We'd better head back," I say. "It's about to get dark."

Agatha and Mór arrive at the castle at the same time as we do. They've been out scavenging for food, which they add to the pile of items we found in the castle: clothes, bedding, weapons, anything we thought might be useful.

At evening meal, Cray, Finn, and Mór joke with one another and tell us stories. Nathara sits with us for a bit and joins in when the others laugh. Agatha is enraptured by the Bó Riders' tales and asks to hear more and more. No one mentions tomorrow's voyage, but it's all I can think about. Anything could happen. Anything could go wrong.

Once we've eaten, Agatha announces that she is going to take the first watch. Cray turns to Mór, who nods and says, "You sure are. Wake us up if you hear anything unusual."

"I will! Don't worry, I—I will!" says Agatha.

"I'll go second," I say. "Wake me up in a bit, Aggie."

"I will do that, J-Jaime."

I curl up in a blanket and close my eyes. The muscles between my shoulder blades throb from my work on the ship; the heat from the fire does wonders to soothe them.

When Agatha wakes me, my first thought is that something is wrong. But she is smiling that big smile of hers and says, "I did it. I d-did the watch, Jaime. It's your—your turn now."

I pull myself up onto my elbows. "Great job, Aggie," I say. "I'll take it from here."

"I'm going to—sleep now. Good night, Jaime," she says. Then, glancing at the others, she repeats in an over-emphasized whisper, "Good night, Jaime."

She lies down on a mattress, which she insisted we help her pull down from one of the upstairs rooms, and closes her eyes. With the blanket around my shoulders, I cross to one of the narrow windows, hoping the fresh air will wake me up a bit. The night is still.

I'm worried that if I sit down, I may drift back to sleep, so I pace the room in large circles. The Bó Riders lie close to one another, not far from the door. Knútr is at the opposite end of the hall, near the skeleton room, tied to a large metal chair. His snores echo off the cold stone walls.

The Badhbh's diary lies tucked away next to where I was

sleeping. I pick it up. It smells of old leaves. I start rereading the final entry. It's been on my mind since I first read it. What it says is very clear: the Badhbh survived. When everyone else died of the plague, he didn't. He doesn't say how he survived, just that he plans to travel west and live in isolation. What I can't understand is that he knew Nathara was locked in the tower, but he still left without her. She was a child, desperate and afraid, and he left her here alone. What kind of monster would do something like that?

A noise outside interrupts my reading. A distant bawl of pain. I put the book down, cross to the nearest window, and squint into the darkness. The sound stops. Or maybe it was never there; it's hard to focus with Knútr snoring in the background. My ears strain against the silence. Nothing. I wander over to the front doors and place my cheek against one of them. At first, the sound is almost imperceptible, but it gets louder and louder: the same whispering we heard when we first approached the castle. The *sgàilean*. Should I wake the others? No, the room is well lit. We're safe as long as we remain inside.

There is another sound, buried underneath the whispering. A slow, repeated scratch, like something heavy dragging itself across the courtyard. It gets louder. Whatever it is, it is getting closer. The door is held shut by a thick plank of wood. I'm not sure how long it would last if someone was really determined to get in. I turn away from the door, but as soon as I do, both of the sounds dissolve away. I count to ten under my breath, as slowly as my thumping heart will allow. Still nothing. I need to take a look. I can do this. I can. I raise the plank from the doors and peer out into the night. There is something in the courtyard, about ten paces from where I'm standing. It's too dark to make out what it is. I draw my sword. Cray has been teaching me how to use it, but I'm not sure I'm ready. Nothing moves.

"Hello?" I say. My voice quivers, but only a little.

There is no answer.

I hurry to the pile of supplies and pick up a torch, then hold it in the fire until it crackles to life. I should wake someone up, but something stops me. I want to do this on my own. I need to prove that I can.

Back at the door, I hold the torch in one hand and the sword in the other, and step out into the courtyard. The gravel crunches underfoot and a raw breeze runs up my spine. I shuffle forward a few paces, all of my senses alert. There is a whispering to my left. I swing the torch and the sound stops. As long as I have the fire, I am safe. *As long as I have the fire, I am safe.*

As I draw nearer to the object, it moves. A twist of its head so that it stares at me with a single glassy eye. It gurgles from the back of its throat. It is dying, nearly dead. I lower the torch and see the bloody stumps where its horns once were. A stag. I've seen one once before on Skye, but never like this. I take another step forward. It is now so close I could reach out and touch it. There are tear marks all over its body. It's missing one of its back legs, and a deep slit in its side reveals struggling lungs, fighting to draw air under a battered rib cage. Its roving eye is both scared and pleading.

"Okay," I say. "It'll be over soon."

I place the tip of my sword on the side of its head and slide the blade in. The relief of death shudders through its body.

The *sgàilean* did this. A food offering for Nathara. It must be them, not her, who hunt the animals she eats. They are doing what they were created for: serving her family.

There's something I've been wondering ever since we arrived at the castle. It's a terrible idea for so many reasons, but . . . what if there was a way we could take the *sgàilean* with us to Norveg? It's drastic and terrifying and awful, but having an army with us would greatly increase our chances of success. They'd be a last resort, only to be used if all negotiations—and then threats—came to nothing. Could it be possible?

The Badhbh wrote in his diary that the *sgàilean* can be both contained and controlled, but he is vague on the specifics. During her more lucid moments, Nathara does claim that they do what she tells them. But the *sgàilean* are also ruthless killers; the body in front of me is a clear reminder of that. It is so mutilated that I am swamped with anxiety. What if I did take them with us and they ended up doing that to me? Or to Agatha? Or, even worse, our entire clan? I can't even consider the possibility unless I know they won't hurt us. Our ancestors were originally from the mainland, so Scotian blood should run through our veins, but they left long ago.

There's only one way to know for sure.

I shut down the doubts in my head and step away from the stag. With shaking hands, I place the torch on the ground by my feet. *Breathe. Breathe. Breathe.* I steady myself long enough to take three deep breaths, then I edge away from the light until my whole body is overtaken by darkness.

"Come and get me," I say. "I'm right here. Come and get me."

The whispering starts behind me. Before long, there is more, from all sides. I glance at the torch, lying just a few paces away. My whole body jolts, fighting the urge to leap back to the safety of the flames. There is still time. I resist. I need to do this. I *can* do this.

The first shadow hits me like a gust of wind around my ankles. Sharp prickles race up my legs and then all at once I am consumed. They are across my chest, through my hair, down my back. What have I done? Goose bumps erupt all over my skin. My vision is obscured as hundreds of *sgàilean* soar across my face. They claw into my ears and invade my nose. I clamp my mouth shut, even though I'm struggling to breathe. The whispering is so intense it blocks out all other senses. I need to get them off me. I need to get away, but I am trapped by their momentum. I can't speak, I can't move, I can't see. Their hatred is overwhelming; they yearn for destruction, to rip, tear, kill, destroy.

But they are not hurting me.

I cling to that realization with the whole of my being. I curl my toes into the ground and repeat it to myself again and again until the clamor begins to mellow. The whispering dies to a low growl and the *sgàilean* drift away.

As soon as the last one is gone, I scramble to the torch and rush back inside, bolting the door behind me. My legs are so weak, I collapse to the ground. Blood is thundering at the sides of my head. I can't believe it. I survived. I stepped into a swarm of *sgàilean* and walked out again unharmed. Our blood protects us; my clan will be safe. It is all I needed to know.

We're taking the *sgàilean* with us.

BEFORE DAWN, I CLIMB THE STEPS TO THE TOP OF THE tower and knock on Nathara's door. There is no reply. I push it open. Nathara is awake and dressed, standing by the far window. I clear my throat.

She spins around and shouts, "Why are you here? It's not for you." She picks up a small wooden box and throws it at my head. It misses by an inch and crashes into the wall behind me, spilling its contents onto the floor: rings, chains, earrings, bracelets, each one inset with precious stones.

"Sorry, I'm sorry," I say, retreating to the safety of the corridor.

"It's okay, Calum, no need to be sad."

She crosses the room and meets me at the broken doorway with an odd smile.

"We're leaving soon," I say. "Do you still want to come with us?"

"I'm not going anywhere. Neither are you. Daddy says don't leave. He'll be mad."

"We've been through this, remember? I need to go on the ship. I have to rescue my family."

She stares at me for a long time and then asks in a slow and precise manner, "Are the horses coming?"

"They don't like going on the water, but we'll come back and see them soon." When she folds her arms and scowls, I ask, "Does that mean you've changed your mind? That you don't want to come?"

She unfolds her arms and pats me on the top of my head. "Of course I'm coming. Don't ever leave me again."

"Okay, I won't. Good. Um . . ." Is this the right decision?

Probably not. I just have to say it. "I want you to bring the shadows too."

"Shadows."

"Yes. The *sgàilean*. To help us fight the bad people."

As soon as I've said it out loud, I'm drowned in a new wave of doubt. I'm putting my trust—and our lives—in the hands of someone who can barely remember her own name.

"Shadows," she says again. She presses her teeth together and curls back her lips.

"Can you make them help us?"

"They're always helping. They want it, they need it, they'll help."

"Good. That's good. But only if you can control them. I need you to prove that to me. You said before that you could?"

"Of course," she says. "If it didn't break when you made me throw it."

She slides back into the room. Is it right for me to be using her this way? It's her choice to come with us, but she has no real understanding of the danger that lies ahead. The *sgàilean* will protect her, I suppose, if she can make them come. I peer around the door frame and see her crouching over the contents of the jewelry box. She picks up a necklace and fastens it around her neck. Hanging from a simple chain is an onyx amulet that rests at the base of her throat. Its vast size is both striking and grotesque.

"Stop shouting," she says to me, even though I haven't said anything. "We're ready to go." She drops onto all fours and scurries down the staircase. When we reach the main hall, she speeds straight past the others, heading for the far doors.

"What's happening?" asks Finn, who is on the final watch.

"I'm not quite sure."

Nathara has the doors open in no time and, standing on two feet again, she strides through the courtyard. I follow her at a half-jog. A misty predawn light covers everything in spiderweb gray.

"Wait!" says Finn. "The *sgàilean*—?"

"It's safe," I say. "I think. . . ."

He pauses, then runs out to join me. Nathara is now standing at the castle's main entrance. The skewed door looms above her, at least four times her height. There is a lever on one side, attached to a pulley system, not dissimilar to the ones used on the enclave gates back on Skye. Nathara pulls on it with both hands. Nothing happens, so she adds her whole body weight. There is a high-pitched creak, and then the wooden door falls with a crash. Nathara steps onto the middle of it and begins to shout.

"*Sgàilean, thigibh a-steach! Thigibh a-steach!*" She says the same words again and again. "*Thigibh a-steach.*"

"Uh-oh, that doesn't sound good," says Finn, his eyes darting back to the open door of the tower.

"What? Why? What's she saying?" I ask.

"It's a command. She's telling them to go inside, or enter. She must mean the tower." He turns to leave but is stopped in his tracks by the foul sound that is becoming increasingly familiar. Everything turns a few shades darker as the light is sucked away from around us.

All my attention is on Nathara. Through the grim haze, she opens the onyx amulet like a locket. She holds it in front of her, repeating the command.

"I don't think she's telling them to enter the tower," I say.

"Surely they can't all—?"

Finn's question is drowned by the sea of whispers. Thousands of sgàilean drift out of the shadows, darker than night and as fluid as water. Finn grabs my arm. We are both transfixed. All at once, they descend on Nathara in a frenzied blizzard and then disappear into the depths of the stone. Nathara shuts the amulet and the whispering stops. The darkness fades. My mouth drops open.

"That was incredible!" I say. "You didn't tell me you could do that. I don't even know how—This is incredible, Nathara, incredible!"

For the first time, the tide is turning ever so slightly in our favor.

"Shhhhh!" says Nathara. "Don't cry or the birds will come and steal your tears."

I am not crying. I am invigorated. "It's time to wake the others," I say.

Cray and Mór are already stirring when we enter the tower. I wake up Agatha and tell everyone what happened with Nathara and the amulet. I also tell them about my plan to take the sgàilean with us. Cray looks impressed when I describe how I walked among them last night. Agatha is unconvinced by the plan, and I have to explain several times how I know they won't hurt us.

Without wasting any time, we carry the supplies down to the harbor. The weather has turned wild again, and the wind seems determined to push me off the gangway as I stagger along, laden with goods. By midday, we are ready to go. We share one last meal, eating meat from the stag that the sgàilean brought last night.

Finn spent the morning roasting it on a smoky fire. The memory of its wild eye lingers in my mind as I eat.

"There's plenty left over," says Finn once we've finished. "If you soak it in seawater and leave it out to dry, it should last you the whole journey."

"Thanks," I say. There is an empty pause, which no one wants to fill. "I guess it's time to go, then."

"I'll fetch Knútr," says Cray, getting to his feet.

"Are you ready to c-come with us?" Agatha asks Nathara.

I expect Nathara to question where we are going again, or complain, or say something incomprehensible, but she does none of those things. She nods, picks up the one item she has decided to take with her—a tatty soft toy in the shape of a pine marten—and leads the way out of the tower. She pauses at the castle's entrance, and doubt flashes across her face.

"It's all right," Agatha reassures her. "Don't be scared."

She takes Nathara's hand and smiles at her. Nathara smiles back, and the two of them leave the castle like old friends going for a stroll.

We follow them around the narrow cliff path to the start of the stone steps. There, I say goodbye to Bras, Sruth, and the other two bulls, rubbing each one in turn on the spot between their horns. I will miss the warmth and protection they provide so willingly. They lean over and watch us as we make our final descent.

The pebbles at the bottom of the steps glint with flecks of silver and crunch against one another as we walk across them. The sound makes me think of grinding bones. When we reach the ship, Mór takes Knútr on board and ties him to the central mast.

Before leaving the dock, Agatha asks Cray, "W-why don't you want to come with us?"

"I would if I could; you know that. But my people need me here."

"I'm going to—miss you," she says.

"I'll miss you too, Agatha." He smiles at her. A gentle smile, not his usual arrogant one. "Here, why don't you take this? To remember me by." He hands her his spear, which she accepts with wonder.

"Thank you, C-Crayton, thank you—very much."

She leans in and kisses him full on the lips. Cray's eyes open wide.

"Well, that's a first!" he says when she finally lets him go.

Agatha grins. "And *that* was something to remember—me by."

Finn bursts into laughter.

"I'm certainly not going to forget it any time soon," Cray assures her.

"Do I get one too?" asks Finn.

"No," says Agatha. "Only Crayton, because he's my f-favorite."

"Fair enough," says Finn.

"But I do—like you and I will miss you, and Mór as well even though a-at first I thought I didn't like her and—and then I did."

"You certainly know how to make a girl feel special," says Mór as she swings down the gangplank, back onto the dock.

I say my goodbyes, touching each of their foreheads with my own. Cray and I touch foreheads for the longest. We've been through a lot.

"You be careful out there," he says to me.

"I'll try."

"I hope you find what you're looking for."

"Me too."

"You're a hero, Jaime," he says without warning. "A hero for even trying. And so much braver than you will ever realize. Foolish too, of course, but mainly incredibly brave."

I don't know what to say to that. I look past the ship at the sea. It swells and surges under the gloom of the sky. So much water. The deepest I have ever seen, with no land in sight. Am I really about to set sail on that? My stomach cramps at the thought. "I don't feel particularly brave."

"None of the bravest people do."

AGATHA

AT FIRST I DIDN'T WANT TO GO ON THE SHIP BECAUSE OF what happened to the other boat when it sank. I was splashing in the water because I couldn't swim and I thought I might drown. Lileas saved me then. Now she is dead because of the nasty deamhan did it. It still makes me so angry when I see him which is all the day now because he is tied to the pole in the middle. I try not to let the angry get too hot because it's what I shouldn't do.

I decided to be brave and go on the ship to show the queen it was all right. She was scared to go on it. She needs me to look after her and I am good at helping people. "It's fun being on the water," I tell her, and now she likes it.

She is a real queen. The nasty deamhan calls her the Mad Queen, but I think she is nice so I call her the Nice Queen. Or I call her Nathara, which is her other name. Sometimes she says things that are funny and I laugh.

We are not going very fast. Jaime says it is hard because it is only me and him to make the ship go and he is not good at it. The nasty deamhan tells us what to do and which way to go. He shouts a lot of things and bosses us. I don't like it and I don't want to do it, but Jaime says we have to because he's the one who knows. I'm the best at doing the sails because I'm good at climbing so that's my most important job and I do it.

It was sad to say goodbye to the bull people because they are my friends now and I miss them so much. I hope I will see them again soon, especially Crayton. He gave me his spear because he likes me and I gave him a kiss because he liked it.

It is always cold on the ship. I don't mind being cold. We put on lots of clothes to make us warmer but it is still cold. I cannot see a single thing except for only so much sea all around us. The sea does not want us to be on it. That is what I think. The waves are big ones and sometimes they come over the ship and get us wet. Me and the Queen Nathara like it when it does that. She screams when she gets wet and is happy.

When I am looking at the sea it makes me remember when I was on the wall being a good Hawk and I did it for all the day. Because it is nearly nighttime the sea is a dark color like purple. It is my favorite color when it is dark.

The shadow things are on the ship as well. That is what Jaime says. They are in the necklace on the Queen Nathara. I don't know about that. As long as they stay in there and do not come out and get me. I do not want them to get me. They are very bad things.

"How you doing, Aggie?" It is Jaime who says that, who is standing at the big wheel that steers the ship which way to go.

"I'm okay," I say. "Do you n-need me to hold your—hand again?"

"I'm all right, thanks. If I look straight ahead, it makes it easier."

He means what happened earlier. It was when he started shaking and then he let go of the wheel and he was kneeling on the floor with his head down and his breathing was all coming out fast and a lot. I said to him, "What is it, Jaime?" but he was shaking his head and his eyes were wide and his breaths were huh huh huh huh. It was the same as when it happened before so I did the helping like Lileas did. I took his hand and put it on my chest where my heart is and said to him to do the breathing slow with me. Soon later his breaths were more normal again and I helped him to stand up. It happened because we can't see Scotia anymore. Jaime told me that. He doesn't like the water when it is so deep. That's okay. It's okay not to like things. It doesn't mean you're afraid. When he feels it happening, he calls to me and I hold his hand again because that is what he says helps. It's because we are friends.

Something runs up my leg and I scream.

"What is it?" says Jaime.

"A shadow thing! It's got me. It's on my leg." Now it is going around my tummy and at my neck. It's going to kill me. It's going to tear me all apart.

"Hello, little fella," says Jaime.

Jaime is looking at my neck where the shadow thing is. He puts his hand up to take it off. When he moves his hand I see it.

Milkwort!

It is not a shadow thing it is Milkwort my friend and the vole. He has come back to me! I take him from Jaime and I kiss him and I scratch him behind his ears.

"You came with us!" I say. "How—how did you g-get here?

You followed us all the way. I knew you wouldn't leave me." I do not say it in my head because I know he will not hear me and that will make me sad and now I am only happy he is here again.

"Don't you run away again," I say to him next but I am not really telling him off.

Jaime is smiling. Milkwort goes down my arm and into my pocket. We are together again now. We will always be together.

"*Dødhai! Dødhai!* Look—there! A *dødhai* comes!"

It is Knútr who is shouting this. He is looking at the other side of the boat. Jaime looks over and I look too.

"What is it?" I ask to him, but then I know it. It is a deathfin. Its spike comes out of the water and it is coming to us. What do we do? If I was on the wall I would know. Deathfins means you have to hit the Fourth chime once at the bottom and then the people in the boats will know and we can use the arrows to help them. But there are no chimes on the ship and we don't have any arrows. Jaime is breathing fast again.

"How do we make the ship go faster?" he shouts to Knútr.

"Untie me and I do it," says Knútr.

"No," says Jaime. "Just tell me what to do. Tell me what to do."

"You cannot outrun it. You do not have the skill. The *dødhai* it crashes ship and it sinks."

"So what do we do?" says Jaime in a really loud scream.

"I tell you: untie me," says Knútr.

The Nice Queen Nathara goes to Knútr and is wobbly when she walks because of the moving.

"I told you not to shout! You'll wake the baby," she says to him.

"*Luk mudr ykar,*" he says, which I don't know what it means. The Nice Queen Nathara giggles at that.

The deathfin is getting closer. Jaime turns to me.

"Agatha—can you stop it?" he asks. "Like you did with the wildwolves. Can you make it go away?"

I don't want to say it but I have to tell him.

"I can't d-do it anymore," I say. "It doesn't—work now."

"What do you mean?" he says.

"Something b-broke," I say.

"Just try, Aggie."

"I can't!"

"You have to try!"

There is no point to try. I go to the side of the ship where the deathfin is coming, but I can't do it and I said I can't do it and I can't.

"I can't do it," I say again and I shout it because I am sad and angry.

"Okay, take the wheel. Keep it straight."

That is what I can do. Jaime jumps down to the middle where Knútr is and pulls out his sword and points it at Knútr and says, "I'm not untying you, so if that thing sinks this ship, you're going down with it. Tell me what to do. Please! Tell me!"

Knútr shrugs and looks away. Jaime leaves him and runs to the side of the ship. The deathfin is right next to our ship now and is going all around it. It is so big and gray and its tail makes it go fast. The Queen Nathara is watching it too and she is smiling but I don't know why. I wish I could talk to it to make it go away. I want to do it so bad. I hold on to the wheel tighter and keep it so straight. My fingers are hard and the wind makes them colder.

There is a bump on the side that is a really big one which is the deathfin. It makes me nearly let go but I don't.

Jaime has gone to below and comes back and he has the spear that Crayton gave me.

"I need to use this," Jaime says to me.

"Yes," I say, "you can use it." Even though it is a special one.

Jaime leans over the side and tries to get the deathfin with the spear. "I can do this," he says to himself. The deathfin is too far away and he can't reach it. He stops trying and shouts to me, "Agatha, when I say, pull the wheel to the right, all the way, as fast as you can."

"Okay, J-Jaime!" I shout back.

"Nathara—hold on to something. Agatha—now!"

I do it. It is hard to do but I am quick and I pull the wheel all the way so quick and it makes the ship tip and I think it will fall over but it doesn't.

"Straighten it up! And go again—now!"

I know what Jaime is trying to do and it is a clever plan. When the ship is tipping he is closer to the deathfin and he can get it with the spear I think.

"And straighten up again."

I know what I have to do now, and every time he shouts, "Now!" I do it. We work together because we are a team and I am helping.

He jabs it with the spear once and then twice and he gets it. It's because it is a good spear. The deathfin goes under and I don't see it again. It is gone.

"You did it!" I say, and I straighten the wheel again. The wheel is stiff and my hands are hurting, but that's okay.

"That was close," says Jaime, who is still looking into the sea. The spear has red on its end.

It is all quiet except for the waves which are hitting on the boat with slapping.

Then there is a big bump and I scream because it is a surprise one. It is so hard that Jaime nearly falls over. The deathfin has come back. It is on the other side. No, there is more than one. The fins come up and there is seven, eight, nine deathfins! They are all around.

"*Dam ort!*" Jaime swears.

"It's not safe it's not safe stay in your room it's not safe" is what the Queen Nathara is saying. She is not smiling anymore.

Jaime runs to the other side of the ship with the spear and when he leans over the side one of the deathfins jumps out of the water so high I don't know how and it is the worst thing I ever saw. It is so big and the sea comes out of its mouth which is a huge open one and it has a hundred teeth that are all so sharp. It is going up to Jaime because it wants to eat him.

"Aaaaaah!" Jaime shouts, and he hits it with the spear in its mouth and it goes all the way in nearly to Jaime's hand and the deathfin closes its mouth and it breaks the spear which Crayton gave me and it smashes it. The deathfin falls into the water and I hope that it is gone forever but I don't know. Jaime moves back from the side. He only has a small piece of the spear in his hand now. I am sad the spear is broken. More of the deathfins are jumping out of the water on both sides and hitting the ship with their tails and I can hear it crack like it is all going to break.

"Keep holding on, Aggie," shouts Jaime. "I'm going to try something." He drops the broken part of the spear and runs up to where I am. The ship is going all ways even though I am holding as hard as I can so it's not my fault. Jaime takes one of the lanterns that is next to me and carries it to Knútr and puts its handle in Knútr's mouth.

"You're going to need this," he says.

Then Jaime goes to the Queen Nathara who is at the front of the ship and holding on and Jaime says, "We need the *sgàilean*. Now. Or the whole ship is going to be destroyed. Can you make them stop the deathfins?"

There is another big bang on the side and it is making my teeth hurt and my head. It is hard to hear what the queen says because of the bangs, but I can see when she opens the black stone on the necklace. What happens next is worse even than when the death-fin jumped up with all the teeth.

It goes darker all around and black shapes are coming out of the necklace. There are so many of them and they come onto the ship and make a horrible noise that is loud. They are the shadow things, I know it. Sometimes I can see them and sometimes I can't. They keep going so I am not sure where they are or if they are there or not. I want to get away from them, but I have to hold the wheel straight so I don't. They cannot hurt me. That's what Jaime says. They only hurt people from other places like Knútr, which is why Jaime gave him the lantern. I am glad there is a lantern near me too so they don't come near me just in case.

There is a swoosh and the shadow things go all together up the pole in the middle of the ship, the one where Knútr isn't. The ship does a jolt and then it starts going fast and much faster.

"Jaime!" I shout, because the wheel is hard to hold now. Jaime comes and takes it from me. "What's happening?" I ask him.

"The sgàilean—they're pushing the sails somehow," he says.

"W-why?" I have to say it loud because of the noise of the shadow things. The noise is in my head like it has got all wasps in it. I don't like it.

"I don't know. I was hoping they'd attack the deathfins, but this is even better!"

He looks behind us and I look too and the deathfins are far away now. They cannot get us now we are so fast.

"If the sgàilean keep this up, we'll reach Norveg in no time."

I do not like the shadow things. I wish they would go back inside the necklace.

"Looks like you won't need to lower the sails after all," Jaime says. "We'll make use of the speed and sail through the night. Why don't you go below and bring up some blankets?"

"Okay," I say. I can do that no problems.

Before I go, I take Milkwort out of my pocket and leave him by the lantern. "You stay here," I say to him. He'll like it by the warm. I do not want the shadow things to get him like they got the stag we ate.

I go down the steps to the middle part. There is something not right. I look up. The whoosh is a fast one and the shadow things are on me. On my face and in my clothes and they want to hurt me and I know it.

"No!" Jaime shouts, and then someone pushes me over and I fall and I am on my tummy and the shadow things go off me and are gone. When I open my eyes I am next to Knútr the nasty deamhan who is too close to me. I lift my hands because they hurt and there is a cut on my arm.

"Agatha, are you okay?"

I sit up. I am by the pole in the middle. Jaime is there. The Nice Queen Nathara comes over too. The shadow things are above me but they can't get me now that I am by the lantern.

"What—happened?" I ask. My knee is hurting too.

"I told you not to touch them. They only want to play. They don't, they don't," says the Queen Nathara, which is one of the things she says that isn't a funny one.

"The *sgàilean*," says Jaime, and he is looking at me with a frown face. "When you stepped out of the light. They all came at once."

"But—but you said they c-couldn't hurt me. You said that, Jaime."

There is laughing and it is Knútr. "This is so good," he says to me.

"What is good?" I say to him. It is not good.

"Stay out of this," Jaime says.

"This is the truth," Knútr says to me. "You think you are from Skye, but it is not true. The killing shadows try to get you, which means only one thing. You are a foreigner." His eyes are all wide when he says it and he licks his lips. "Just like me."

PART THREE

NORVEG

JAIME

THE *SGÀILEAN* ARE BACK ON THE SAILS, PUSHING US forward. It's a risk, keeping them out after what they tried to do to Agatha, but she's safe as long as she stays under the lantern light. I was struggling to sail the ship on my own, so we need to make the most of the *sgàilean* while we can; the sun will rise soon, and then I'll ask Nathara to call them back to the amulet. The speed eases the tension in my chest, which started when we lost sight of Scotia and was made a hundred times worse by our encounter with the deathfins. The sooner we reach land the better.

I keep wondering what made the *sgàilean* attack Agatha. Was Knútr right when he said she isn't from our clan at all? How could that even be possible?

A faint glow of light appears in the distance. Norveg. There must be fires in the harbor to help guide ships in during the night. Even with a spyglass, it's too dark to make out anything specific.

Knútr calls out, "Give me *skyggert* so I see."

"You mean this?" I ask, holding up the spyglass.

"Of course this," he says.

I step down to the middle deck and hold the spyglass to Knútr's eye. "This is good," he says. "We sail good. Go a little west. When the sun comes you see two islands to east. Past them you see Stórangr port. This is where we go."

"And then you'll take us to the king?"

"Then I take you to king."

I return to the top deck and alter the ship's course in line with Knútr's directions. The reality of what we are about to undertake starts to sink in. I grip the wheel tighter. The salty air is good for my lungs. I let the *sgàilean* propel us in for a little while longer and then wake up Nathara.

"We're nearly there. It's time to call the *sgàilean* back in," I say.

"Does Mummy say so? If not, she will be cross."

"Yes, Mummy definitely says so."

She stands up. Her long hair has tangled around her body during sleep, giving her the appearance of a feral creature. She opens up the onyx amulet and calls out the same words as before.

"*Sgàilean thigibh a-steach! An-dràsta! Sgàilean thigibh a-steach!*"

Nothing happens. She tries again, and this time, when she calls, the ship thrusts forward. The *sgàilean* remain on the sails.

"What are they doing? Why aren't they coming down?"

"They don't want to play with me," she says.

"You need to call again. Keep trying."

Her next attempt is more lackluster. The *sgàilean* push forward harder still, spraying water all around us.

Agatha wakes up and laughs, enjoying the speed. "Jaime, w-we're going so—fast!" She rubs her nose and her ears.

"How do we slow them down?" I ask Nathara, but she has no answer. This was not the plan. I taste bile in the back of my throat.

I pull down hard on the wheel. The ship responds and we start to curve. If we circle until the sun rises, the light will force the *sgàilean* down, and I'll regain control. There is a tug in the opposite direction, and the wheel spins back to its former position. What—? I try to pull it back, but whatever force is keeping it straight is too strong to overpower. Some of the shadows must have slipped down and altered our course from the rudder mechanism in the hold. Even with Agatha's help, I cannot budge the wheel.

The two islands that Knútr described slide into view and then speed past soon after.

I abandon the wheel and turn to Agatha. "We can't slow the ship down, so we're going to have to prepare for our arrival. At least the darkness will give us a little cover. There is a knife with the food supplies, in that chest behind you. Put it in your belt and keep it there at all times. Once we're on land, if anyone tries to hurt you, you hurt them first, understand?"

She nods and starts rummaging in the chest. We are hurtling toward the shore now. Several deamhan longboats are moored in the port to the west of us. They look the same as the ones that were used to attack our enclave. On our current course, we are set to crash into the shoreline about a mile farther south. The only way I can think of to keep that from happening is to cut down the sails, but if I do that, we'll be stranded in the water and an easy target once the sun comes up. I leave the helm and jump down the few steps onto the main deck where Knútr is.

"We're going to hit land south of the port. How far is that from where we need to go?"

"Less than half a day walking."

"Fine. If you try anything—anything at all that makes me think you're betraying us—you'll regret it. Do you understand?"

"The little boy thinks he is so tough now. Do not worry. You have your people soon." His smile causes thick lines to crease all of the tattoos on his face.

The shoreline is only a few hundred yards away now. Agatha is leaning against the wheel with the dagger in her waistband and a piece of meat in her mouth. How can she think about eating at a time like this? She spots the remains of Cray's spear by her feet and adds it to her belt.

"We're going to hit land soon. Hard. Hold on to something with both hands and prepare for impact."

Both Nathara and Agatha do as I say. I grab hold of the mast supporting Knútr; if he breaks free during the crash, I want to make sure he doesn't get far.

There is a small fishing vessel in our path. We collide with it head-on, smashing it into driftwood. Our ship doesn't break speed. If anything, it seems to be moving even faster. Land looms nearer, and I brace myself for impact. Three, two, one—

The shock of the ship slamming into the coastline shatters the bow to pieces and splits the hull in two, the momentum carrying its top half skimming across the terrain. My head is whipped backward. I cling to the mast with both hands as we thunder along, torn splinters flying in all directions. Nathara wails, the noise drowned out by the annihilation of wood against stone.

We come to a juddering halt. The air is peppered with dust, which gets stuck in my throat and makes me cough. My cheek is grazed where it hit the mast at the moment of impact, but other than that I am not injured. I check on the others. Knútr is still secure, and Agatha is helping Nathara to her feet, dusting down the older woman's clothes. I release a long breath.

There is a rustling above me and I look up just in time to see the entire *sgàilean* army leak down from the sails and disperse onto the land.

"Wait, no. Nathara—the *sgàilean*! Why are they leaving? You need to stop them!"

Nathara shakes her head as she watches them go. "They have waited a long time for this," she says.

"But you said they would follow you. The Badhbh said—they serve the royal family. They're not supposed to leave. Why have they gone?"

Nathara doesn't give me an answer. I beg her to try and call them, but she insists they're not coming back. Did she know this was going to happen? Did she *let* this happen? This is everything I had feared and worse. Our greatest weapon, our best hope. Gone. Not only that, but I've unleashed an army of assassins on an entire nation. *Guilty by association* is how the elders would have explained it. *All life is precious* is what Cray would have argued.

"What do we do now?" asks Agatha.

"The plan is still the same," I say, choking on my own disbelief. "We go to meet the king. Take one of the lanterns with you. The *sgàilean* will come back to us. They are still on our side." I hope.

I draw my sword and cut Knútr loose, ensuring that his hands are still tied, then stand behind him and place the sword across his throat.

"Lead the way," I say.

We step off the remains of the ship, onto moist grass. My first impression of Norveg is how flat it is, especially compared to Scotia. It also has a very distinct smell: the freshness of seaweed, mixed with something smokier.

There is no one around as we start our walk inland. Knútr limps from the wound in his leg. Cray kept his word and healed the infection, but it's still causing him pain.

It takes a long time for the sun to rise, and when it does, it is trapped behind a shroud of fog. There is enough light, however, to make out a settlement ahead of us. Their bothans are smaller than ours and made out of wood rather than stone. Something moves between two of the bothans; the deamhain are waking up.

"We need to take a detour," I say.

"Too late," says Knútr.

He's right; some of them have already noticed us, and word of our presence soon spreads. Small groups of deamhain start walking toward us, striking their chests and yelling threatening words from their blue-lipped mouths. Some call Knútr by name. They're all covered in similar blue-and-red tattoos, although each design is unique.

"Stay back!" I say, pressing the blade tight against Knútr's throat. I make Knútr translate to ensure they obey. We must make quite a spectacle: a prince held hostage, a filthy woman with ankle-length hair, and Agatha, who—if Knútr is to be believed—would have been killed at birth if she'd been born here.

They stay back as instructed, but it doesn't stop a growing number of them from following us. Many of them are holding weapons. As the crowd grows, it starts to feel less like we are being followed and more like we are being pushed.

"How much farther?" I ask Knútr.

"Close," he says.

We walk over a hillock, and a snow-capped mountain range appears ahead of us. Knútr stops when he sees it.

"Why have you stopped?"

"The one in the middle. It is Sterkr Fjall, the home of the king."

"Wait—the king lives *inside* a mountain?"

Knútr nods. "The king lives inside the mountain."

The path leading up to it skirts around a loch, which contains the clearest water I have ever seen. The reflection of the mountains is almost mirror-perfect. I glance over my shoulder to make sure the group of deamhain is still keeping their distance.

A dark opening appears at the base of the mountains; a tunnel at least six feet wide. As we draw nearer, Knútr's pace starts to slow. I nudge his back to encourage him to keep walking. When we reach the tunnel's entrance, I pause.

"Inside is where your people are," says Knútr, sensing my uncertainty. "It is only way to see the king."

"Fine," I say, "but no one enters with us."

"Dvelið útan," he calls out to the deamhain who have followed us here. They remain where they are, and we enter the mountain alone.

The moment we step inside, an aching chill washes over my body. Knútr leads us along the passageway, which slopes upward toward the heart of the mountain. There are torches fastened at regular intervals, which glow with a strange blue flame. Water drips down the walls. It smells of salty mold. We walk past many junctions and sharp bends. The tunnel gets narrower as we wind higher into the mountain, and I can't shake the feeling that we're heading into a trap.

After a time, the sound of people talking trickles toward us. It grows louder as we turn more corners, and then the tunnel opens up into an enormous chamber. It is full of deamhain. So many deamhain, all of them armed. I stand my ground, my sword still at Knútr's throat. When the deamhain see us, they plummet into silence.

Someone starts clapping, a slow, patronizing clap. I search the room for the source of the sound. It is coming from a man on a large throne at the opposite end of the chamber. The respect he commands leaves no mistaking who it is: Konge Grímr, the Norwegian king. Several layers of animal fur are wrapped around his shoulders, and he wears a pair of antlers on top of his head, giving him a monstrous appearance. Unlike those of Knútr and the other deamhain, the braids in his hair are meticulous, and his silver beard is braided to three perfect points. His tattoos are denser than those of anyone else in the room.

He stops clapping and motions for his people to step aside. They obey, leaving a path all the way to the throne.

"Stay in your room stay in your room stay in your room stay in your room," Nathara starts saying.

"Shhhh!" says Agatha, and Nathara obeys.

We edge forward, Knútr and me in front, Agatha and Nathara just behind. As I walk, I take in my surroundings. Eight spiral pillars twist up from the floor, carved to look like the trunks of great trees. Where they meet the ceiling, they branch out into a canopy of chiseled leaves, which rain down the mountain walls, transforming into scenes depicting fierce battles and bloody hunts. The same blue fire that lit the tunnels shines out of hundreds of lanterns, hung from chains at different levels throughout the chamber. Their light gives the engravings a soft, ethereal glow.

The cavern tapers to what must be the natural peak of the mountain, for, at the top, diamond-shaped holes have been cut through the walls, letting in a spattering of natural light. Above the holes, the highest point is covered in a blanket of white. At first, I mistake it for snow, until a few drops break away and swoop around the chamber. *Great snow bats.* I've heard about them before. They only live in the coldest regions.

I stop when we are about ten paces away from the king.

I swallow. Twice.

"I am Jaime-Iasgair of Clann-a-Tuath, the free people of Skye. You un*dùth*fully enslaved our clan. I am here to demand their immediate release."

Konge Grímr stands. The blue light swims across his dark face like moonlight on mud. He ignores me and addresses Knútr.

"*Minn sonr, ak hugjisk dervar død,*" he says.

"What did he say?" I demand of Knútr.

"I said I thought he was dead," says Konge Grímr. He speaks our language much better than Knútr but still with a heavy accent.

"Yes. It is miracle, Father," says Knútr. Is there a slight hesitancy in his voice? "Release his people and I am free."

Konge Grímr considers this for a moment and then addresses me. "Jaime-Iasgair, of the free people of Skye, you say?"

"That is correct."

"Sadly, no. That is not correct. You see, 'the free people of Skye' no longer exist. Nor does your home, as it is now occupied by our acquaintances from Raasay Island. The whole plan was theirs, in case you were wondering. They watched us invade Clann-na-Bruthaich and feared the same thing would happen to them. So they approached us with a proposition. It worked out rather well, don't you think? They're enjoying their new enclave, and your clan has been given a new life here. You should be thanking me. I have removed your people from the worthless existence they once knew and given their lives meaning, as servants to the great Øden, protector of us all."

"Øden?"

Before replying, Konge Grímr takes a long pause, as if to digest my ignorance.

"Øden the Almighty: he who created the universe, he who controls the world. The One True God."

"But gods don't exist," I say without thinking.

The king's face, which up until now has remained impassive, erupts with rage. "I will not have you blaspheme in this mountain!"

The deamhain around us reach for their weapons. Konge Grímr holds up a hand to restrain them, and his former composure returns.

"You have so perfectly demonstrated what a heathen you are," he says. "All of your people are heathens. That is why Øden sent us to show you the truth."

Is he crazy? I know that in the past some clans used to worship invisible entities, but they never used them as an excuse to murder and enslave people.

"Release my people or I will kill your prince," I say. My voice sounds more confident than I feel.

"Will you, now?" says the king.

"I mean it. I'll kill him right here in front of you." My threat sends ripples through the gathered deamhain. Knútr shuffles. "Just like you did to Lileas," I add in his ear.

"And then what?" asks Konge Grímr.

"What do you mean?"

"If you kill him, you have no hostage, nothing to bargain with. Stuck in the heart of a mountain, surrounded by one hundred of my greatest warriors. You think you will fight your way out?"

"I'm hoping it won't come to that."

"Three people against one hundred? Not even three people. One child, one old lady, and *that,* which I would not even call a person."

"Say that again and I will tear—tear out your eyes!" Agatha shouts. "I am not afraid."

The deamhain laugh at her.

"I like her," says Konge Grímr.

"This is your only son, is it not?" I say.

The laughter dies.

"It is," replies the king.

"The prince of Norveg, your only heir. If the great Øden ordained that you should be king, then surely he granted you this son to rule after you when you die. Do you really want him murdered in your own chamber? While you do nothing to stop it from happening? Murdered by the clan that your great Øden commanded you to overcome? Do you really want that to be your legacy?"

That came out better than I expected. This might actually work. The king winds his fingers around the central braid of his beard while he thinks.

"You are right," he says at length. "He is my only son. I should be thanking you for returning him to me."

Yes. Finally. "Then let us discuss the terms of the trade," I say. "You will release my clan immediately. All of them. And provide us with enough longboats to sail back to Skye, plus food and supplies for the journey. Only when everyone is safe on board will I release Knútr. Understood?"

But Konge Grímr has stopped listening. He turns to the deamhan next to him and reaches out his hand. The deamhan hands him an ax. The glint of its blade flashes in the firelight. The king weighs the ax in his hand and then launches it straight at me.

The ax lands in Knútr's head, splitting his skull in two, covering me in his brain. His body becomes dead weight, and I have no choice but to drop it. It falls to the floor in an ugly mess. I stare at it, at him, my mouth agape.

"You see," Konge Grímr says, "my son, the esteemed Prins Knútr, may have informed you that he was the only heir to my kingdom—which is true—but what I'm sure he failed to mention was that he was also cowardly, irresponsible, and disrespectful of my authority. Which is why I ordered him to be thrown over-board and left to drown. I would rather have no heir than leave everything I have spent my life fighting for to someone as unworthy as him. But I must thank you for returning him to me. I thought he was already dead, but it was much more satisfying to kill him myself."

I can't breathe. My chest is a knot, weighing me down.

"Take these creatures out of my sight. Tonight we will witness their execution. In the name of Øden and all that is holy. *Takan frott þeim!*"

Rough arms grab me. Someone thumps my hand, making me drop my sword. I let it fall. Agatha screams, but the sound is far, far away.

I offer no resistance as I am dragged out of the chamber.

AGATHA

I AM THINKING WHAT I CAN DO. I DON'T LIKE IT IN HERE.
It is so dark and I have to get out or they will kill us. That is what
the man king said. He had antlers on his head which was stupid
and he killed the nasty deamhan Knútr. It was an ax in his face
and it was horrible to see it, even though I hated him.

I don't know where Jaime is or the Queen Nathara. They are
in a different place. I called their names but they didn't say anything which means they aren't here. Maybe they can't hear me
because of the walls. I am still inside the mountain. The room is
dark and a small one. I can't remember well when they brought
me in because they were holding me and I didn't like it so I was
trying to get them off and screaming and trying to bite when they
covered my mouth. I'm not supposed to do bad things when I'm
angry but it is different with the deamhain and I couldn't stop it
and I didn't even want to stop it or care. Then it was dark when
they closed the door and I cannot see a single thing. They took
my knife away and also the piece of spear that was a present from

Crayton and I wished they didn't do that. I moved all around to find the walls which is how I know it is a small room and that no one else is here. I tried to find the door by hitting on all the walls but I couldn't find it and it doesn't open because it is locked.

I do a lot of shouting but no one answers. I sit down on the floor which is cold and also wet.

"Have you quite finished?" says a voice that is quiet.

"Who's there?" I say. I am not scared.

"You mean you don't recognize my voice?" the person says. "Forgotten about me already, have you?" I can't hear it very well. It does sound a bit like I know it.

"Where are you?" I ask, and I stand up and move my hands around even though I know the person is not in the room with me because I checked.

"Outside your cell. These walls are thick, but sound penetrates them well enough. So I had the pleasure of hearing your wailing."

The person does a humph and then I know who it is.

"Maistreas Eilionoir!" I shout. I cannot believe it. "It's me, Agatha!"

"I'm well aware of that, my dear."

"We thought you were d-dead! We saw all your heads that were spinning," I say. It was horrible to see.

"That was the other elders—*caidil gu bràth*—and the seventh was one of the Moths. She had already fallen, so I placed my elder chain around her neck to fool the deamhain. How did you get here? I thought *you* were dead."

"I came on a sh-ship with the Mad Queen but she's not really mad and J-Jaime and the bull people helped us because I had to stop the wildwolves and I rode all the time and the—the shadow things went but that—it wasn't the plan and when I screamed I couldn't—the king killed him and we were trying to—he was a nasty one and we came but they grabbed us and I can't find the door I—I—"

"Shush your mouth! Stop that. How do you expect me to understand when you speak such garbled nonsense?"

I knew it was coming out wrong but I couldn't stop it. It happens like that sometimes.

"Now, tell me again how you came to be here. And this time slow down and speak properly."

I tell her everything and I say it slower and in the right way.

"Sounds like you've had quite an adventure," she says when I have finished.

"We came to—rescue you," I say.

"I always knew there was more to you than meets the eye," she says.

"Where is everyone else?" I ask.

"Our people are slaves here, Agatha. And it's not just us; the king has enslaved thousands of people from many different places and is forcing them to carve out the mountain behind this one. It is to be a temple—the greatest the world has ever seen—all in honor of his wretched *god*. The deamhan are victims of their own made-up stories, which the king uses to manipulate his subjects and increase his power. Every day, more and more people die from exhaustion and disease. It is dreadful to behold."

It is not right. The king is a very bad man.

"W-why are you here and not in the other—mountain?" I ask.

"They do not know that I am alive. The whole time we were traveling across the sea, I pretended to be a helpless old crone—which I suppose is not that far from the truth. . . . Then I collapsed during our first work shift and pretended to be dead. They dumped my body in a pit containing hundreds of bodies—not a smell I'm going to forget in a hurry—and left me to rot. I have been hiding in the tunnels ever since, stealing food to feed the prisoners, keeping their hope alive, waiting for the right moment. And now you have arrived. This is our chance. Tell me more about the power you have harnessed."

"Uh?" I say, which is because I don't understand.

"I may be all rags and bones and filthy as slush mud, but I am still your elder. Do not make uncouth guttural sounds at me."

"What did you m-mean, though?" I ask.

"Tell me more about what you can do. About the animals you can control."

I knew she would ask me that. I didn't say it all before because it makes me sad to think it.

"I can't—I can't do it anymore," I say.

"What do you mean you can't do it?"

"It went away after the w-wildwolves. When I screamed in the tree all the wolves in my head made me go black and I f-fell out of the tree. After that it wouldn't do it anymore."

"Hmmm," she says. She doesn't say anything for a little bit and then she says, "As you know, the elders do not encourage the practice of such things, so my knowledge is limited. I do know, however, that it is not a skill that can be taught, so I do not believe it is one that can be lost. You were born with the ability; it is part of what makes you who you are. Trauma may have blocked it, but that does not necessarily mean it has gone away forever."

That is a good thing! It means maybe I will do it again.

"How do I do it again?" I ask.

There are footsteps coming.

"I have to go," says Maistreas Eilionoir, "but I'll come back. Think about what I have said. You've come this far; don't give up now."

I do not want her to go. The footsteps stop and there is talking I cannot hear. Then the footsteps go away again.

Now there is no sound.

"Maistreas Eilionoir?" I ask. "Are you still there?"

She does not reply so she is gone. I am alone again.

Could it really be true what she said? I wished she could have said some more. I also wanted to say to her why Knútr said that I am a foreign person like him. It is not true. I am not like him.

I take Milkwort out and hold him close to my face. It is so dark I can't even see him. Maistreas Eilionoir says maybe I can still do it so I try. *Milkwort,* I say in my head. *Milkwort?* I say it again and again and again, but it is no good. Maistreas Eilionoir is wrong. I will never do it again. My eyes are crying because I am sad and I can't even stop them.

I wait for Maistreas Eilionoir to come back but she doesn't come back. I do not want to be here anymore. I want to be in the enclave which is my home and I wish none of this ever even happened.

THE NEXT TIME THE STEPS COME THEY OPEN MY DOOR. IT is so bright I cannot see and then I can. There are three deamhain there. One looks like Knútr but it is not him because he is dead. The other two ones are women ones and they have long axes.

"Come with us," says the man deamhan. "Do not struggle or we will hurt you."

I do not want to be hurt and there is too many of them to get past them with their axes anyway so I have to do it what he says. They pull my hands behind my back and it hurts and I say "Ow!" but they don't say sorry. Then they put something on my head and I can't see again.

"I don't like it," I say. "I want to see. Take it off my head please." But they don't take it off because they are mean.

It is hard to walk when you can't see anything. I only know where to walk because one of them squeezes my arm too tight and makes me go which way by pushing me. We go a long way. When they take off what it is on my head I can see again now and I know where we are. We are in the big mountain room where we were before. It is darker because it is night now so it is only the blue fires that make the light. The two deamhain holding me make me climb up eight steps and I know it is eight because I count them. Now I am on a new bit that wasn't there before. It is in the middle and made higher. The shape is a square and there is blue fire in the corners. I can see everything from where I am on top. The king with his antler head is sat on his big chair. There are even more deamhain than the last time. Too many for me to count them. Maybe it is all of them in the whole world.

Someone else comes up the steps and it is Jaime with two more deamhain who are holding him. When they take his hood off he can see me. He looks at me but he doesn't say anything. He is sad, I know it. The deamhain holding him make him stand on the other side of me.

We are going to be killed. That is why we are here. I try to think of a plan so that we won't be. I cannot think of one. It is too hard when they are holding me so tight and there is so many people looking at me.

There is screaming from a person which is the loudest I ever heard. I can't see who is doing the screaming. It looks like the ceiling is falling down but it is not. It is the bats who don't like the screaming so they fly down and are making lots of noise. It is the Queen Nathara who is doing the screaming. They bring her onto the platform next to me.

"Off! Off!" she shouts at them. "It never rains but it pours, and then you'll be sorry you were ever born."

One of the deamhain pulls the hood off her head and she smashes her face into his. Crack! It is a big one. The deamhan falls down and his head bleeds where she did it.

The other deamhan slaps her on her face. It is very hard.

"Leave her alone!" I say.

The deamhan spits next to my feet. "You will be next," he says.

The Queen Nathara does not scream anymore. She looks at me and says, "Agatha." Her eyes are wet because of some tears.

"Yes, Queen Nathara," I say. "It's me."

"I do not like it here," she says.

"It's okay," I say, which is a lie because it is not okay. I only say it to try and make her happy.

She is on one side of me and Jaime is on the other. Two deamhain are holding each of us on our arms. They hold our arms so tight that we can't go anywhere because we are trapped. The king with the antlers on his head stands up and everyone is quiet.

"Welcome back," he says to us. "I trust you had an enjoyable day?"

"No," I say. "It was dark and boring."

The king laughs and so do some of the others. "It was a rhetorical question," he says, which I don't even know what that means or care. "Before we proceed, there are a few guests missing. *Lergjað fangir ina!*"

More deamhain come in and they are with people in chains and it is Lenox and other people who are my clan and Flora as well.

"Jaime!" shouts a girl. She is from our clan and an Angler.

Jaime does a breathe in.

"Aileen," he says. "I tried—I—"

"Silence!" shouts the king. "I have brought a select few of you here to witness the execution of your would-be rescuers. I want you to know that they attempted to save you, and to witness how unsuccessful that rescue attempt was. Let this be the end of all hope for you, and a lesson that this is what to expect should any of you try to cross me in the future. Accept your fate with honor, as *húskarda* of Øden, the One True God. His will be done."

"You're insane," shouts Jaime. The king looks at him angry.

Jaime keeps talking. "Stop hiding behind your 'god' and accept that you are committing murder for nothing more than to feed your disgusting ego."

"Kill the boy last," says the king, and he sits down. "And make it slow."

Someone walks up the steps with a clunk clunk and when they come up it is a deamhan with a very long sword that is rusty. It is the sword that is doing the clunking. The deamhan man is old. His eyes are under lots of lines so I can hardly even see them.

"For the attempted murder of a prince of Norveg; for attempting to blackmail His Supremacy the king; for attempting to liberate the servants of Our Lord; and for blaspheming against the One True God within the Hollow Mountain. Of these crimes you are found guilty, or guilty by association, and are hereby sentenced to death. In the name of Øden—may he always guide us. *Má hann dafjan oss visájr.*"

"*Má hann dafjan oss visájr!*" shout all of the deamhain, and they hit their chests and chant something that's like "Dud, dud, dud, dud."

The old deamhan with the eyes that I cannot see stands in front of the Nice Queen Nathara and lifts the sword above his head. I try to move but I can't. I need to think of a clever plan and I wish I could think of one.

"*Død! Død! Død! Død!*"

"I don't think Mummy and Daddy are here," says the Queen Nathara.

The sword deamhan swings the sword above his head once and twice and I can only watch it with my eyes and do nothing to stop it. He pulls it back but before he can use it the Queen Nathara twists her body and bites one of the deamhain holding her on his shoulder so hard. The deamhan shouts loud and lets go of her. She tries to get free but there is still one more deamhan holding her. She turns her head to bite him too but he won't let her. The sword deamhan goes to stab her with his sword. The Queen Nathara leans back and lifts her legs up and kicks the sword on its side with her feet. The deamhan with the sword stumbles over. I think he's going to drop it but he doesn't. He grips it harder and swings it around and he is too quick this time. Before the Nice Queen Nathara can kick again he pushes the sword into her. It goes all the way through and out the other side. She screams even louder than before and the deamhain roar louder and the king is smiling. There is too much in my head that is anger and sad and hate and there is no room for it all. The white bats are flying around so mad with the noise. I am screaming too. I do not want it to be happening.

There is another sound I know. It is a horrible one and it's at the top of the mountain room. The shadow things. They have come back. They heard it when the Queen Nathara screamed is what I think. They want to come in through the windows but they can't because of all the fire.

The deamhan pulls the rusty sword out of the Queen Nathara. Her head is down. The sword deamhan wipes off the blood from the sword with his arm.

I am not scared. I will die brave. I look at Jaime and show him I am brave. Then I look at Flora and Lenox and the others to show them I am brave too. The sword deamhan has finished cleaning the sword and moves next to me.

There is pushing and shouting in the deamhain. Someone is there who is trying to get past. The cloak falls off her head and it is Maistreas Eilionoir! Why is she there? Run away or they will get you! They are grabbing her now. She throws something onto the platform. It lands by my feet and goes all around. The deamhain grab her tight.

"Agatha!" she shouts, and she is looking at me. "It is within you. You are stronger than them all."

She tries to pull away but they are holding her too hard.

"Get your grubby hands off me, you filthy—" One of the deamhain hits his elbow into her head and she goes knocked out so she can't talk anymore. The deamhain drag her away.

I look at the floor and look down harder to see what Maistreas Eilionoir threw at me. It is all around my feet. It is seeds. What? Seeds cannot help us.

Oh. Oh. I know why the seeds. She threw them to remind me. About when I had to sort the seeds and not be angry. And then I know it. I don't know how I know it but I do. It is the angry that made my head break. When I was in the tree, all the wildwolves were in my head and they were the most angry ever because they hated the screaming and I was so angry too because I hated it all and it wasn't fair. All of the angry together made inside my head go black and that is why I couldn't do the talking after. I can still feel the angry. The wildwolves' angry is still inside me. If I can make it go away maybe I can do the talking to the animals again.

I close my eyes so I cannot see the antler king who I hate or the other deamhain. It is easier if I cannot see them. I know what I have to do. I do a big breath in and think about the place inside my head where the wildwolves were, then I breathe out and try to make their angry go away. It is hard to do it. I try again. And one more time again. Please come on let it work. The next time is my biggest yet. There is something like water in my head that is a little trickle and then it is more and then it is a big river going fast inside. It feels different again now.

I open my eyes. The sword deamhan raises the sword above his head. I need to be so quick. *Hey,* I call to the white bats that are flying near me, and then I say, *Excuse me,* because it is manners. I say it to all the bats because there are so many of them and they are going too fast to say it only to one. Their voices fill my head. I can hear them!

I need your help! I shout. They hate the deamhain as much as I do, I can hear it. But there is not enough time. The sword goes in a circle once and then twice. *He is going to kill me,* I tell them. The deamhan lowers the sword and he is going to put it into my middle, just like he did to the Queen Nathara.

One of the white bats comes down from above and lands on the sword deamhan's head and grabs on his horrible hair with its claws.

Yes, yes! Thank you, yes! I say. Then other ones are landing on him too and pulling at him and flying in his face. He tries to get them with the sword but they are too fast for it. He goes backward and waves his arms and he does not know the edge is there and he falls off.

I thank all the bats because they made me not get stabbed with the sword. The deamhain cannot believe what happened and they do not know why. Now I have another plan and it is a clever one. It is my best plan ever. The only thing that is not clever is that it means I will be dead. But I have to do it. For Jaime who is my friend and for my clan to be rescued.

"Put out all the fires!" I shout, and then I remember that I need to say it in my head so I say it in my head loud so all the bats can hear me. My head is going to hurt again to say it to so many but I have to do it because it is the plan. *Help us and you can have this mountain,* I tell them. It is what they want.

The white bats are talking to each other with so much screeching. They decide they will do it. They are scared of the fire but they will do it. They knock the torches off the walls and start to blow out the lanterns by using their wings. The blue fires are going and the mountain room gets darker. The deamhain are still holding me but it is not tight anymore. They are watching the bats and cannot even believe it. The one holding the Queen Nathara drops her and leaves the platform to try and stop the bats. One of the fires on the platform goes out. The Queen Nathara is on the floor and she is not moving.

Milkwort, can you hear me? I ask him, and he can! It makes me so happy to do it. I tell him he needs to leave the mountain room so quickly and find somewhere to hide. He understands and climbs out of my pocket. There is no time to say goodbye. He runs down my leg and off the platform. Please let the deamhain not step on him.

At the top the horrible noise is louder. It is my plan and it is working. The fires are going out so the shadow things can come in. They come all down the walls to get the deamhain. They want to tear them all apart.

And they want to do the same to me.

JAIME

SGÀILEAN POUR DOWN THE WALLS LIKE A DARK WATER-
fall. The first wave hits the deamhain, and pandemonium erupts.
The deamhain try their best to fight, but their enemy is merciless
and almost invisible.

"Drep ina meyla völva!" Konge Grímr bellows, pointing at
Agatha. The shout attracts the attention of several bats. They
shriek in his face and claw at his eyes. His arms lash out amid
their flurrying wings. The antlers slip from his head and topple to
the floor. His agony echoes around the chamber.

One of the deamhain holding Agatha pulls out a knife and
turns toward her with bloodthirsty eyes. I have to free myself. Now.
I bend my knees and push all my weight into the deamhan on my
left. I'm not strong, but I catch him off guard, and he stumbles.
Using his momentum, I force us closer to the nearest fire stand
and swing my leg at it. I miss. The deamhain are trying to pull me
back. I swing again. This time, the side of my foot clips the stand,
shifting half of its base over the edge of the platform. It teeters.

Come on, fall. Fall! It's tipping. Yes! It plummets over the edge and our corner of the platform turns black. A flicker of a shadow later, unseen hands reach up and snatch the deamhain from either side of me. They are too shocked to call out as they disappear.

One of them dropped a sword, which I grab as I stand. The deamhan with the knife is staring at the space that used to be occupied by her kinsmen. I swing the sword at her knife hand and chop it clean off. She stares at the stump, her mouth a black circle. I'm staring at it too. Did I really just do that? I blink in disbelief, then her howl shakes me back to my senses. I charge into her with my shoulder and shove her off the platform.

There's only one deamhan left on the platform now. He throws Agatha to the floor and squares up to me, pulling an ax from his belt. I retreat to where there's no light, hoping he will follow. He hangs back; he saw what happened to the others.

Agatha slides over to Nathara and cradles her in her arms. "I'm here for you, N-Nice Queen, I'm here for you. Please don't die," she says. Nathara does not respond.

The deamhan flips the ax in his hand, preparing to throw it. I raise my sword, ready to defend myself. There is a loud screech behind him as several white bats fly down and start beating their wings at the fire on his right.

"Å *nein!*" he says, swiping at them with his ax. It clips one of them on its wing, but it does not deter them. They flap even harder, until the fire dwindles to nothing.

Only one fire remains on the platform, behind where Agatha and Nathara are lying on the floor. The deamhan strides over to it, puts the ax between his teeth, and lifts the entire fire stand. He makes it look so easy. He stalks toward me, holding the fire above his head.

"Agatha—find some light!" I say, as she slips into shadow.

Once he is within reach, the deamhan flicks his head, flinging the ax from his mouth straight at me. I thrust out my sword in front of me. The ax rebounds off it, sending tremors down my arms. The deamhan bares his teeth like a savage dog. Still holding the stand, he jumps in the air and kicks me square in the chest. Something cracks and pain floods in. I tumble backward, dropping the sword, which slides over the edge of the platform. The deamhan towers above me. He is easily twice my size. He lifts the fire stand, preparing to bring it down and crush my skull. Veins pulse along his arms.

I whip my legs around and slam my feet into his ankles. He drops the stand, which misses my head by a crow's breath. The fire spills, scattering flames onto the ground below. The platform is now completely dark. The deamhan's eyes widen, and his breath catches in his throat. He knows what is about to happen, and he is powerless to stop it. *Sgàil* hands wind around his ankles, then force him down with a silent shudder. As he falls, he reaches out and grabs my shoulder, pulling me down with him. I hit the ground below the platform with a thud, crashing my teeth and rattling my skull.

The deamhan is lying next to me. His eyes lock onto mine. We both see the dagger at the same time. It is in the space between us. I make a grab for it, but he is quicker. Its blade catches the last of the light as he raises it into the air. Pain pins me to the floor. He drives the dagger down, toward my head. All I can do is stare.

At the last moment, I whip my arm in front of my face. The dagger collides with something metallic and slips away from me. My eyes focus on my wrist, on the bracelet that has just saved my life. The deamhan lifts the dagger for another strike, but before he gets a chance, his body starts convulsing. A *sgàil* has taken hold of his waist. He stabs at his own sides, trying to release its grip. The nails of his other hand scrape along the ground, resisting the pull. Every muscle in his body clenches, but the *sgàil* is too strong. A moment later, he is gone. His wailing drains away as he is dragged out of sight.

I stand up, sucking in shallow breaths. Dark outlines clash and struggle all around me. I can scarcely make out which are deamhain and which are *sgàilean*. My ears ring with the chaos of clanging weapons, tearing flesh, final breaths.

Agatha! She was left in darkness. I have to get to her before the *sgàilean* do. I push past warring bodies, trying to find the steps leading up to her.

I circle the platform once, possibly twice; it's hard to tell in the dark. The steps are no longer there. I raise my arms to pull myself up, and pain explodes in my rib cage where the deamhan kicked me. I grit my teeth and heave. It takes three attempts before I manage to swing a leg over and drag myself up. Two bodies lie on the opposite side of the square, neither one moving. I rush to them and shake the first I reach. Nathara doesn't respond. I put my hand on her heart. Nothing. She is dead. My eyes sting, but I blink it away. There is no time for remorse. I reach over to the second body.

"Aggie, it's me," I say, shaking her shoulder.

She fights to open her eyes. "J-Jaime!" she says. "You came back for me."

She is drenched in blood. I'm too late.

"Of course I came back," I say. "We're a team, remember?" She tries to smile, her face contorted in pain. "We need to get you away. Into the light."

No sooner have I said it, than the final lantern is extinguished and darkness swallows us all. I drop beside Agatha and wrap my arms around her, trying my best to cover her with my body.

"Stay with me," I say.

The sounds in the chamber intensify: vicious whispers, high-pitched squeals, furious cries.

Agatha tries to speak. Her voice is weak.

"What is it, Aggie?"

"Th-thank you for being my friend, Jaime," she says.

"You don't need to thank me for that."

The whispering creeps in on us. I hold her even tighter, pressing her into my pain.

There is a tug at her feet, which becomes stronger and more persistent.

"Leave her alone," I shout, kicking at the air.

"I am not afraid, Jaime," she says. "I am not afraid."

A final pull rips her from my arms.

I scream, scrabbling in the darkness.

"No. No!"

She is gone.

JAIME

THE CHAMBER IS SILENT. HOW LONG HAVE I BEEN ASLEEP?
I don't remember closing my eyes. The fires are still out, but the
high windows let in just enough daylight to see by. The platform is
surrounded by more bodies than I can count. They lie sprawled at
all angles, their faces torn and pleading.

One of those bodies is Agatha's. I can't tell which.

An abyss of sadness opens up inside me that I know will
never disappear.

Cold water runs beneath my fingertips. I lift my hands, but
they are not wet. It is the *sgàilean,* flowing across the platform. For
once they make no sound at all. They gather at Nathara's body and
swim in her blood.

More *sgàilean* join, until there are so many that her body is
completely obscured. The click of the onyx amulet cuts through
the silence and, one by one, the *sgàilean* slip inside it. When the
last one disappears, I reach over and snap the amulet shut. It

hangs limp at the side of her neck. It is some relief, at least, that the *sgàilean* are once again contained.

With the utmost care, I straighten Nathara's body and place a single kiss on her forehead.

"May you find peace in endless sleep," I say.

I stand up on weak legs. I need to find Agatha's body as well, but the thought of looking for it is too unbearable right now. I'll search for my clan first, then return for her on my way back through.

What happened to Aileen and the others who were brought in to witness the executions? I lost track of them when the fight broke out. The *sgàilean* shouldn't have harmed them, but what if the deamhain did? A sudden panic forces me into action. I jump down from the platform. My ribs still throb, but the pain is bearable. I pick my way across the room, trying to look down as infrequently as possible.

The sound of footsteps stops me midstride. People are approaching the chamber from one of the tunnels that feed into it. It must be deamhain from outside, returning to reclaim the mountain now that the sun has come up.

I dive behind the nearest pillar. The footsteps get louder. There are voices, all talking at once. I peer out as the first people emerge from the tunnel.

I gasp. I cannot believe it.

It is my clan. All unchained, all unguarded.

And at the very front, leading them, is Agatha.

I almost fall over in my haste to get to her. I throw my arms around her. She hugs me back, squeezing tight.

"Be careful of Milkwort!" she says.

The vole looks happy enough, perched on her left shoulder.

"I thought you were dead," I say.

"I'm not, J-Jaime. I'm not dead."

"Well, I can see that! But the *sgàilean* took you. You were covered in blood."

"They took me away but they didn't hurt me this time. And—and it wasn't my blood. The blood was from the Nice—the Nice Queen Nathara." Her voice falters as she says her name. "She's dead, isn't she?"

I nod and we hug again.

Maybe Nathara's blood prevented the *sgàilean* from attacking Agatha somehow? That's the only explanation I can think of.

"Where did you go?" I ask her. "I was worried about you."

"When the noises stopped, you were being so—sleepy and sleeping so I went to find our clan, Jaime. And look—look, I found them!"

I stare at the many hundreds of faces around us, at everyone we have saved. People I never thought I'd see again. And it is not just our clan who are there; Agatha has freed all of the prisoners in the mountain.

"How did you—?" I ask.

"It was easy for me," she says. "Milkwort showed me the way. There wasn't even anyone g-guarding them."

The guards must have come running into the chamber when the battle started and then suffered at the hands of the *sgàilean*. Either that or they ran away. Many of the freed prisoners look similar to us, but some look completely different. Some even look like deamhain, only without any tattoos.

Maistreas Eilionoir steps forward and covers both my fists with her hands. There are flecks of crusted blood in her hair, where the deamhan hit her.

"You've come a long way, Jaime-Iasgair," she says in a slow, raspy voice, "and overcome many hardships. Clann-a-Tuath will forever be indebted to you." Then she leans in close and whispers into my ear, "You truly are the bravest of us all."

"*Guma fada buan*, Jaime! *Guma fada buan*, Agatha!" someone shouts from the crowd. It becomes a chant, and before long, everyone is shouting our names in praise. The echoes reverberate to the top of the mountain, where they disturb the white bats from their slumber. They glide down majestically before returning to their perch.

Everyone wants to greet me and clasp my fist. I am turned from person to person, from smile to smile. Exhilaration courses through my body.

"You still wearing that ugly hunk of metal on your wrist?"

I spin around.

"Aileen!"

She launches herself at me, and I fail to hide the wince as she knocks my chest.

"Are you hurt?"

"It's nothing."

She looks different. Older, maybe. But she still has the same spark in her eyes.

"You're alive," I say. "I came for you."

"It took you long enough." She punches my arm.

I twist away from her and smile.

I smile so much it hurts.

"It is time for us to leave this damned-awful place," Maistreas Eilionoir calls out above the hubbub. Everyone falls silent to listen to her. "Pick up arms from the fallen enemy; we do not know what to expect when we leave the mountain. Jaime, do you have a plan?"

"Ask Agatha," I say. "Her plans are usually the best."

Agatha beams. She runs the tip of her tongue over her bottom lip and then says, "We should go to where their boats are. We will take their boats and go—go home!" Everyone raises their fists in the air. "Follow me and J-Jaime. We are not afraid!"

Another huge cheer breaks out. Agatha looks at me and I nod in agreement. I can't believe it. We're going back to the enclave. We're going home. Who knows what we'll find when we get there? If the islanders from Raasay think it belongs to them now, they've got another thought coming. It's ours, and we're taking it back. The way I feel now, there's nothing we cannot do.

People break away from the crowd and arm themselves with whatever weapons they can find. I ask some of them to help me lift Nathara's body down from the platform. Then, with Aileen by my side, we all move as one, through the chamber and down the tunnels that will lead us out of the mountain, never to return.

AGATHA

EVERYONE HAS TO ROW ON THE LONGBOAT. THAT IS HOW they go. I don't have to because I am the hero. Maistreas Eilionoir said it. I was so clever to have the plan and I did it and it worked. I didn't even die which I thought I would. Now we're going home. Everyone is so happy and we did it.

The only sad thing is that the Queen Nathara is dead. That is why I wished I did my plan sooner so she didn't get killed. That is the only thing.

When we got to the boats there were deamhain there who didn't want us to take them. They weren't the ones from inside the mountain. They were different ones. Maistreas Eilionoir said to them, "Your king is dead. Your prince is dead. The people in the mountain have either perished or fled. We are no longer your prisoners. Let us go in peace and we will be merciful. Try to stop us, and it will be the end of you all."

After that the deamhain let us take the boats because they knew they couldn't stop us. Also maybe they heard about the shadow things and they were scared. The shadow things are back in the necklace now and wouldn't have come out because it was the daytime, but the deamhain didn't know that. The other prisoners went on different boats because they are from different places.

I didn't want to do the rowing but I wanted to do an important job so Maistreas Eilionoir said I could be the lookout from the front of the boat like a Hawk, the most important one. My face is always salty and I lick it. I can see the land which Jaime says is Scotia again. We are not going across it like before. We are going around the top of it in the boats.

I wonder what Crayton and the bull people are doing. I hope we will see them again one day and I can tell them that we beat the deamhain. They will be so happy to hear it.

"How about here?" asks Jaime. He is standing next to me at the front of the boat.

"Yes," I say. "Here is a—good place."

We have been looking for somewhere to say goodbye to the Queen Nathara. We are going to put her in the sea because she liked it when it did the splashing. Jaime holds his hand up to the rowers to stop and they do. The other boats stop too. Four people carry the Queen Nathara's body to the front. It is on a piece of wood like a bed. She looks pretty because I stroked her hair and put flowers in it from before we left.

"None of you knew Queen Nathara," Jaime says, "but it is because of her that you are all here now. Keep her name in your hearts and remember her forever. *Caidil gu bràth*, Nathara."

"*Caidil gu bràth*," everyone says, and I say it too. It is one of the things in the old language that everyone knows. It is what you say when someone dies, and it means I hope you sleep forever with peace.

Jaime bends down.

"Where's the necklace?" he says. He looks around her neck and inside her clothes.

"What necklace?" asks the man who was one of the ones carrying her.

"She was wearing a necklace. A locket with a big black stone," Jaime says. "Where's it gone?" He means the necklace with the shadow things inside.

"She wasn't wearing it when we lifted her onto the boat," the man says. "At least I don't remember seeing it."

The other people who carried her shake their heads to say they didn't see it too.

"So where is it?" Jaime looks at Maistreas Eilionoir. "We agreed to bury it at sea. If it ends up in the wrong hands . . ."

"It is no longer our concern," Maistreas Eilionoir says. "The sgàilean cannot hurt us."

That is not true. They tried to get me once. I was lucky that they didn't get me in the mountain, too. Jaime says it was because I had the Queen Nathara's blood on me so they thought I was like her. I think it was because they realized I am Clann-a-Tuath and that I am not a foreign person like Knútr said. I do not like that necklace or the shadow things.

Jaime stands up and nods at the people who carried the Queen Nathara. They pick up the piece of wood and lower her over the side of the boat. I look over so I can see it. She stays floating for a little bit and then she starts to sink. I wave goodbye to the Nice Queen and I say I'm sorry that I couldn't save you.

Some birds are making squawk noises in the sky. I look at them and they are flying all around. When I look back at the water I cannot see the Queen Nathara anymore.

"What happened to the necklace?" I ask to Jaime.

"It must have fallen off at some point, back in Norveg," he says.

"I'm glad we left the shadow things behind," I say.

"Don't worry," he says. "They won't get you again." He puts his hand on my shoulder.

I shiver a little bit because it is cold. It is time for us to go now.

Everyone starts to row again and the water splashes on both sides. In front of the boat, a gannet goes in and out of the water. It is the one with the Queen Nathara's soul, I think. I hope it takes her somewhere nice.

We follow it for a long time. It is leading us home.

EPILOGUE

THE BEAST SNARLS, PULLING AGAINST THE CHAINS ON ITS neck. A thick line of drool leaks out of its mouth onto the floor.

"What's it saying?"

"It's hard to tell, Your Majesty. Wildwolves are tricky at the best of times."

"I was told you were the best in the land."

"I'm the *only* one in the land, Your Majesty."

"So ask it again. A thousand wildwolves don't come running that far south for no reason."

The man leans forward until he is mere inches from the wildwolf. Its foul breath warms his face. He stares deep into the animal's eyes. They are intense: one of them bright yellow, the other ice blue. Its lips peel back to reveal raw gums and razor-sharp teeth.

"Bloody hell," the man says several moments later. He stands back up and faces the king.

"What is it?"

"It says there was a fight. With people in the north. Really far north, if you catch my drift."

"Not Scotia?" says King Edmund, his misty eyes bulging out of their sockets. "Impossible. No one was left alive."

"That's what it said, Your Majesty. And . . . there was something else."

"What?"

"I'm not sure I completely understand. . . ."

"Spit it out!"

"Something about a girl. A girl who hurt them in their heads, all at the same time."

For a long time, the only sound is the wildwolf's growls and the clink of the chain as it struggles to pull itself free.

"A girl who hurt them in their heads," says King Edmund, gritting his ancient teeth together. He sucks in a long, wheezy breath. "I think we need to find this girl. I think we need to find her straightaway."

A NOTE ABOUT THE LANGUAGES

THE "OLD LANGUAGE" THAT IS REFERRED TO AND USED IS, for the large part, Scottish Gaelic. I was assisted in this by Gaelic expert Liz Macbain, who did a fantastic job of tweaking many of my original suggestions. Occasionally, I made alternative choices for artistic reasons or in order to aid the reader, so any errors or inconsistencies are mine alone. In addition, some words—such as *bothan*—have been integrated into the clan's contemporary language, hence the plural of *bothan* being *bothans* (rather than the Gaelic *bothain*).

The language spoken by the deamhain is a fictional one, inspired by Old Norse.

ACKNOWLEDGMENTS

I USED TO WONDER HOW AUTHORS HAD SO MANY PEOPLE
to thank in their acknowledgments, but now—having experienced
what it's like to have my own book published—I've come to realize
it truly is a collaborative process. This book would not have been
possible without the following people, and I am extremely grateful
to each and every one of them.

Firstly, to my agent, Claire Wilson at RCW: you are the best.
I've said it before and I'll say it again. THE BEST. I cannot thank
you enough for your belief in this book and in me, and for all the
wisdom and support you have imparted. Thank you.

To my editors Annalie Grainger at Walker Books UK and Susan
Van Metre at Walker Books US—thank you for always pushing
me to make this book the best it could possibly be, and for being
so understanding and responsive to any concerns I've had along
the way. I have learned so much from you both and am excited to
share the next chapter of this incredible journey with you.

Extended thanks to the whole team at Walker—both in the

UK and America—including Megan Middleton, John Moore, Maria Middleton, Maria Soler Canton, Anna Robinette, Rosi Crawley, Kirsten Cozens, and Jamie Tan. Also to my copy editors, Betsy Uhrig and Maggie Deslaurier, my proofreaders, Matt Seccombe and Emily Quill, and to Amy Silverman and Andy and Sarah Merriman for their invaluable and extremely insightful sensitivity reads. For assisting me with the Gaelic in the text, thanks to Liz Macbain, Màiri N. Reid, Rebecca MacLennan, and Jayne MacLeod. And a big hug to Donna MacLeod for my lesson on Gaelic pronunciation. You're a smasher!

The Balbusso twins—Anna and Elena—you have created one of the most stunning pieces of cover art I have ever seen. I can't believe it's on the front of my book; every time I look at it I smile.

A huge thank-you to early readers Layla Daer, Poppy Merton, Bex James, Sue Bellew, and my siblings Tom, Elizabeth, and Kate Elliott. Your enthusiasm gave me strength when I needed it the most.

To my awesome debut buddies, especially Katya Balen, Savannah Brown, Aisha Bushby, Sam Copeland, Holly Jackson, Sarah Ann Juckes, Kesia Lupo, Struan Murray, Lucy Powrie, and Yasmin Rahman—you have taught me so much and kept me sane on this crazy roller-coaster ride that is the world of publishing. (Sidenote: their books are all brilliant, and you should definitely buy them all right now.)

To the staff and students past and present at College Park School in Westminster: you are where this story began. Thank you for inspiring me and for all the great memories.

Additional thanks (I'm writing the word "thanks" too much,

aren't I?) . . . Additional "gratitude" (thanks, Thesaurus.com) to Cerrie Burnell, Cat Doyle, Kate Potter at the Down's Syndrome Association, Zoe Nelson, Miriam Tobin, and Sam Coates. Sorry to clump you all together in a didn't-know-where-else-to-put-you list . . . Doesn't mean I'm any less grateful, promise.

I am ridiculously lucky to have the most amazing family and friends, whose collective pride and excitement for this novel has been completely overwhelming. To my grandma, Janice "Red Grandma" Smith: if you're reading this, then yes, it is *finally* finished. Sorry I made you wait so long! And to my parents, Gill and Tony Elliott—you have always supported my artistic dreams, and I cannot thank you enough for that. Padge—sorry for all the times Mum is going to embarrass you by telling total strangers that her son wrote a book. Mum, keep spreading the word—I'm counting on you to get my sales up. I love you both very much.

Finally, to my husband and best friend, Richard. I almost can't put into words how much you have done to help create this book. At various stages, you have been an editor, a proofreader, a sounding board, and a source of inspiration. For your constant encouragement and unwavering belief in me, and for staying up until 2 a.m. that one time to help me redraft, I thank you from the bottom of my heart. This book is for you.

SIGRID

MY FACE IS ON FIRE, BUT I'M NOT GUNNA SCREAM. I DON'T think I could even if I tried. I need water but can't ask for it. My mouth doesn't work no more. I knew it was gunna hurt. It's *sposed* to hurt. Still, I didn't know it was gunna hurt as much as this. Somethin's gushin down my cheek. I dunno if it's ink or tears or blood or what. Praps it's a mix of all three.

"I'm movin on to your neck," ses the man. "Keep still."

As if I'm gunna move with that hek massive needle close to skewerin me. I grip the sides of the stool, lettin its splinters dig into my skin. One of the stool's legs is shorter than the others, so I gotta hold my weight slanted to stop it wobblin. Evrythin's hek skittin in this shack. I knew soon as I came in that this was a bad idea, but it was too late by then. Mamma'd already paid him.

He looms over me, his breath harsk as milkreek. Dark blue ink drips from the end of the needle. I close my eyes as the stabbin starts again.

A forever time later, the man pulls away and tosses the needle on the side.

"Done," he ses.

I'm hot all over. Swear Øden I never been so hot. Even breathin hurts.

"Þokka," I say, although it seems hek foolin to thank him, given how he's done nothin but stab me with a needle for the last however long.

My mother is waitin for me outside. Soon as I step out, the man slams the shack door shut without sayin goodbye or nothin.

"Well," ses my mother, "let's see it." She grabs my head to steady herself and leans in for a better look. Her face is too close to mine. Bits of sweaty hair are stuck to her forehead, and her eyes are faraway and wild. "Ha!" is all she ses.

"What?" I say. "What's wrong with it?"

"Nothin," ses my mother, but she's smilin wicked. She could at least pretend it looks all right. It was her what convinced me this was a good idea, after all. I was far too keen, but who wouldn't want their first ink early? This wasn't how I imagined it happenin, though. All of my mother's ideas are bad ones; you'd of thought I would've learnt that by now.

"Did it hurt?"

"Yes," I say. No point in lyin.

"It'll heal soon," she ses, pretendin she cares.

The walk back to our shack is a blur of throbbin. The ground's sodden from where it's been spewin all afternoon, and the wet finds my toes through the holes in my shoes. I tried fixin the shoes yesterday, but I guess I didn't do a very good job. I'll try again tonight, do them better.

Soon as we're back, my mother crashes on her sleepin mat and asks for water. There's a mirror by the water bucket, so while I'm fillin up the horn I see my new ink for the first time. The mirror's cracked, which doesn't help none. Has been ever since I knew it. Probly my mother did it before I was born, or maybe it was my pa before . . . Well, before what happened to him happened. One of the mirror cracks goes right through my reflection. My face is diffrunt now. I keep starin at it, but I can't find the person I was before. First inkin is sposed to make you look brave. On me, the way that sickweasel done it, it doesn't look nothin but ugly. There's no other word for it. It's swollen red and crusty with blood. Mamma thinks he was lyin about used to bein a *tatovmaðr*. I coulda told her that. He woulda told her anythin to get his greedy hams on our money.

The ink's sposed to be a raven. Mamma let me choose, probly cuz she couldn't be bothered thinkin of somethin herself. It don't look nothin like what I was hopin, though. It clings to my neck with its head stretchin over my jaw like it's tryin to peck out my cheek. It looks dead, like someone clean snapped its neck. It looks like it's cryin on my cheek but it's not got no tears. Oh well, isn't nothin I can do about it now. We just gotta hope it's good enough to fool whoever my mother's plannin on showin it to. Now I'm inked I should be able to get work on one of the larger farms, diggin up crops or somethin. It'll be hard grind, but I don't mind that none. Anythin's better than spendin all day bein pushed around by Mamma.

I cross over to her now and hand her the water horn. She takes it without sayin nothin and doesn't even open her eyes. I try to slip out, but of course she hears.

"Where you goin?"

"Granpa Halvor's," I say.

"What you goin there for?"

"I wanna show him my ink." That's a lie. He's gunna be hek grieved when he sees it. I shoulda told him we were gunna do it. I didn't cuz I knew he'd tell me not to.

"You spend too much time with that old man," ses my mother. "It's not normal." She doesn't hardly speak to Granpa Halvor. I think cuz he reminds her too much of my pa. "Don't be long. My head's throbbin and I'm hungry," she ses.

I'm already out the door before she's finished speakin. Granpa Halvor's shack isn't far from ours. Close enough to run to when my mother's turned sour from neckin. I knock on his door and, soon as he opens it, first thing he ses is "What has she done to you?"

"She didn't do nothin," I tell him.

"She may not have held the needle, but I bet it was her idea."

His face is tight with so much concern, I feel my own face crumplin. "I shouldn't of done it," I say. "It's my fault. I knew it was a sickrotten idea."

"Hey, shush, girl. Come inside and I'll make you some sweetmilk."

He puts his arm around my shoulders and leads me in. Granpa Halvor's shack isn't nothin like ours. It's hek poky, but everythin's put neat and tidy clean. Best of all is the twistknot rug on the floor what's nearly as big as the whole place. Granpa made it himself when he was a kidlin out of bits of old clothes and scraps. He cleans it every day so it isn't never dusty. I sit on it and run my fingers through the scruffs.

He brings me over a bowl of sweetmilk, and while I'm drinkin, he dabs at my face with a wet rag. I hold in the wince that's wantin to come out.

"Who's the grotthief what did this to you?" he asks me.

"I dunno, Granpa," I say.

"Sure as hellfire wasn't no proper *tatovmaðr*."

"I know, Granpa."

"How much'd you pay him?"

"I dunno, Granpa."

"It wouldn't of come cheap, gettin him to do it with you bein only twelve and all. What was your mother thinkin? What's her game? And what sort of a lyin, thievin scoundrel would do this to a girl? I feel like trackin him down and . . . and . . ."

I can't help smilin at that. The thought of Granpa hurtin anyone is hek smirks.

"What you laughin for?" he ses. "If I was twenty years younger . . . I'll have you know I was a force to be reckoned with in my time."

"Sure you were, Granpa," I say. I slurp down the rest of the sweetmilk. It's hek creamin on my insides. "I thought you didn't agree with fightin anyways?"

"Depends who's fightin and what they're fightin for. If it's sendin away our kidlins to be slaughtered on foreign lands for nothin but pride and power, then no, I don't agree with fightin one speck."

He's talkin about his son, my pa. I don't hardly remember him. He died over the seas somewhere when I was a little kidlin, fightin for the king in some bloodsplash invasion.

"What about if Mal-Rakki came back?" I ask. "Would you fight for him?"

"That's diffrunt and you know it. His fight has purpose. The day he returns, I'll be the first to stand by his side."

What if Mal-Rakki never comes back? I think, but I don't say it. I draw lines in the dregs of the sweetmilk with the tip of my finger.

"Here, I got this for you." Granpa Halvor throws somethin at me.

I catch it quick, and my gawpers open hek wide.

"Where'd you get this?" I ask. The plum is bright yellow, soft as a babkin's foot, perfectly ripe.

"I pulled it out my nose hole; where d'you think I got it?"

"But I thought you had to give them all up to the king?"

"I did, but I sneaked one away, just for you."

I smile, and for a speck I forget about the wreckmess of my face and all its hurtin. The tree behind Granpa's shack is a scraggin old knot, but it grows the most hek *rìkka* plums in the whole of Norveg. I bite into the one in my hand and it's good—so good! Its juice trickles down my arm, and I lick it up, not wantin to waste none. I take another bite, then offer the rest to Granpa.

"No, girl, it's yours. I want you to enjoy it," he ses.

I don't need tellin twice. I put the rest of it in my mouth, stone and all, and chew down, lettin the sweetness burst inside my cheeks. I should slow down, take my time scrammin, but it's too good for bein slow. Once all the flesh has gone, I keep the stone in my mouth, suckin on it for any last drips.

"I think you enjoyed that," ses Granpa Halvor.

I nod. "Thanks, Granpa." I spit out the stone and bury it in one of my trouser pockets. "Once I'm earnin, I'll buy us fruit evry day."

"What you talkin about, earnin?" His forehead creases, makin the ink rabbit what's there crumple into a slackdead heap.

Granpa's got hek loads of ink, but the rabbit on his forehead has always been my favorite.

"Mamma says I can earn good pennies workin on one of the big farms. That's why I got the ink done."

"You don't wanna be workin down there. You'd have to get up before the sun to arrive on time. Earnin isn't evrythin, Sigrid. Specially when the king's men come take it all from us anyways."

"What choice have I got?"

"What do you mean what choice? There are always choices. It's knowin which are the right ones that's the hard part."

I dunno about that. Far as I see it, I haven't got no choices, sept doin what Mamma tells me. Which reminds me . . .

"I gotta go, Granpa," I say. "Mamma's not feelin too good. She'll be hek skapped if I'm not back cookin somethin soon."

Granpa scowls hard, like a beaver what's been bit. He's always scowlin when I mention Mamma. "Well, don't let her talk you into no more brainrot plans," he ses. "And keep that ink of yours clean. If it gets any redder, come straight back to see me."

"Yes, Granpa."

Before I go, he holds my chin between his thumb and finger and turns my head sideways to get another gawp at my ink. "My little Sigrid, growin up," he ses. "A raven was a perfect choice. He may not have been no real *tatovmaðr* what done it, but I think he did a good job. I like it."

He strokes my other cheek with his knuckles. It's nice of him to lie.

ABOUT THE AUTHOR

JOSEPH ELLIOTT is a British writer and actor known for his work in children's television. His commitment to serving children with special education needs was instilled at a young age: his mother is a teacher trained in special needs education, and his parents provided respite foster care for children with additional needs. He has worked at a recreational center for children with learning disabilities and as a teaching assistant at Westminster Special Schools. The heroine of *The Good Hawk*, which is his first book, was inspired by the many incredible children he has worked with, especially those with Down syndrome. Joseph Elliott lives in London.